Taking Flight

Senior
Fiction

About the author

Sheena Wilkinson has won many awards for short fiction and has a Masters with Distinction in Creative Writing from Queen's University, Belfast. She teaches English in Belfast and lives in County Down where she spends far too much time writing and reading. A lot of the ideas for this book came to her when riding her pony in Castlewellan Forest. *Taking Flight* is her first novel.

Taking Flight

Sheena Wilkinson

First published 2010
This edition published 2013
by Little Island
7 Kenilworth Park
Dublin 6W
Ireland

www.littleisland.ie

ISBN 978-1-84840-949-1

Cover design by Inka Hagen
Inside design by Claire Rourke

Printed in Poland by Drukarnia Skleniarz

 Little Island receives financial assistance
from The Arts Council (An Chomhairle
Ealaíon), Dublin, Ireland.

10 9 8 7 6 5 4

For Mummy, John and Rhona with love;
and in memory of Scarlet, the best pony ever

Acknowledgements

It seems a long time since I first started scribbling the notes that became *Taking Flight*. I am grateful to Malorie Blackman who, at an Arvon course, saw the potential of an early version, and especially to Lee Weatherly, mentor extraordinaire, who is unfailingly generous with advice, criticism and encouragement.

I am indebted to the English Department at Queen's University, Belfast, partly for the full scholarship which enabled me to do the Masters in Creative Writing in 2008/9, and also for the guidance and support of the Seamus Heaney Centre staff, especially Glenn Patterson and Ian Sansom.

The Tyrone Guthrie Centre at Annaghmakerrig never fails to work its magic and I am thankful for the part it plays in my writing life.

Thanks to all the readers – friends, family, critiquing partners – who have ploughed their way through numer ous drafts. My sister, Rhona Wilkinson, checked all the showjumping details.

The aptly named Faith O'Grady, and Lauren Hadden, have given me all the support a writer could wish for from her agents. Finally, a huge thanks to everyone at Little Island, especially Siobhán Parkinson and Elaina O'Neill, for believing in *Taking Flight*, and helping me to make it the best story it can be.

Chapter 1

DECLAN

First the crack of bone, then the gush of blood. I never knew blood came out that fast. I flex my fingers. 'That's the last time you call my ma a slag, McCann.'

Emmet McCann doesn't say anything, just stands there in the playground with his hands up to his nose and blood spurting through his fingers. The knot of boys and a few girls who two minutes earlier had been egging us on with, 'Fight! Fight! Fight!' now mutter, 'Payne's coming!' and melt away. Seaneen Brogan is last to leave. 'Good on you, Declan,' she says.

Payne looms up and Seaneen scrams.

'Fighting again, boys?'

Emmet mumbles and splutters and points at me but he can't talk.

'Sir, he started it. He called — well, he was saying stuff.'

'*Saying stuff.*' Payne sighs and gives me his usual you're-a-piece-of-dog-turd look. 'Your articulacy never fails to astound me, Kelly.'

I rub my fist on my school trousers.

'McCann – school nurse; Kelly – my office. Now.'

He can't drag us – they're not allowed to touch you – but he marches between us back to the main building. 'Another phone call home,' he says in a bored voice as if he has better things to do.

Emmet turns to me before he goes into the nurse's room. 'My da'll get you for this, Kelly.'

'Oh, I'm so scared.'

'Enough!' roars Payne. 'In here, Kelly.'

Mr C. Payne, Deputy Head (discipline) makes me stand while he lets on to be doing something dead important at the computer on his desk. He's probably playing solitaire or looking up porn. It's just one of his techniques, making you wait. Making you sweat. I am sweating, but only because I've just been fighting and maybe a bit because I'm thinking about Barry the Bastard McCann and what he might do when his precious wee Emmet tells him Declan Kelly broke his nose. Cause I'm pretty sure it is broken. I can't help smiling at the memory of that sickening, satisfying c-r-a-c-k!

'Take the smirk off your face, Kelly.' Payne stops looking up porn and reaches for the phone on his desk. 'Didn't have the pleasure of seeing your mother at last week's Year Twelve parents' evening, did I?'

'No.'

'No, *sir*.'

'Sir.'

She never comes up to the school. Or anywhere else these days. At first I thought it was better than having her hang round Barry's flat all the time, sometimes for days, but now I'm pissed off with it. Every day, sitting in front of the TV, sometimes still in her jammies at tea time. I imagine the phone ringing in the living-room. She won't answer. I glance at the clock on the wall. Five to two. She might not even be up yet.

When Barry first dumped her, she used to leap on the phone every time it rang, but it was never him.

Payne puts down the receiver and gives me a dirty look. 'Does your mother work, Kelly?'

'No ...' I leave it as long as I dare. '... sir.'

'This is not the first time you have assaulted a fellow pupil, Kelly.'

Assaulted. Payne is so far up his own arse. 'Sir, he called my ma a slag.'

Payne winces, like I just dirtied his precious office. 'Kelly, it is not helpful to bring these' – he sniffs – 'domestic issues into school. Now, I have been familiarising myself with your record. Not terribly impressive, is it?'

I shrug. 'Dunno, sir.'

He raises grey eyebrows behind gimpy specs. 'Oh, let me assure you, Kelly. Very unimpressive indeed. Poor work; anger issues. Then, of course,' he sneers, 'let us not forget last year's little ... eh, holiday.'

They always bring it back to that. It wasn't a holiday and it was nothing to do with school. But there's no point saying anything.

Payne's starting to sound bored. 'You know the punishment for fighting as well as I do, Kelly.'

Should do by now, he means.

'Suspension, sir.'

'And reintegration *only* following parental interview,' he snaps.

Whatever.

Payne taps a few keys and the printer whirrs and hums. He must have a letter on file and just changes the names – there's fights all the time at our school. He makes a big deal out of sealing the envelope and thumping down on it just to make sure. 'Take this home to your mother *now*. You are suspended pending parental interview.'

I stuff the envelope in my blazer pocket. At least I'll get out of the Friday afternoon boredom – Personal Development with Mr Dermott (bearable) and English with Psycho Sykes (not).

The corridors are quiet, just a few after-lunch crisp packets and chip papers drifting in corners.

'Oi, Declan!' It's Seaneen Brogan again, heading out of the photocopying room with a pile of papers that look like very like Mr Dermott's PD worksheets. 'Where are you going?'

'Home. Suspended.'

'God, Declan, you're an eejit.'

'Thanks.'

She clutches the pages tighter to her chest. She has massive tits. 'You know Emmet McCann's da'll be after you for this?'

'So?'

'*So* he's a psycho. Seriously, Declan – watch your back.'

'Go on back and suck up to Dermie. He must be missing you by now.' I lift the top worksheet. 'What am I missing? "Assertive, not aggressive." Christ. God love him, he tries, doesn't he?'

'He'd need to. See ya, Declan.' She wiggles down the corridor, arse and curly pony-tail bouncing.

'See ya.'

I sling my bag over my shoulder and head through the main doors. The shiny silver Jeep – BAZ 67 – crouched outside makes my stomach nosedive and I press myself back into the doorway until it's gone. Barry must be taking Emmet to casualty. I make sure the Jeep's well away before I carry on, head down against the rain.

I'm dead.

When I get to the top of our street I do my automatic check to see if the curtains are open. No. Shit.

She's staring at the TV – some daytime crap; she'd watch anything. When I flick on the light she jumps. 'What are you doing here at this time?'

I fire the letter at her. 'It wasn't my fault,' I say while she rips it open. 'I just got the blame as usual.'

She explodes of course. I zone out. Heard it all before. Can't cope; you're out of control; can't hold my head up in the street after the last time …

Sure she's never in the bloody street.

'And I'm going up to no school,' she finishes. She ties her dressing gown belt tighter, like she's getting ready for battle. There's a tea stain down the front of it. 'I'm not having them tell me I'm a bad mother.'

'You're not a bad mother.' I sit down beside her and try to slip a fag from the packet in her dressing gown pocket, sort of joking, but she slaps my hand away, hard. I catch the greasy stink of her hair.

'Don't you try and get round me. I've had as much as I can take.'

'Mum, you're overreacting.'

'And don't you dare patronise me! You sound like our Colette.'

The phone rings. She hesitates, then picks it up. From the look on her face I think I'd be as well to hide out in the kitchen. Maybe even make her a cup of tea.

But when she slams into the kitchen five minutes later she goes straight for the vodka cupboard.

'Mum, it's only three o'clock …'

She swings round. The glass trembles in her hand. 'You never told me who it was!'

'Does it matter?'

'Course it matters!' She slams the glass down on the fridge then reaches for it again. 'How d'you think I felt? That snobby get saying they wanted to keep domestic issues out of school. He knew all my bloody business.' Her voice shakes.

No he didn't. And neither do you. You don't know what Emmet said about you. *Drunken slag* – and me denying it! You're a crap mother. I hate you. I wish you were dead.

I think these things. I don't say them.

'So how long am I suspended for?'

'You have to write an apology letter to Emmet and take it with you on Tuesday.'

I laugh. 'Well, they can piss off. I'm not writing it.'

She shakes her cigarette at me. A lovely whiff of ash. 'You'll bloody write it.'

'Make me.'

She hits me. Across the face. Not hard but her rings catch my cheekbone.

So I do say the things.

All of them.

Out in the street it's still raining and I've run out without my coat so I don't think I'll be hanging round too long. Just enough to let her calm down. I reckon I've got a couple of hours while Barry and Emmet are safe in casualty. Christ, it's boring though, walking round in the rain. No one's about. I head up onto the main road, past the chippie, the chapel where Gran used to go, the book-ies, the waste ground where we burned that car out –

yeah, it was stupid, far too close to home. I'd know better now. Maybe not the best place to hang round now. I'd better head on back. She could be sorry by this time – she might even let me go for chips.

The silver Jeep is parked outside our house.

I can't go in. But I have to.

As always his belly is the first thing I notice. His T-shirt stretches across it like a blown-up balloon. My mum had sex with this man.

'Och, Barry,' she goes, 'it's just boys being boys. Sure, you used to fight the bit out when you were that age.'

'Never mind "boys will be boys".' He jabs a fat finger at me. 'That wee toerag broke our Emmet's nose. And they can't even set it till Monday, it's so swollen. Four hours sitting in casualty!'

You can't have been, it's not even five o'clock, I think, and if it was anyone else I'd say it.

'He started it,' I say instead. I hate the way my guts have curdled. I hate the way my voice just came out, higher than I planned.

'If I have to take him private' – he swaggers a bit at 'private' – 'you can pay for it.'

'Och, Barry, come on now. Let them sort it out between them; they're only kids.'

'Oh aye, don't you worry. Our Emmet'll sort him out as soon as he's fit. And *he's* got plenty of mates.'

I want to think, *you are pathetic*. A forty-year-old man threatening a fifteen-year-old boy cause he gave your son a bit of a thump. But I can't. His voice, the way he slaps his keys against his thigh, the smell of his aftershave, all make me shrivel.

'Barry, would you not stay for a wee drink? For old times?' Mum is sucking round him so hard I could scream.

'I think you've had enough already, love.' The way he says 'love' turns it into an insult. He looks round the room and I can see his piggy eyes snapping up the closed curtains, the overflowing ashtray, a couple of days' worth of dirty plates. 'Let things go a bit, haven't you?'

Mum's hand flies up to smooth her hair, and she moistens her lips – God, it's sad to watch her – but there's nothing she can do about the grubby dressing gown.

'Let *yourself* go, too. No, I'll not be staying.'

As soon as he's gone she starts to cry: ugly, snottery sobs making her face hideous. She blunders into the kitchen to pour another glass and I follow her.

'Yeah, Mum, that'll really help. If Gran –'

'The less you say about your gran the better!'

I head up to my room. Stupid cow. Let her drink herself into a stupor if that's what she wants. I put on some music and lie on my bed and wonder how I'm going to keep away from Barry and Emmet. My fist still throbs when I remember it smashing into Emmet's face. Was it worth it? I thought so at the time but now … Nobody messes with the McCanns.

The CD finishes and I can't be bothered to get up and change it. The room goes darker and darker round me till I can only make out shapes. All the stuff on top of the wardrobe morphs into humps and shadows. How will I stand a weekend of this and then a long, empty Monday?

I wake up to hear Mum crashing around. Doors creaking. Shouting. Tomorrow she'll be as sick as a dog, spend half the day in the bog and yell at me for breathing. And then that'll be her off the drink for ever – till next time. I just hope she makes it up to bed. Once, I had to step over her, passed out on the stairs, and there was puke all down the wall. If Gran was alive … But that's a bad thought for the middle of the night, so I stop it right there.

Later I wake up again and hear snoring. It annoys me so much that I get up and close her bedroom door and mine.

When I wake up the third time the sun's shining through the curtains and the house is quiet. I go to switch the light on but nothing happens – that means the electric's run out. If she's still out of it I'll have to get the card and some money out of her purse and top it up at the shop. And I'm starving. So while I'm at it I'll go to the chippie.

No sign of life in the living-room. I open the curtains to let a bit of light in. There's ash spilled on the floor and an envelope of photos on the sofa. I pull some of them out. Mum and Colette and my dad laughing outside the chippie. Around my age. I remember Gran showing me these one time. 'Was my dad nice?' I asked her, and she said he was, he was lovely. I wonder why Mum was look-ing at them. I put them back on the sofa and rifle through her purse for the money and the electric card.

There's a new bit of graffiti on the wall of the commu-nity centre. SUICIDE KILLS. Ha ha. Fat Frankie's is empty and I shovel the fry into me like I haven't eaten for twenty-four hours. Then I realise I haven't. I never got any tea last night and I spent lunchtime breaking Emmet's nose. I'm so full after that I walk up the main road for ages. It feels safer there, but I can't keep away for ever.

A couple of guys from my class are hanging round outside the Spar – Kevin Walsh and Chris Reilly. I just go 'alright' to them and push past. Most of my class are well in with Emmet McCann. I get a two litre bottle of Coke. She goes mad for Coke when she's been on the drink.

Getting close to home, the plastic bag handles cutting into my hands, I do my automatic curtain check. Open. Yay. Then I remember I opened them before I left.

I race down the street, fish my key out. It doesn't matter – I wouldn't expect her to be up yet, after a night on the drink. I just have a feeling.

I pause outside her bedroom door. Nothing. I remember the snuffling snores of last night. But now – silence. I push the door open. She's lying on the bed, half-slumped over the side. Her face is a bluey colour and when I touch it the skin's cold.

I hit her.

Nothing.

Shout at her.

Nothing.

Something takes over and throws me back down the stairs, shoves the phone into my hand and finds the 999 buttons. I'm outside watching myself. I see my fingers shake. My voice sounds scrambled but I must make some kind of sense because the voice at the other end says an ambulance is on its way. It asks me if I know how to put her into the recovery position. I keep saying it's too late and the voice says stay calm, it'll be with you in a few minutes. 'Stay with her,' it says.

But I can't go back in there.

I make it as far as the landing. Stand outside the door. Why didn't I go in last night? I just closed the door to shut her up. I squeeze my eyes shut but the image of that room the way I just saw it is scratched onto my eyelids. The rumpled bed. Mum's face hanging, collapsed.

And something else, something weird – what was it? The bottle of tablets on the bedside cabinet. Jesus!

Sickness floods me. Bathroom. White tiles. Hands grip something cold and hard. I'm still spitting up bits of sausage when I hear the loud rap at the door.

Chapter 2

VICKY

'D'you miss me at weekends?' I asked while Mum was cutting my sandwiches.

She paused, mid-chop. 'Sort of. Well, *yes*. But I know you're happy with Dad and Fiona.'

'And Flight.' I didn't mention Molly. 'Can I take some of those apples for him, Mum?'

'They're Pink Ladies – far too good for a horse! There's a bag of carrots in the fridge.'

'Nothing's too good for Flight!' But I rooted in the fridge. It was a huge bag. Mum was pretty nervous around Flight but she didn't mind buying him stuff. 'Oh Mum, I can't believe I got asked to be on the senior team!'

'And you're sure you're ready for it?' She looked anxious – horses had that effect on her.

A little worm wriggled in my stomach while I shoved the bag into the rucksack I always took to Dad's. 'Well, he's a showjumper. He's bound to be a bit more – well, complicated, than a pony. But Cam thinks I can do it.'

And that feeling of not bonding with Flight – maybe I was imagining it.

'Well, she should know, darling. And Flight's a very good horse. He'd need –'

'I know, he'd need to be, the amount Dad paid for him! So you've said about a million times.'

She laughed and set my lunchbox on the table. 'Hurry up, love. It's past eight and you haven't dried your hair yet.' She ran her fingers through her own short, dark hair.

'Can I use your straighteners? We're going to the Rowan Tree for Fiona's birthday tonight, and it is *so* posh.' I didn't tell her my main reason for wanting to look my best – that Rory from three doors down had a part-time job there.

'Go on then.' Her voice was a tiny bit tight. Maybe she minded me talking about Fiona's birthday. Fiona was thirty, a barrister, though she was on maternity leave now.

I squeezed Mum's waist on the way past. I'd been taller than her for ages.

'Hurry up if you want a lift!' she called after me.

Swinging out of the driveway we saw Rory out for his run. He stepped back onto the pavement to let us pass and waved.

'He likes you,' Mum said.

'Mu-um! He'll hear.' I felt my cheeks catch fire and hoped Rory hadn't noticed.

As I waved goodbye to Mum outside school I thought she looked sort of small in her blue Golf. I wondered if she *really* didn't mind me being away all weekend. Fliss kept saying she couldn't understand why Mum didn't have a boyfriend yet – after all, she and Dad split up five years ago – but she only thought that because *her* mum had a new guy, on average, every six months. My mum wasn't like that. Thankfully. Because that was about the worst thing I could think of. I swung my rucksack and pushed my cuddly Tigger down out of sight. With luck Fliss and Becca would be at the lockers already and we could get a good gossip before tutor group.

They were both there, leaning against our special bit of wall, talking about going into town the next day. Becca looked tired; she'd probably stayed up to revise for our French test. Her mum gave her a hard time if she didn't get straight As.

'You up for it, Vic?' asked Fliss, blotting her lip-gloss with a tissue to get it to just the right level of naturalness to keep Mad Max off her back.

'Sorry. Got to practise jumping.'

'You're always doing that!' Becca complained. 'You're never around.'

'I am!' I protested. 'But you know I'm on the senior school team – the first show's next week!'

'What've horses got to offer that your best friends don't?' Fliss started on her eyeliner. It was green, the same as her eyes.

'Oh, try fun, excitement, glamour, the odd gorgeous boy rider in skin-tight jodhpurs. Not much, really.'

'Oh, when you put it like that!'

'Seriously, though. You two should come and watch me next week.' I tried to keep out of my voice just how much I would love them to. They looked at each other and then at me, with identical 'no way' expressions.

The bell for tutor group made us all groan and shuffle our stuff together. I shoved my rucksack into my locker and had to slam the door to get it closed.

Dad's silver Merc was waiting at the gates at 3.30 p.m. I

called goodbye to Fliss and Becca, swung my bags into the back seat and myself into the front.

'Hi Dad!' I hugged him as best I could in the car.

'Hello, darling. Good week?'

I'd talked to him most days on the phone but this was part of our Friday ritual, part of sliding back into being Dad's daughter instead of Mum's. Or as well as.

'OK. Bashed my leg at hockey today. Otherwise, pretty good. I got 48 out of 50 for my English oral work – I had to do a speech. I did foxhunting. That's an A *star*,' I added, in case he didn't realise how good it was.

'Good girl! That's the old legal brain. You must get that from me.'

'Maybe.' I could have said 'Mum did law, too,' but unlike Dad, she had only studied it for less than a year. Dropped out of university, pregnant with me, before her first year exams, after being the first person in her family to go to university – first in her whole street, probably, I thought, thinking about the horrible estate where Mum came from. I never used to think it was horrible but that was when Gran was there. And now Mum worked in a library.

'I can't wait to jump Flight tomorrow.'

Dad's eyebrows crinkled in puzzlement. 'But darling, I thought you knew?'

'What?' My stomach turned to water. 'Oh, my God, what's happened?'

'Calm down! He's absolutely fine. But he and Joy got their flu jabs yesterday. And you know that means no riding for a few days. I thought Fi told you.'

Tears of disappointment sprang to the backs of my eyes. 'But they weren't due for a couple of weeks!'

The road crawled past and Dad beeped at a cyclist

with a death wish. 'I know, darling. But the vet was at the yard to see another horse and Fiona thought it was a good chance to save on the callout fee. You know he charges a fortune.'

'But that's not fair! It's OK for Fiona; she never rides Joy these days, but what about me?'

'Well, I suppose Fiona forgot about the show. There's always next week.'

Next week! Next week *was* the show! How was I ever going to be ready?

* * *

'Champagne?'

I glanced up into Rory's gorgeous blue eyes and smiled. 'Lovely, thanks.' To my amazement my voice came out sounding normal. When he bent over me I caught a wave of coconut shampoo. He turned to fill Dad's glass and I saw his tight black waiters' trousers and nearly fainted into my salmon. He played rugby for the boys' grammar school and it showed.

I touched the sleeve of my new white top. Fiona had bought me it for no reason, 'because I thought you'd like it'. It was quite low-cut and I wished I'd more to fill it with.

I was the only person at our table under thirty. Apart from Dad and Fiona there were Fiona's parents – 'call us Henry and Pamela', they always said, as if making it clear that I wasn't to be confused with their *real* grandchild, but somehow I never could. Mr and Mrs Ross wasn't quite right either so I just never called them anything. Of course Molly, when she learned to speak, would be calling them Granny and Grandpa. Dad's parents had moved to Spain when they retired and Gran – Mum's mum – well, it was over a year since she'd died, even if it didn't feel like it.

'To Fiona!' everyone chorused and I sipped my champagne. The fizz made it easier to drink than most alcohol and I decided I could develop a taste for it.

Fiona laughed. She looked sparkly and happy. Usually she just slopped around in jeans but tonight she wore a blue dress. Only I knew that she'd had to lie on the bed to get it zipped up. I'd used Mum's straighteners on her blonde bob and helped her with her make-up.

Dad coughed when everyone had set their glasses down. 'I have another little surprise, darling,' he said.

Fiona looked at the new sapphire eternity ring on her left hand. 'Peter! You've given me enough.'

'Just a little treat,' said Dad, and held out a blue envelope.

I couldn't believe what it was – tickets for a weekend in Paris.

'Time we had a little break,' he said and gave her a really soppy smile.

'And we're having Molly, darling,' said Henry. 'So you and Peter can have a proper second honeymoon.'

Suddenly the champagne felt cold and gassy in my stomach and the salmon on my plate looked greasy and too pink. Ever since Dad moved out I had spent every weekend with him – first in the apartment on the riverside and then in the house he and Fiona had built on the site Henry and Pamela had given them for a wedding present. OK, I'd probably missed the very odd one – but basically that was what I did at the weekends, and I liked it. I didn't want *anything* to change.

* * *

Fiona swung her legs against the gate we were sitting on and sighed – a happy sigh. I tried to catch her mood. In the field a few horses in their winter rugs nosed the bare ground for the few bits of grass still sticking up through the mud. The greedier ones, like Joy, Fiona's mare, hogged the feeders at the gate, chewing on haylage. Flight, his rug splashed with mud where he'd been rolling, was standing still, eyes fixed on something in the distance. His lovely chestnut head was alert, ears pricked.

Look how lovely he is and how lucky you are, I scolded myself. Never mind that the show is only a week away. It'll be *fine*.

Fiona turned and smiled. 'You can't imagine what a treat this is,' she said. 'Just sitting here looking at the horses. No one demanding attention.'

'But you love Molly!'

'Course I do. To bits. But being someone's mother – well, it's just so full on. Nothing prepares you.'

Fiona always talked to me like that – like I was grown up. She never tried to do the stepmother thing, thank goodness. But she was nowhere near as much fun as she used to be. She used to give me riding lessons and show me how to do really good make-up and let me stay in her bed and watch DVDs with her when Dad was away. And all my friends were like, 'Your stepmother is just so *cool*.' But this was the first time since Molly was born that she'd been to the yard with me. And I was glad of her – there wasn't anyone my age at the yard. Cam was too busy to chat on Saturdays, and Tony didn't work weekends so there was just old Jim who always looked at me as if I was a spoiled brat just because he was paid to clean up after my horse.

'It might get harder when she's a stroppy teenager.'

'She won't *be* stroppy,' Fiona said firmly. 'She'll be charming, like her big sister.' She grinned.

Big sister. It still sounded strange. What would Molly be like when she was sixteen? I would be older than Fiona was now. Weird. It was hard to think of her as a person. I wondered if they would get her a pony when she was old enough. I wondered if Dad loved her more than me.

I didn't allow myself that thought *ever* so I was glad to have my attention caught by the slow clopping of unshod hooves. A small, plump woman led a dark brown cob with a bandaged foreleg round the yard below the field.

'Look,' I said. 'There's Sally with Nudge. Is she getting better?'

'Well, the vet said she could lead her in hand for twenty minutes a day. Let her stretch her legs. But it's still fifty-fifty whether she'll ever be sound again.'

'And if not?' I curled my foot tighter round the bar of the gate to keep my balance.

'She could breed from her – at least she's a mare.'

I tried to think of keeping a horse for years without being able to ride. No shows, no jumping, just a lame horse hobbling round a field. I shivered and looked for reassurance at Flight, healthy and sound, trotting up the field now as he caught sight of Nudge, who had always been his mate before the accident with barbed wire which had mangled her leg. He nickered and the cob lifted her head and squealed back.

'I thought of asking Sally to exercise Joy,' Fiona said. 'I'm not going to have time for a while.' She shifted on the gate and I remembered her talking about having stitches after Molly's birth. Gross. 'All Sally's spare cash goes on Nudge, and her vet's bills are horrendous. She might be glad of something to ride for nothing. Come on, let's go and ask her.'

I let my hair fall forward to hide my face. Cam had already asked *me* to let Sally ride Flight during the week, to keep him fitter for me to jump at the weekends. I'd said no. I hoped she hadn't told Fiona. 'Hold on, there's my phone. It's Mum. I'll catch you up.'

I'd already spoken to Mum at lunchtime. It wasn't like her to phone twice on a Saturday. Maybe she really did miss me.

But it wasn't that.

'Vicky,' she said, her voice really serious, 'I have something to tell you. Something bad.'

Chapter 3

DECLAN

The nurse is outside in the main ward but I catch most of what she's saying into the phone. 'Your sister-in-law, Theresa Kelly … alcohol … tablets …'

I can't hear Colette's half of the conversation. Just a long silence.

'Oh, no … got her in time … serious but stable …'

Silence.

I imagine Colette in her posh house, frowning at the phone and thinking, 'what has this to do with me?' I don't know. But they've kept asking me who they should contact and she's the only one I could think of. And when the nurse comes into the side ward where Mum lies wired up and twitching she says, 'Your aunt's on her way.'

Picturing Colette getting into her car and driving up here stops me thinking about Mum. A bit. I should sit nearer the bed. Touch her. But I can't. All those wires and drips. They keep telling me she'll be fine but she looks terrible. Not bluish any more but yellowy. I wonder how long until Colette gets here? She lives on the Malone

Road. That's dead far. I look at Mum. Look away. Cream walls, grey floor, sink. Twist a Coke can round in my hands. Concentrate on the coldness of it. Feel the stickiness where the Coke has spilled. Don't think.

The doorway fills up with them. The nurse, big and bossy; Colette, small, dark, uncertain-looking.

'They've pumped her stomach,' says the nurse. 'Just as well we got her in time.'

I don't meet Colette's eyes. I focus on Mum, marooned on the bed in the middle of the room. I sense Colette trying not to stare at the tubes and machines. Feel her eyes on me. The nurse's eyes on me. Asking, why did she do it? What did *you* do?

There's only one chair and I'm sitting on it. I turn my Coke tin round and round in my hands. Make myself look up and nod. I haven't seen Colette for ... must be more than a year. I'm always out when she calls round. Running the streets, as Mum would say.

She speaks first. 'Did you find her?'

I nod. Don't think. Don't remember.

'Did you phone for the ambulance?'

'Yeah.' I can't think of another thing to say. Is she here to see Mum or to take me to her house or both?

The nurse fusses round and then says, 'I'll leave you with her for a while then. But I think the doctor would like to speak to you.' She means Colette.

'OK,' says Colette.

'You have the chair,' I say, uncurling myself. My legs and back ache when I stand up. Colette is the same height as me.

'I'm sure there's another one somewhere. I could go out and have a look in the corridor.' She sounds like she wants out already.

'No, I will.'

Mum moans and mutters a bit, making me jump, but she doesn't open her eyes. I have to get out. 'I'll get the chair.'

I walk to the end of the ward even though there are plenty of chairs nearby and when I get back there's a man talking to Colette. I hover in the doorway, holding the chair in front of me like a shield.

'We'll keep her in for a few days,' he says. His words – tests, liver function, psychiatric assessment – wash over me. Is Colette going to take me home with her? I know they won't let me stay home on my own even though I'd be fine.

Colette pushes back out past me to find the nurse. I listen. She's giving her her phone number. 'I think I'd be as well taking him on home,' she says. 'There's nothing we can do here.' She comes back in and smiles at me. 'So it looks like you'll be coming home with me for a day or two.'

'Is that OK?'

'Course.' Her voice warms up a bit. 'We'd better go and pick you up some stuff.'

Walking out of the hospital is like leaving a dungeon. But out in the real world, driving up the Falls where the street lights are on, and on out to our estate, the facts come crashing back in. *She tried to kill herself.* Not that anyone's *said* that. They've said 'overdose' and 'alcohol' and 'sleeping tablets' but that's all. What will Colette tell Princess Vicky?

Mum's told me all about growing up next door to Colette. How she thought she was too good for everyone else in the street. How she stayed in and studied and never went out to play. They were best friends till Colette went to the grammar school and didn't bother about her any more. They sort of got back together when Mum started going out with Colette's brother – my dad. Gran always said Colette had brains to burn and I used to think that was a funny thing to say, like why would you burn your brain?

Colette turns off the main road. I always think our estate looks kind of unfinished even though it was built before Mum was born. It looks like someone just threw it at the side of a mountain and it clung on.

Our house is the same as every other house in the street. Maybe a bit scruffier. It never looked like this when Gran was here. It has a sad, empty look, but that's just because I know what's happened here. A *dead* look. I wonder what we'd be doing now if she *had* managed to kill herself. I shiver. I notice Colette noticing the long, trampled grass. A few crisp bags hang sadly around the doorstep.

Colette grew up in this house. What does it feel like, coming back? You can't tell from her face. In the hall she nearly trips over the Coke I bought earlier. I think about picking it up and putting it in the kitchen but it seems like a massive effort. If I bend down I think I'll just lie on the floor and not get up.

The living-room is dark now; the streetlight shining through the window doesn't show up the dirt but I can see Colette's eyes taking everything in. The grubby duvet without a cover, spilling onto the dirty carpet. An ashtray spewing butts on to the sticky-ringed coffee table. Smoky air. Bet Colette's house isn't like this.

'She sometimes sleeps down here,' I say, as if Colette has asked me a question. I pick up the duvet and back out of the room, hugging it. 'I'll take this upstairs and get my stuff.'

'What about turning on the light?'

'You need to punch in the code to the electric meter.'
I remember getting the card topped up. Feels like days
ago, not hours. I do it, then go up and grab a few things
and shove them in a plastic bag. When I come back down
she's in the kitchen. The light's too bright. The surfaces
are all crumby and slimy and the floor crunches under
my trainers. The pile of clothes on the floor in front of
the washing machine stinks. I want to tell her it's not
always like this but what's the point? She frowns at the
plastic bag and I narrow my eyes at her. Snobby bitch.

'You haven't brought much,' she says.

'You said it wouldn't be for long.' I try to keep the
hope out of my voice.

'No. But what about school?'

I can't tell her the trouble I'm in. So I go and get my
uniform.

All the way to Colette's house my throat gets tighter
and tighter. It's so obvious she doesn't want me. She's just
the type of person who does the right thing.

I've forgotten how huge their house is. In a posh, quiet
street with trees up the footpath. I trail behind Colette,
not sure where to put myself. The house is so clean it
makes me feel filthy. Bookcases, hippy sort of rugs, flowers. I follow her into the kitchen and she fusses around,
puts the kettle on. I'm knackered. The big clock on the
wall says it's nearly five but it feels like the middle of the
night. My eyes are gritty and when I slump into a chair
at the table I wonder if I'll ever have the energy to get out
of it again.

'I'll just go and sort out the guest room, Declan,' says
Colette. 'Make yourself at home.'

I force myself to stay awake and look round. It's a big

room, bright and clean but sort of cosy too. There's a row of cookbooks on a shelf. The kettle clicks off. If I don't stand up and walk around I'm going to fall asleep at this table. I trail over to the window. Big garden. Trees. There's a photo on the windowsill. Princess Vicky. On a horse. I forgot she had a horse. Imagine having your own horse. Spoiled bitch. She looks spoiled too: all tanned and blonde and hefty.

But the horse. Oh Jesus, the horse is amazing. Bright gingery-brown with a proud look. It's half turned away from the camera, a secret look in its eye. No one would mess that horse around. It shines too. Like a conker. I wonder what it feels like to touch.

'Oh, there's Vicky's pride and joy.'

I haven't heard Colette come back. I set the photo back and catch myself on. Horses. Gay.

'D'you want a cup of tea?'

I nod. My throat's so swollen that I can't speak.

'Something to eat?' Colette goes on, pouring water into a teapot.

I shake my head. 'No, I'm OK,' I manage to say. I don't think I'll ever eat again.

'Vicky won't be back until tomorrow evening. She goes to her dad's every weekend.' Her voice is too bright. 'That's where she keeps Flight – the horse. Well, at a livery stable nearby. Maybe she'll take you up to see him.'

What the hell's a livery stable? When she mentions Vicky she drums her fingers against her cup. I want to see Flight but not Vicky.

'Do you want to take your things upstairs? Maybe you should try to get a bit of a sleep. You look shattered. The guest – your room's the second on the left. Bathroom's just opposite. I've left clean towels on the bed.'

I force my legs upstairs. Step by step. All the doors on the landing are closed. The bathroom is so shiny I'm nearly scared to take a piss. The guest room is yellow, everything matching, a girl's room. I collapse on the fleecy bedspread and bury my head in a pillow. It's cool and smells like fresh air. I should take my trainers off, I think. But it's too much effort.

Chapter 4

VICKY

'It'll be fine, Vicky,' Fiona said when she hugged me goodbye, a bit awkwardly as she was trying to calm down a grizzling Molly at the same time. 'You might even enjoy having someone your own age in the house for a change.' She sounded *exactly* like Mum.

But Dad should know better.

'Come on, darling,' he said when the Merc purred to a smooth stop at the end of our driveway and I made no move to get out. I sighed and leaned back in my seat. He ruffled my hair. 'I don't suppose it will be for more than a few days. And who knows, maybe the charming Declan will have improved with age.'

Yeah, I thought, turning round to haul my rucksack out of the back seat. I bet! I wasn't sure exactly how much Mum had told Dad about Declan's little run-in with the law last year.

'And if he hasn't gone by next weekend at least you can escape to us,' Dad went on.

'*You'll* be in Paris,' I reminded him. I grumped out of

the car and up the drive. I didn't look back. Usually I waved until the car was out of sight. I hitched my rucksack higher on my shoulder, made sure Tigger was squashed down out of sight and let myself in through the back door.

The kitchen was warm and herby with the smell of Mum's special homemade pizza. She and The Hood were at the table.

'Hello, love.' Mum turned to smile at me. 'Here's Declan. I told you he was here for a few days.' She made it sound like he was on his holidays.

'Oh yes,' I said, as if I had just remembered. I hadn't planned how my voice should be and I was glad it came out cool and distant.

He nodded at me. 'Hiya,' he mumbled. I'd forgotten how rough his accent was.

I plonked my rucksack down.

'Good weekend?' Mum asked.

'So-so. Can you take me to the stables on Wednesday for a lesson? Oh, and Dad's going to Paris. So can you take me to the show as well?'

'Yes, I suppose so.' Usually she moaned at having to take me to the stables midweek, and she *hated* pulling the horsebox.

Declan had had his ear pierced since I'd last seen him. The thing that hadn't changed was how much he looked like Mum. Other than that, he just looked exactly like those steeky boys hanging round the bus stops, all shaved hair and shiny tracksuit bottoms.

Mum kept giving me a *haven't-you-forgotten-something?* look. I guessed what she was after – she wanted me to ask how Theresa was. But I didn't *care*. I hadn't even seen her since Gran's funeral. Before that, when Gran used to mind me sometimes, Theresa was always out. And I suspected Mum wasn't that keen on her either, even if she did have this thing about them being old friends and sisters-in-law and all that.

Declan kept his eyes on his plate. I noticed how little he'd eaten. *Would you feel like eating if your mum was lying in hospital?* asked a cool little voice in my head, but I didn't want to listen.

* * *

Monday morning, usual scramble. Except it was so weird, trying to do my normal getting ready for school stuff with him in the way. Mum had an en-suite so I was used to having the bathroom to myself. Today I suddenly remembered *he* was around and I had to dive back into my room and put my dressing gown on. Then when I got downstairs he was in the living-room with a bowl of cereal, watching TV. *I* was never allowed to do that! So I just went and got *my* cereal and took it into the living-room too, and by the time I realised Mum was having a private conversation with him it was too late to back out.

'Well, I'll phone your deputy head today,' she was saying. 'You should have told me earlier. But I don't suppose a day off will do you any harm.'

He was getting a day off school for no reason!

'Come on, Vic, love,' Mum said, turning round and looking at me properly. 'You'll be late.'

I didn't tell *anyone* at school, not even Fliss and Becca. If I didn't talk about him maybe he wouldn't exist. But when I got home there he was, sitting in the living-room watching TV as if he hadn't moved all day. And it was the corner of the sofa *I* liked, the nice squishy bit.

When I went upstairs to get changed, Mum was putting clean clothes away in my room for me. 'Try to make him welcome, Vic,' she said.

'I am.'

She gave me a look. 'How would you feel if *I* was in hospital and you had to go to stay with Theresa and Declan?'

'I'd go to Dad's. I wouldn't go *there* and you wouldn't even want me to.'

'You used to go all the time.'

'When *Gran* was there.' I yanked off my school tie and stepped out of my revolting green skirt. My shirt felt sticky even after one day. I threw it over the chair and Mum picked it up.

'I don't like the way you're behaving.'

'But he's *horrible*.' I had my back to her when I said this, rummaging in my drawers for my favourite old jeans. Then I remembered I'd left them at Dad's – I hated it when that happened. I threw on old trackies and a top.

'Don't be ridiculous, Vic. You've hardly said a word to him.'

'He doesn't speak to *me*.' I got out my French books and plonked myself down at the desk. She sort of gave up on me and I stayed upstairs until she called me for dinner. Spag bol. My favourite. I wondered if it was for my benefit or *his*. My phone bleeped and I got it out of my back pocket to look. 'WANT 2 MEET ME & BECS @ STARBUX? F xxx.' I read it out and was going to text back yes when Mum totally wrecked everything!

'Why don't you bring Declan along to meet your friends?'

I couldn't believe her! To be fair to him, he grunted something like 'Nah, you're alright.'

'Then no,' she said. 'It's a weeknight and your mocks are in a few weeks. And *if* you expect to go to the stables on Wednesday …'

I knew what that '*if*' meant – I was going to have to start being nice to him.

Chapter 5

DECLAN

Seven o'clock Tuesday morning. I scrabble under the pillow for the exercise book I shoved there last night and stare at the blank page. How do you write an apology letter? *Dear Emmet*. *Dear* is the kind of word you use for someone you like. I lean back against the headboard, chew the pen and look round the bedroom. All clean and yellow in the light from the bedside lamp. This is the third morning I've woken up here. I wonder how much longer I'll be able to put up with Princess Vicky without breaking *her* nose. *Dear Emmet*. I'm not sorry – Emmet McCann deserves more than a broken nose – but in a way I am. Because hitting Emmet was how it all started. Right, here goes. *Dear Emmet. I am sory that I hit you. Declan Kelly*. Short and sweet. And sort of true.

When I get to school I go straight to Payne's office.

He looks at me over his specs and holds the letter at arm's length. 'Two Rs in "sorry", Kelly. Not exactly fulsome, is it?'

I bite my lip.

Then he seems to get fed up. 'Registration,' he says. 'I'll see to this. And *don't* let me see you back in my office this term.'

School. Scuffed walls, smell of crisps and polish and feet. All the noise – teachers shouting names, pupils replying – is behind classroom doors. I push open the door of our classroom and Mr Dermott's voice trails off when he sees me. From the way some people look at me I know they know about Mum. Half the people in my class live round our way. I slink to the back and sit beside Cathal Gurney. I can see the ribbons of snotters and his wet, red, open mouth. No wonder no one ever wants to sit beside him.

When the bell goes I grab my bag as usual but Mr Dermott puts his hand out to stop me.

'Just a minute, Declan.' At least he calls me by my name. The likes of Payne just call you by your surname which is stupid because there's three Kellys in our class. I hang back. 'Sit down,' he says, pulling out a chair beside his desk.

I sit.

He pulls at his earlobe. He looks a bit like Homer Simpson, only ginger. 'Umm, Declan, just wanted a bit of a word.'

I get ready for the usual pep talk about fights.

'I had a phone call yesterday from your aunt. She ... well, she told me about your mum being ... um, in hospital.'

'Oh, right.' My cheeks burn.

'Don't worry,' he goes on, 'nobody else has to know. But if you're finding things a bit difficult, well, come and find me and we'll see what we can do.' He sounds embarrassed too. I wonder how much Colette's told him. I know I'll never in a million years go and find him, no matter what happens.

Seaneen Brogan is leaning against the wall opposite twisting a bit of hair round her hand. When she stands like that the first thing you notice is her tits in her tight school blouse. 'Right, Declan?' She walks beside me. 'Heard about your mum.'

'Not you too.'

'Sure you know my granny misses nothing.' Seaneen lives round the corner from me but her granny lives right across the street. She smiles at me and pulls her ponytail tighter. She has all this curly hair that she scrapes back off her face but wee frizzy bits always escape. 'Granny says she saw you going away in a blue car.'

'I'm staying with our Colette.' I might as well tell her.

'Her that married a Prod?' Without waiting for an answer she goes on, 'Is your mum going to be OK?'

God, what is it with this girl? I can't shake her off. She's on her way to Technology, like me, and she's obviously going to walk every step of the way with me, talking non-stop. But in a way I don't mind. Colette has been pretty nice to me but she's hardly mentioned Mum; it's like she doesn't exist even though she's the reason for me being there in the first place. And at least Seaneen doesn't look at me the way Princess Vicky does, like I'm *nothing*. She's prettier than Vicky too.

I see Emmet in the playground at break, surrounded by his mates, as usual. I wonder if he got the letter yet. I wish I hadn't spelled 'sorry' wrong. He gives me what I *think* is meant to be a dirty look, but it's hard to see what his fat gob is doing because his nose is still spread all over it. I hope it never goes back to normal. He's an ugly bastard anyway – you can tell he's going to be just like his da. Barry stubbed out a cigarette on the back of my hand once, when he found out I squealed on Emmet to the peelers. I still have the scar; why shouldn't Emmet?

Don't know what Mum sees in Barry. I know she gets cheap drink and fags and that off him, but I can't believe that's enough to make her keep going back to him. I don't make eye contact with Emmet. Even when one of his mates looks over, says something to him and they both laugh.

The bell goes at last and I trail in behind everyone to English with Psycho Sykes. *Macbeth*. Crap. But there's just this one thing that stays in my head. *What's done cannot be undone*. If I could undo breaking Emmet's nose. That's what started all this. If I hadn't done it ... if Barry hadn't come round to the house ... if I'd known Mum wasn't just sleeping off a hangover. If if if. I know it's all my fault. And Mum does too. Why else would she not even want to see me? She's been in three days and I haven't seen her since the first day. Colette tried to tell me it was the doctors' decision, that she should be left in peace or something but she's only saying that.

I can't think these thoughts. I shove them as far away as I can. It's like I have a wardrobe in my head, a really tall one, and I pile all these horrible thoughts on top of it, out of sight. I try to make sure they stay there by paying attention in every class, which makes the teachers give me very funny looks.

Chapter 6

VICKY

'You haven't forgotten about taking me up to Cam's tonight?' I asked Mum as we pulled out of the driveway. She had been giving me a lift to school all week, but early, so she could get across town to take Declan to his school. It was called St Something-or-other's – I'd never even heard of it – and you should have seen their uniform – cheap, nylon blazers with the badge tacked on with big stitches, and trainers instead of shoes.

'No, that's OK. But,' she went on, with a glance in the rear-view mirror at Declan in the back seat, 'Declan and I are going to see his mum after school. So it'll be a bit of a rush. You need to be ready, homework done and everything, when we get back.'

'Oh.' I hated coming home to an empty house. Then I thought it wouldn't be much fun for Mum either, hospital visiting. 'What about tea?'

'I'll leave something ready. A chilli or something. You might have to put it in the oven, though.'

'Did you remember to ask Dad about the horsebox?'

'Yes.' She sighed. If Mum hated towing the horsebox there was at least one thing she hated more: phoning Dad. Not that she'd ever said, but when I heard them on the phone their voices were weird. Sort of super-polite. It was hard to imagine they'd been married to each other for years.

We turned into the road where my school was. All you could see were lines of girls walking down the hill. Green skirts and grey blazers everywhere. Wool blazers.

'You don't need to take me right to the gate,' I said.

Mum looked puzzled. She could be slow to catch on. 'But sure I have to go all the way down anyway to get on to the Lisburn Road.'

'Yeah, well, I want to walk.' I caught sight of Fliss's long, dark pony-tail. Even with high heels on – Mad Max was always catching her but she kept on wearing them – she was tiny beside Niamh, who she was walking with. Niamh was tall, like me, but skinnier. 'Look, there's Fliss. I have to ask her about the physics homework.'

Fliss was looking at something on Niamh's phone. They were giggling. No way did I want them to look into the car and see *him* sitting in the back seat with his nylon blazer and his earring and his wee hard man haircut.

Mum sighed. 'OK, OK, I can pull in here. I'll leave you a note on the table if I need you to do any cooking. Don't forget to check. See you later, love. Got your PE bag?' She turned round to Declan. 'You might as well jump out and get in the front. No point in you sitting back there all the way to school.'

'See ya!' I leaped out and grabbed Niamh's arm before The Hood would have the chance to get out and be seen. 'Hey,' I said. 'That your new phone? Oh, you got the pink one. Cool.'

Niamh shot me this weird look. 'Duh. You saw my phone already. I got it last week.'

'Yeah, but I never looked at it properly.'

'Who's that getting into your car?' asked Little Miss Observant Fliss.

I sighed. 'Long story. You don't want to know.'

'He's a bit of all right, though, Vic,' said Fliss. 'Your mum got a secret toyboy or something?'

'Oh, you're so funny.'

Mum pulled away just then, but it was too late.

'He's just someone my mum's giving a lift to,' I said.

'So why've you gone all red?' pestered Niamh. 'Hey, I wish my mum gave lifts to good-looking boys.'

'Yeah, I like that dark, dangerous-looking type, don't you?' said Fliss.

'Thought you liked Niall? He's blond.' This was a bit mean because Niall was Niamh's twin and she wasn't meant to know Fliss had a crush on him.

'Hey, talking of boys, hope you've invited plenty of fit ones to your party,' I said. Niamh and Niall's joint birthday parties were legendary and her sixteenth was next week. The phone was an early birthday present.

'Yeah, is *Rory* coming?' Fliss asked, nudging me, getting her own back.

'Rory Marshall? From my street?' I tried to sound casual but it was my turn to blush.

'Yeah, he's on the rugby team with Niall. He asked Niall if he knew you.'

Wow! As far as I knew, no boy had ever been aware of my existence before. I'd had a crush on Patrick Scott at Pony Club Camp the summer before last but every time I saw him I used to get my reins tangled up and lose my stirrups.

'Hey, Vicky, you're going to walk into the gate. Too busy thinking about Rory? Tell your mum to come too and bring her toyboy,' said Niamh and they both giggled.

The party wasn't till next Friday, twenty-third of November. Today was only the fourteenth. There was no way he would still be with us.

Chapter 7

DECLAN

All day my guts shiver at the thought of seeing Mum. I want to. Don't want to. Don't know what I want. Except for Mum to be better and not drinking. And for Barry never to come near us again. And for me not to have made all this happen. *What's done cannot be undone.*

Seaneen Brogan hangs round me again. 'Is your ma getting home soon?'

'I dunno. Piss off. You're a nosy cow.'

Seaneen laughs. She has wee spiky teeth. 'I know,' she says. I think you would have to try pretty hard to offend her – not like Princess Vicky. Seaneen doesn't piss off either. She sneaks out at lunchtime to the chippie – not Fat Frankie's but the one at the school gates.

'You coming?'

'Nah.'

'God, you're no fun these days, Declan Kelly,' she says but she brings me back some chips and a cigarette. I haven't had a fag for ages. Smoking that cigarette is about the only time I forget about going to see Mum, but when

I get out of school there's Colette in her shiny blue Golf, sitting outside. I can see people giving me funny looks. A few people in our school get picked up in fancy cars – Emmet McCann for one – but not me.

'Good day?' she asks when I get in.

I shrug. Half the time I don't know what to say to her so I end up saying nothing.

She doesn't give up, though. 'Homework?' she says, starting the engine.

'Nah. Don't really get homework.'

'Lucky you. Vicky gets about two hours a night.'

'There's no point giving us homework. Nobody would do it.'

This is the longest conversation we've ever had. Too soon, though, she's parking the car in the big hospital car park.

'D'you want me to give you some time on your own with your mum?' Colette asks as we get near the ward. My legs get heavier with every step.

'Don't mind,' I say, which is a lie. I need her to stay.

'Well, I'll come in with you to say hello, and then we can see what you feel like.' Colette's carrying a Marks & Spencer's bag. I don't have anything.

Mum's in a normal ward. She still has a drip and she's a funny yellow colour but she's sitting up. I hold back from hugging her. I'm scared I might hurt her and I don't know if she's still annoyed. The last time I spoke to her I told her I wished she was dead. The last time I saw her she was unconscious. I keep *trying* not to replay those minutes before the ambulance came, when I thought she was dead, but sometimes I can't make them stay on top of the wardrobe where they belong.

'Well,' she says. Her voice is flat.

'Well,' says Colette.

'Alright, Mum,' I say.

Colette hands over the bag – it's got magazines and a nightie and stuff. Mum says thanks and they start on that boring women-talk, about the food in the hospital and how good the nurses are. I zone out and try not to stare at Mum. She hasn't met my eye yet.

Then Colette says she'll leave us on our own for a bit and here we are.

'I'm sorry,' I say. *Two Rs in 'sorry', Kelly.*

Mum's eyes fill with tears. I bite the insides of my cheeks hard. Please don't let her cry. Or me.

'Och no, love, *I'm* sorry,' she says. 'I didn't mean – I was just a bit depressed. Everything will be OK when I get home.'

'When?'

'They won't tell me. But you're OK, aren't you?' She gives me her pleading look.

'Yeah, fine.' I search for my most 'fine' voice.

'Colette feeding you well?' asks Mum, who half the time doesn't notice if there's nothing in the fridge.

'Yeah.' This isn't the whole truth. Colette's food is OK in a vegetably way but my throat tightens every time I try to swallow.

'And what about Vicky?'

'She's OK.' This isn't even a tiny bit true. Vicky is a Class A Bitch. 'She's taking me up to see her horse tonight. We're going to some showjumping thing on Saturday.'

'Showjumping!' For the first time her voice loses that flat, dead tone. 'Where's that at?'

'Dunno.' There's no point asking me things like that. I never know where anywhere is. Until last week I always thought the Malone Road was about ten miles away.

Sometimes Colette used to phone Mum and invite her over to her house, and Mum always used to say the same thing, 'Aye, it's OK for her with her fancy car. How could I be trailing away over there?' So I grew up thinking it was really far. Plus I thought it was all Prods but there's a big Catholic church and all so it mustn't be.

'And what about school?'

'Haven't been in any trouble.' This *is* the whole truth. I don't mention Emmet and neither does she.

'Good,' she says. Her face is all pulled down with tiredness. I wish Colette would come back. Mum closes her eyes and I pick up one of the magazines and read some crap about Victoria Beckham. Mum is as skinny as Victoria Beckham. You can see her bones at the top of her nightie. It's minging.

At last we're on our way back to Colette's. It seems far because we get stuck in loads of traffic jams.

'She looks a bit better, doesn't she?' Colette says when the silence gets too loud.

Better than what? I think but she's doing her best so I just go, 'Yeah.'

Colette looks at the clock on the dashboard. 'God, this traffic's terrible. Vicky's supposed to be at the stables for seven. I hope she got my note about putting the chilli in the oven.'

When I think about going to the stables I feel two things. One, that it's going to be *crap* having to go some-where with Princess Vicky; and two, that tonight I'm going to see a horse. For some reason, ever since I saw that photo of Vicky's horse, I've kept on thinking about it. When those memories of last weekend threaten to fall off the top of the wardrobe, I imagine riding the horse. Going faster than anything.

It's a rush to get out of the house again after the chilli and Vicky moans the whole way there that she doesn't like riding straight after tea.

'So, how's your mum?' she asks me, but not as if she cares, just as if she wants to know how soon she can get rid of me.

I shrug. Not going to talk to her just because she suddenly decides to talk to me.

It's about fifteen minutes' drive to the stables. I don't see where we're going because it's dark but pretty soon we're on twisty, up-and-down roads with no street lights.

I thought the stables would be big and posh but we drive into quite a small farmyard sort of thing. Horses start neighing when we get out of the car.

'Flight, baby!' says Vicky, leaping ahead of us into this big shed thing.

Colette turns to me and smiles. 'OK?' she says. 'D'you like horses?'

'Dunno,' I say. I get out and follow her across the yard into the shed.

In real life Flight is even better than in the photo. I've hardly ever been near a horse before. Only once but I didn't get up close because one of the gypsies came out and chased me. It was one time I had a fight with Mum and I took off. After a bit I sort of forgot about the fight and I just wanted to see how far I could run. I left the estate behind and ran on and on. Way up on to the Glen Road – further than I'd ever been. I was only about eleven. And I came to the gypsy camp. It was a real tip, all rubbish and old cars. But there was a horse. It had a rope tied round one of its legs and it was just standing there eating grass. I crossed the road to go and see it. It was a nice horse, black and white with big hairy feet. It looked round at me with a bit of grass hanging out of its mouth and I slowed down in case I scared it. Then I heard someone yell, 'Oi, you! Clear off, you wee shite!' I ran back down the hill. That's the last time I saw a horse.

Vicky's horse is sleek and shiny. He looks down his nose at me over the stable door. I stretch out my hand to let him sniff me and he curves his neck to reach down into my hand. When he sees it's empty he sort of loses interest in me, but he lets me stroke his face. His face is like velvet.

'Isn't he gorgeous?' Vicky says. For the first time she smiles at me.

'Yeah. He's ...' I want to say amazing, unbelievable, beautiful. 'He's OK.'

Colette and I do a bit of standing about getting in the way while Vicky fusses around Flight, brushing him and putting on his saddle and that. I try to look bored.

A thin woman with short red hair comes up leading a tiny black pony. 'OK, Vicky?' she says. 'Ready in the school in five minutes? I'm just putting Hero in and I'll be straight down. Warm him up, both reins, while you're waiting.' She talks fast but posh. She nods at me and Colette and strides off with the wee pony.

Vicky comes out of the stable, wearing a riding hat, and Colette and I jump sideways to give her space to swing herself up on to Flight's back. When I see her sitting up there, all easy like a cowboy, I'm so jealous I could kill her.

For a balls-freezing hour Colette and I lean on the gate of a big sandy field thing with spotlights all round it and watch Cam making Vicky and Flight do stuff. Some of it looks easy – just going round in circles – but I guess by the look of concentration on Vicky's face when she's doing the smallest circles that it's harder than it looks. Then Cam puts up some jumps. They look huge to me but Flight clears them all with a flick of his tail. After some of them he kicks up his heels as if he's enjoying himself.

'OK, I'll put these up to a metre,' Cam shouts. 'Now watch the stride coming into the gate.'

I've only seen horses jumping on TV. Vicky looks nicer when she's on Flight. Half the time I forget it's her and just enjoy watching the horse jumping. Then I remember what a bitch she is and that's when I get so jealous I could run up and pull her off the horse and gallop off on him myself.

Except I haven't got a clue how to.

Chapter 8

VICKY

After tea on Friday I settled down to give my tack a good clean. Mum and Declan were at the hospital so the house was quiet, making being there on a Friday evening instead of at Dad's seem even weirder.

As I rubbed soap into my bridle I had snakes in my stomach thinking about putting it on Flight next day at the show. There was something so scary about jumping as part of a team, with everyone relying on you. I saw myself falling off, forgetting the course, having three refusals at the first jump – every disaster you can imagine.

I heard Mum and Declan come in, then him going upstairs – good; I could have some time with Mum.

She looked into the kitchen. 'Any chance of getting in to make a cup of tea?'

I looked round. Bits of leather were draped over every chair back and the air was sweet with oil and saddle soap. 'Just need to put my bridle together again and polish my boots.'

'Give me the boots and I'll do them for you.'

Mum pretty much kept out of the horsey side of my life but I quite enjoyed chatting to her while we polished and rubbed.

'Nervous?' she asked.

I nodded. 'But Flight was brilliant on Wednesday, wasn't he? Did you see the way he cleared the gate?' When I remembered the feeling of Flight and me jumping on Wednesday, like we understood each other for the first time, like we were a team, I had a blast of confidence.

'Well, it always looks terrifying to me.'

'Mum, can you take me to the yard really early? Like eight o'clock? Wainwright says we have to plait.'

'Your hair?' Mum wrinkled her face in surprise.

I giggled. 'Flight's *mane*.' I tried not to let the nerves creep into my voice. I'd never plaited Flight before and I didn't know if he would stand OK. Normally Fiona did all that sort of stuff for me. 'Will you *hate* coming to the show tomorrow?' I asked.

'Course not! I'm really proud of you. I just get so nervous watching you go over those huge fences. And you know I never know what to say to that horsey crowd. But at least I'll have company. '

'What d'you mean?'

She rubbed hard at my black leather boot. 'Declan, of course.'

The snakes wriggled back into my stomach, only this time they had fangs. 'Mum! I'm not jumping with him watching.'

'Don't be silly' Mum looked at me in surprise. 'I can't just leave him here on his own all day.'

I spat on Flight's bit and started rubbing a cloth over it hard to shine it. 'You mean you wouldn't trust him?'

'*No*, I mean it'd be a very rude way to treat a guest.'

I tried a different tack. 'Well, he'll *hate* it. You know how much hanging around there is.'

Mum shook her head. 'He seemed to enjoy watching you on Wednesday. Anyway, he's coming and that's that. Maybe he can help you with Flight. You know I'm useless.'

* * *

'*Stand*, you big pig!' I felt pretty useless myself. I tried to jerk on Flight's headcollar rope, but my fingers were sweaty with trying to get the tiny rubber bands round the uneven red plaits I had *finally* managed to coax his thick mane into. He pulled away and laid his ears flat and the last plait sprang out into a useless frizzy pompom. I dropped the plaiting bands.

'Damn!' I could have cried. This was just too difficult. I couldn't manage without Fiona. How was I going to survive the show? The snakes started somersaulting inside me.

'Having trouble?'

I stuck my head over the half-door of Flight's stable. It was Sally. 'I need to plait him for Mossbrook. We're jumping in the schools' provincial league,' I explained. I hoped she would be impressed.

She looked in and laughed. 'Not with those plaits!'

'I've never done it before,' I admitted. 'Fiona's away and Cam's busy.'

'I'll help.' She was already in the stable, pulling out my pathetic attempts. Flight looked at her in a long-suffering way. 'Poor old son,' she said. 'It's a bit boring, isn't it? Never mind, we'll soon have you looking gorgeous.'

She made it look easy. Flight had been as jittery as a rabbit with me but with Sally he just stood with his lip drooping and never moved a hoof. I handed her the mane comb and bands when she asked for them.

'I've been riding Joy this week,' Sally said.

'Oh yeah. Fiona said.'

I felt a bit guilty thinking about how much I didn't want her to ride Flight.

'OK, all done.' She slapped Flight on the shoulder. He looked amazing. He flexed his neck as if he knew it and Sally gave him a Polo mint.

'Thanks, Sally, I owe you one,' I said. I'd ask Mum to get her a bottle of wine.

'No worries.' She went off to see to Nudge.

Old Jim came grumbling into the yard pushing a wheelbarrow. 'You still in that stable?' he called.

'Well, it is *my* stable,' I pointed out.

'I need to get the beds finished. Can't muck out if you're standing there.' He frowned at me over his wheelbarrow.

'You can do it later. I'll be away pretty soon. I just have to –'

'I won't have time later. If I can't get in to do it in the next five minutes you can do it yourself.' Grumpy old git.

'That's not what my father pays full livery for,' I said. Jim looked at me with his mouth open and my cheeks burned. Where had that come from? That's the sort of thing I *thought* from time to time, but never actually *said*. And I'd never have said it to Cam.

It was probably lucky that I looked up to see Mum's car pulling into the yard.

She had her usual panic about getting the box hitched up. 'I can never remember what goes where,' she admitted when Cam, thank goodness, took pity on us. The back of the car was packed with Flight's stuff – gleaming tack, sweat rug, boots – and my show jacket, white jodhpurs and stuff like that. I was paranoid about forgetting something. Declan would just have to fit in round it as best he could.

I'd only had Flight in the box a few times, and he'd loaded OK, but of course today was the day he decided to make a fuss. And Cam was late for a private lesson so she had to leave us to it. We tried everything – a bucket of feed, a lunge whip – but he just kept pulling back and digging his feet in.

Mum stood around looking nervous.

'Mum, could you help?' I begged. 'I'm going to try a rope round his backside.'

She drew back. 'Vicky, you know I'm not very –'

Declan stepped forward. 'I will.'

Well, I didn't have much choice. I showed Declan what to do and whether our teamwork defeated Flight or whether he just got bored fighting, he gave in and sauntered up the ramp.

'Brilliant!' I said. Declan grinned at me. It was the first time I'd seen him smile.

It was already half twelve and then we lost another five minutes before we even got to the end of the road, as Cam's neighbour Stanley's cows had got out and were mooing and crapping all over the road. Even from the front seat I could hear poor Flight neighing in alarm.

Mossbrook was an hour away, cross-country round all the wee twisty roads. If I'd been with Dad or Fiona as usual we'd have chatted the whole way about who might be there and how Flight might jump and what the course might be like, but obviously I couldn't do that with Mum.

Apart from that it was only about the third time she'd pulled the box. Her fingers looked tight on the wheel and her mouth was tight too, with concentration I supposed. She is doing this for *you*, I reminded myself. There must be a million things she would rather do on a Saturday. I wanted to turn and tell her how much I appreciated it, but I couldn't, not with *him* there behind me.

Mum was driving the car like a hearse. The wipers swished like they had all day – but *we* hadn't!

'Mum, we need to get there *today*,' I pointed out. 'You're only doing forty five.' So much for being grateful. I knew I sounded like a brat. But the team would be waiting for me. And I was so scared about letting them down, letting Flight down. I imagined having to phone Dad in Paris and tell him we'd had three refusals or forgotten the course or demolished everything. I could imagine him reminding me that Flight had cost four thousand pounds. I shivered. Was I really ready for this?

Chapter 9

DECLAN

The car park is packed with lorries and trailers. Horses in bright, fleecy rugs are backed down ramps, snobby girls – and a few boys – with loud voices and shiny boots run round with saddles and stuff and over it all there's the noise of hooves and shouts and shrill neighs. It's like the Grand National or something. Colette backs away when two huge horses nearly go over the top of us, but I'm not scared. There's too much to see. Colette dashes off to find Vicky's teacher. Vicky hauls Flight out of the trailer and ties him up.

He looks round with goggling eyes and screeches at the other horses.

'Quit it!' yells Vicky. 'Look, can you hold him while I tack up?'

She thrusts a rope into my hand. She says it like I'm her slave, but I take the rope. Flight pulls a bit; I have to hold on really tight. Not one of the horses milling round is a patch on him. I stroke his neck while Vicky tries to fasten these boot-like things round his legs. His skin is warm, darkening in the rain. He paws the tarmac and Vicky hits him a slap that makes him poke his nose into the air and lay his ears flat against his head. I wonder if he likes Vicky. Do horses like people?

She doesn't say a word to me, not even thank you. She just grabs the reins and springs up. Flight prances off before she has her other foot in the stirrup and she swears and then kicks him into what I think is a trot.

I don't want to follow her but I don't know what else to do so I lock the car and mooch along behind her. She's riding round a big sandy field like the one at Cam's. I lean on the fence. There are about six horses in it already and they're all flying round really fast and jumping two big fences. Flight pounds up to the first fence and stops dead. Vicky goes up his neck, hauls him round and gives him three ringing whacks on the arse. I don't want Vicky to think I'm interested enough to watch her but what else do you do at a horse show? A big black horse with hairy legs trots past, nostrils flaring red. A boy's riding him. They leap the fences like they could clear a house and the boy hardly moves in the saddle.

'Hey.' I turn to see Colette. 'I've got her number. Mrs Wainwright says she can jump last. She's too late to walk the course but she can watch the others.'

None of this means anything to me so I just go, 'Oh, right.' Flight's jumping now but he and Vicky still don't look the way they did at Cam's on Wednesday. Vicky pulls up beside us. Flight is sweaty and I can feel his hot breath on my cheek.

Next minute we're surrounded by three girls on gorgeous horses. Like Vicky, they're all dolled up in black jackets. A posh, wrinkly teacher joins them. 'Vicky, we're the next team to go,' she says. 'Mansfield have just started. Come in and watch them; you need to learn the course. And *hurry up.*' I try to imagine Payne or Sykes spending their Saturdays with their pupils and I can't. Dermott, though – he would. Not that our school would have a showjumping team. Maybe a joyriding one. They all ignore me and as they ride off together I hear the tallest girl, whose horse is pure white, say to Vicky, 'That your boyfriend?'

'Piss off.'

Colette and I follow them into this huge barn thing. Half of it is taken up by a ring full of coloured jumps like something off the Olympics. There's sandy, sawdusty stuff on the floor, a smell of horse shit and the pounding thump of hooves as a brown horse flies round the jumps. Someone opens the gate and the horse storms out past us, making Colette shrink back. Its nostrils are red and it's huffing like a dragon.

'And that was a lovely clear round for Jamie Spence on Bumblebee,' says the commentator. It's like I've stumbled into a different world. It's weird but I like it: the noises and the smells and the amazing speed and power of what's happening in the ring.

Vicky leans on the ringside fence, her legs massive in tight white trouser things, muttering, 'Upright, rustic, down the middle for the double, number 4, number 5, that's a tight turn.' She doesn't even notice us. Her teacher holds Flight, rubbing his pink nose.

'You want a cup of tea, Declan?' says Colette. 'Vicky'll be on soon.'

'I don't mind.' I don't want to leave the horses, but I'm freezing. 'Will I keep our places here?'

'Good idea.' She smiles at me. 'Plenty of milk, no sugar?'

'Yeah.'

A week ago she wouldn't have known that's how I like my tea. Probably in another week I'll be back home and she'll have forgotten.

'And last to jump for Mansfield Grammar is Patrick Scott on Dan.'

It's the black horse. He trots past me, quiet, ears pricked. Next to Flight he's my favourite. I like his shaggy legs. He looks like a carthorse until he gets going and then he looks magic. Patrick Scott hardly moves in the saddle even though Dan is flying round at a gallop and clearing every jump with masses to spare. He pulls up at the gate, puffing but obedient, and I wish I was Patrick Scott.

'So it's clear all the way for Mansfield. And that looks like the team to beat. The next team to jump is Elizabeth Brent School. First to go is Katie Maguire on Lucky Clover.'

'There you go.' Colette pushes a polystyrene cup into my hand. It's lovely and warm and the tea, even though it's minging, heats me up.

Katie Maguire looks pretty good. There's one moment when her horse skids but she gets it back on track and jumps everything clear. The next girl goes so fast I can hardly see what's going on but the commentator says, 'Clear round.'

'Only one more before Vicky.' Colette blows on her tea.

'D'you hate watching her?'

'I think about all the things that can go wrong. I know I shouldn't but it always looks so dangerous.'

Just then the horse in the ring – a black and white one – collides into a jump, knocking it flying. The girl scoots up its neck, swings in mid air, then lands in the middle of the poles with a crack.

'Ugh. See what I mean?' Colette looks away.

'It's OK. She's getting back on.'

'Blast!' It's Vicky's teacher. She and Vicky are just behind us now. 'OK, Vicky, we'll have to discard Aoife's round. So you *must* go clear if we're going to have a chance.'

'Just put the pressure on!' But she's smiling, stroking Flight's sweating neck.

'And that's a very unfortunate elimination for Aoife Martin. Next to go is Victoria Moore on Flight of Fancy.'

Colette gives a wee shiver beside me. Flight is shiny and prancy in the ring. They have to trot round for ages while people fix up the scattered jump, but finally a bell rings and they're pounding down the far side of the ring to the first jump. Easy. Next one. Flight hesitates, Vicky kicks and they're over. Now she turns down the middle and the next jump is towards us. Over. And the next. Every time they land safely Colette sighs a little breath of relief. Gran used to watch me playing football years ago. I wonder if she used to breathe like that. But I suppose football's not dangerous like showjumping. A rattle, a gasp and 'That's four faults,' and Vicky rides out past us, looking back over her shoulder at the jump. I don't know if she's glad to have only four faults – why four? This seems a very complicated sport – or annoyed not to be clear.

'Sorry,' she pants. 'Got the stride wrong coming into the second part of the double.'

'You'll need to work on doubles before next time,' says the teacher, but she looks pleased enough. 'OK, so we finish on four. We need to finish on nought next round, or we've no chance. If we finish on nought and Down College get at least eight faults, we could be second.'

They do it all again, and this time the girl who fell goes clear and so does the speed merchant, but Katie's horse stops at one jump which, for some reason I can't understand, is three faults. Then it's Vicky again. I can see by the way her mouth is set that she's determined to go clear. And she does. Trotting out of the ring, out of breath, her face is grinning. If you didn't know her you would think she was nice.

'Well done, love,' says Colette. 'Well done, boy.' She reaches out her hand to pet Flight's neck, a bit gingerly. Flight blows down his nostrils at us. I *wish* Vicky would let me ride him. Oh well, this time next week I'll be home in Tirconnell Parade and forget all about horses. It's been OK, today, but it's not *real*. It's not my *life*.

'Well done,' I say anyway, and Vicky looks at me like she's surprised.

'Oh,' she says. 'Thanks.' And she actually smiles.

Then there's a lot of hanging about talking about scores and willing the other teams to knock fences down and in the end Vicky's lot do come second. Vicky tries to explain it to Colette on the way back. 'You see, we're second in the league but that's only the first show. There's two more. We *could* win the league, with a bit of luck.'

The yard's dark and deserted when we get back. We have to do loads of stuff to get Flight ready for bed. He's sweated up again on the journey. There's shit all over the horsebox and Colette says Vicky had better clean that out tonight too.

'I haven't *time*. I need to do his *feed*.'

'I'll do it,' I hear myself saying. I don't know anything about horses but even I can hose shit out of a horsebox.

'No,' Vicky says. 'Mum will. You walk Flight round until he's dry.'

I take the rope and lead Flight round and round the yard. When I'm walking away from them it's like there's just me and Flight in the world. Our breath is like smoke in the dim light from the open shed. Flight walks quietly with his head down. I suppose he's knackered after all that jumping. I could walk him round all night but after ten minutes Vicky says, 'He'll do now.' Then, as an afterthought, 'Thanks.'

Turning into their street half an hour later I realise that I haven't thought about Mum for hours, without having to *try* not to.

As soon as we get home, Vicky dashes up for a shower.

'Come and help me make a salad,' Colette says. 'We're just having pasta.'

She gets me to chop these weird pepper things. They have a sweet, wet smell and for the first time in ages I'm starving.

Then she says, 'Declan, there's something I need to talk to you about.' She sounds dead serious. 'It's your mum.'

The knife freezes in my hand. My heart slams my ribs.

'I had a word with her doctor yesterday. Declan – I'm sure you must know your mum has a problem –'

'She's a drunk.'

'Well, um, the doctors feel she's not quite ready to go home yet.'

'So does she have to stay in the hospital?' I push the peppers into a neat pile on the chopping board.

'Not exactly. They're going to transfer her to a special unit.'

'The *mental*?'

'It's a psychiatric unit, yes. They specialise in addiction.'

'How long for?' My voice comes out croaky.

'The programme is a month.'

A *month*! 'Do I have to stay here?'

'Well, yes.' She smiles. 'I mean, your mum would like you to, and so would I, of course.'

I don't know if she means it. But I know one thing. 'Vicky…?'

'I haven't told her. Not before I'd told you.'

'She won't like it.' Might as well say what we're both thinking.

Colette looks at the lettuce she's chopping. 'She might be a wee bit jealous. She's used to having me all to herself. But it isn't for long.'

How can she say a month isn't long? Vicky isn't just *a wee bit jealous*. She hates my guts. And I hate hers. I hand Colette the peppers. I'm trapped. A month of Vicky treating me like shit. A month of trying to be invisible. While Mum –

'Did Mum really say she wanted me to stay with you?'

'Yes. I phoned her this morning. She says you told her you liked it OK here.'

I shrug.

'Declan, I know this is hard for you. You don't know us very well. I'm not as close to your mum as I used to be. Maybe this will bring us closer again.'

'You used to come to our house a lot. Gran used to mind Vicky.'

'Yes, when I was doing my library training. *And* before that. We grew up together, really.'

'I know.' I can hear Vicky scrabbling about upstairs,

doors opening and shutting. I have to ask before she comes down. 'Will she get better?' I sound like a child.

'I don't know, love.' She's never called me this before. 'But she'll get specialist help. Counselling and therapy. She *wants* to go, Declan. She's admitted there's a problem.'

I hear the thumps of Vicky running down the stairs.

'Don't tell her in front of me!'

Colette smiles. 'OK. Hi, love.' She keeps the smile on as Vicky flings into the room. 'I thought we'd have some bubbly to celebrate your success.'

'Champagne?' Vicky looks impressed.

'Well, sparkling wine with cranberry juice. It's in the fridge.'

'Cool.'

It's cold and fizzy and gushes out the tops of the glasses. They both laugh. I wonder if Vicky'll be laughing so much when Colette tells her I'm going to be around for another month.

Chapter 10

VICKY

'A *month*!' I stared in despair at the wet, Sunday-quiet road outside the car. 'No *way*!'

'I'm not asking you; I'm telling you.' Mum indicated right into Fliss's road.

'But *you* don't even want him.'

She didn't deny it. 'He's family.'

'*Family*! God, Mum, you sound like someone from *EastEnders*.'

'And you, miss, are going to have to start being nicer to him.' The 'miss' meant she was seriously pissed off.

'It just *spoils* everything.' I thought she was being nice, giving me a lift to Fliss's in the rain, but it was only a chance to capture me and talk about *him*.

'It's much harder for him, you know.'

'How?' I knew how, really. It was like there was Nice Me – normal me, that is – and then there was Nasty Me. And I knew it was Nasty Me saying 'how?' like that. I just didn't know how to shut her up.

'Oh, come on, Vic. His mum's in hospital; he doesn't

really know us; you're treating him like a leper. Do you not feel even a *bit* sorry for him?'

'Nope.' I yanked off my seatbelt. We were nearly at Fliss's and I wasn't going to hang around and listen to this for a second longer than I had to. 'Anyway,' I said, 'I don't think he cares about his mum. He's too –' I tried to think of a word. '*Hard.* Like the other day, you were talking about his mum and he just kept on watching TV. He was just like, *whatever.*'

'People can feel things without showing it. I remember when my dad died.'

Oh no, I thought, please don't!

'It was so sudden. Just like Gran. I cried for days. I cried till my face was raw.' She stopped the car and gave a sort of artificial little laugh.

'And?' Images of Mum or Dad dying crowded into my mind. Horrific. I tried to push them away. Mum was only thirteen when her dad died.

'And Gerard didn't. Not a tear. You should have seen him, Vicky. He handed round tea at the wake, talked to people. He even did a reading at the funeral. And all Mum and I could do was cry. But then a week later Theresa and I sneaked out to the shed – Dad's shed, we always called it – for Theresa to get a smoke and there he was, in the middle of all the junk and dad's tools and stuff crying his eyes out.' She sounded so sad – I didn't know if it was thinking about her dad or about Gerard, who died in a car crash when he was twenty two and Declan was a baby. And in a minute she might start talking about *Gran* dying. Declan had cried enough at Gran's funeral but that had probably been guilt. I had a sudden memory of it, my only time in a Catholic church, watching Declan, Mum, Theresa – everyone but me – say all the prayers and stand up and kneel and everything all at the right time, and me feeling totally out of it. Even though she'd been my gran too.

Anyway. 'Can I get out now?'

She wouldn't let up. 'I'm serious. For a start, you can take him with you to the yard. Otherwise' – as I opened my mouth to argue – 'I won't take you near the place.'

'But Cam's giving me a lesson on Wednesday. Mum, that is *so* unfair!'

'I didn't say I wouldn't take you. But Declan's going too. I think he's taken to Flight.'

That was another thing I didn't want to think about. The way he looked at Flight yesterday. Like he *wanted* him. Then I remembered how he'd helped me – and I'd hardly even thanked him. I knew I couldn't win. 'Well, I suppose. Can I go now?'

'Yes. But remember – well, just remember. And back for tea. I want you to come with us tonight.'

Then she let me go, finally.

* * *

I sat in the back of the car, plugged into my iPod and ignoring Mum and Declan in the front, though it was clear I wasn't exactly missing much.

Mum parked the car in a lay-by opposite a tatty terrace of houses. It was so different from Sandringham Park that it felt like a different city. It was still raining which didn't make the streets any nicer, though I guessed they would look grotty even on a sunny day. The sun would just show up the graffiti more, and the litter and the bricked-up houses. They weren't all like that – some of them were actually very smart, with fresh paint and immaculate gardens, the way Gran's had been. A little statue of the Infant of Prague used to sit on the windowsill and I always thought he was welcoming people. I wondered where the Infant of Prague had gone. There was nothing like that in our house. Mum seemed to have given up on religion when she married Dad, I suppose with him being a Protestant. Not that he was religious either.

I sighed my way out of the car after Mum and Declan. It didn't take three people to pick up more of Declan's manky stuff.

'OK, let's go,' Mum said, clicking the remote to lock the car. She shot an uneasy glance at a couple of steeky-looking lads hanging round on the corner.

We trooped up the path to the peeling front door. Declan was holding Mum's old gym bag, banging it against his legs.

'What about her, love?'

We all swung round. An old lady shuffled to the gate of the house opposite. She had a snipey face and a bad greyish-ginger perm. Declan and I both shrank in behind Mum – it was the closest I'd ever been to him – while the old bag leaned on her gate.

She was a nosy old cow but Mum told her as little as she could – just that Theresa wouldn't be home just yet and that Declan would be staying with us.

'And where is it you are exactly these days, love?'

'Malone.'

'Oh. Very nice.' Then her harsh voice went all creamy. 'Och, it's a pity of her too, isn't it?'

Mum made a non-committal noise.

'Sure her and our Mairéad used to be as thick as thieves. Our Mairéad would still call to see her, you know; sure she's only round the corner. But she says she'd got a wee bit *funny* lately. You know, not answering the door and that. I think she was a wee bit depressed.'

Well, Nobel Prize for psychology to you, I thought and I felt an unexpected stab of sympathy for Declan having to listen to this. I took out my phone and started texting Fliss to show I wasn't earwigging and kind of jiggled my feet a bit to encourage Mum to hurry up.

'She liked a man around, didn't she?' the old woman went on.

'I really couldn't say,' Mum said, all prim.

Declan leaned against the front door and shot the old bag a pretty mean look. I didn't blame him.

'And how are you getting on at your auntie's?' she asked him.

Declan grunted.

Mum leaped in. 'Fine. Vicky here is just the same age.' She made it sound like the Waltons.

'Look, can I go in?' Declan said. 'I have to get my stuff. Only you have my key —'

'Here you go.' Mum handed him a key and he let himself in.

As soon as Declan was away the old bag lowered her voice – like she was getting down to the *real* gossip – but as she wasn't exactly softly spoken I didn't miss a word.

'Och, I think *he's* settled down a bit since the trouble. That lad who was with him, now, he was bad news – that Emmet McCann.' She sniffed. 'But your Declan seems to have kept his nose clean.' She sounded like she regretted this. 'Mind you, the kids round here's desperate these days. I was only saying to our Mairéad the other night...'

'And how *is* Mairéad?' Mum interrupted.

I left them to it and went into the house. The hall

smelled of smoke and cooking fat and seemed to have shrunk in the last year. The stairs rose straight up to a narrow landing. I could see an open door and a light so I supposed Declan was in his bedroom. The living-room was tidy enough but the flowers on the wallpaper clashed with the pink flowers on the three-piece suite. They must always have done, but I'd never noticed.

'It's not as nice as when Gran was here,' I said to Mum when she *finally* followed me in.

She looked round. 'No,' she said. 'I suppose Theresa has her own ideas.' *Ideas?* Looked to me like the only idea Theresa had was to do as little as possible. I picked up a photo from a shelf to change the subject. 'Is that you?' It was a wedding group. Mum was the bridesmaid in a salmon-pink dress that did nothing for her.

She looked. 'Hmm, Theresa's wedding. Theresa and I are the only people still alive from that photo.'

'Mum! That's a bit morbid.'

'It's true, though. Look, isn't Declan the picture of his dad?'

'I suppose.' I set the photo back. 'So, how come Theresa lived with her mother-in-law? Is that not a bit weird?'

Mum shook her head. 'She moved in after Gerard was killed. Declan was only a baby. I suppose they looked after each other.'

I followed Mum's gaze around the poky room. 'It's a bit grim, isn't it?'

'Shh!'

'It's OK, he's upstairs. And I don't mean it in a horrible way.'

'Well, don't let Declan hear you,' Mum warned.

'I'm glad *you* moved away from here.' I didn't just mean the house; I meant the whole skanky estate.

'I was luckier.'

'You weren't *just* lucky. You told me you worked dead hard.'

She smiled. 'I did. But I was clever too. I passed the 11+. And I don't know why but somehow I always wanted out of here. Gerard and Theresa both liked it OK.'

'So why doesn't Theresa get a job and move somewhere nicer?'

'Well, maybe she will when she's better,' Mum said. She didn't sound convinced. 'But sweetie, next time you feel like being mean to Declan or putting that snobby face on, just remember this is what he'll be going to back to next month.' We were both whispering.

'OK! God, Mum! Lighten up a bit.'

'I'm just going upstairs,' she said.

I turned on the huge TV – it was the only new-looking thing in the room – and settled down to flick through the channels.

Chapter 11

DECLAN

Feels like months since I was in my own room. I sit on the bed and look round. The dark patch on the blue carpet where Emmet and I spilled the whiskey he nicked from his dad when we were twelve. The torn bits of wallpaper behind the bed that I pick at when I'm bored. Part of me wants to crawl under the duvet until all this is over. The other part can't wait to get out. That stupid old bitch, saying all that crap about Mum. I get up and cross to the window. Backyards. Roofs. The streetlights of the street behind this one. The neon sign of Fat Frankie's – only the sign says The Golden Fry. All I can see from the guest room at Colette's is her garden and the one behind it.

Footsteps on the stairs. Colette in the doorway. I haven't got very far. The bag she gave me is sitting empty on the bed, gaping like an open mouth.

'This used to be my room,' she says. 'Your dad had the big one. I used to say it wasn't fair because he was never in and I was never out.' She laughs. 'God, the hours I used to spend studying in here.'

I have the smallest room because Gran had the other one. When she died Mum said I could move into her room but I didn't like it so I moved back in here after a couple of weeks.

'Does it look the same?'

She looks round. 'I didn't have a TV. Or football posters. I had Duran Duran.'

'*Who?*'

'Long time ago.'

'I don't know what to bring,' I say.

'Do you have a warm coat – a fleece or something? And didn't you say you had to pick up your football boots?'

'Oh yeah.' I dive under the bed for them.

'Books?'

'In my schoolbag.'

'I meant … Oh look, a guitar!' She must have seen it on top of the wardrobe. I shoved it up there months ago. 'D'you want to bring it?'

'Nah. Mum gave it to me last Christmas. It was lying around the house. But I've never learned to play it.'

'You could start. It might give you something to do.'

She says this like she's noticed how bored I am at her house. I don't suppose she'd stop me going out and just walking about but I don't want to. Which is stupid cause they must be dead safe, those posh streets.

'Nah.' I shake my head.

'OK.' But she reaches up for it. She sits on the bed and cradles it and strokes the dust away from its front, like she's stroking someone's face. 'Gerard's guitar.' It's a remembering voice. 'God, he loved that when he was your age. Drove us all mad strumming and trying to sing. He and Gary Brogan were meant to start a band but nothing came of it.'

I never knew any of that. Mum just said I might as well have the guitar because it was only gathering dust. I thought she gave it to me because it was cheaper than buying me a proper present. I did sort of know it was my dad's but I never thought of him loving it or anything. Maybe I would have felt differently if I'd known that. Maybe I'd have tried to learn it. I mean, probably not. But maybe.

I start grabbing stuff fast and shoving it into the bag.

* * *

As soon as Mr Dermott says, 'Right, you lot. Off to assembly,' Seaneen makes a beeline for me. No one else does. Most of the boys in my class are either friends with Emmet McCann or scared of him. Emmet has connections. Well, his da has. Seaneen Brogan's OK. It's just that she's nosy. And a girl.

'My granny says she'd a great chat with your Colette. So you're living it up on the Malone Road, then?' She says 'Malone Road' in a pretend posh voice.

'Yeah. It's all showjumping and champagne.'

'What?' She screws up her face. She has dark stuff smudged round her eyes. Vicky puts that stuff on every morning in front of the mirror in the hall.

'Joke.'

'Oh right.' She feels in the pocket of her blazer. 'Damn. No fags. You got any?'

I shake my head. 'Nah.' I remember the chips she gave me last week. 'I've got money, though. Colette gave me a tenner. I'll buy some at lunchtime.'

'They won't serve you if you're in your uniform. I know who's got some though. Emmet McCann.'

'Well, I'm not buying off him.'

'Oh yeah.' She narrows her eyes. She's the only person I know with green eyes like a cat. 'I forgot. Does his da not still go with your ma?'

'*No*. Piss off, Seaneen.'

'Declan Kelly. Seaneen Brogan. Get to assembly.' Mr Dermott pads up behind us in that sneaky, teachery way. He mustn't have heard me saying piss off. Or maybe he just ignored it. Sometimes he lets on to be deaf.

'Right, sir.'

He locks the classroom door and follows us down the corridor so there's no chance of mitching off assembly. 'Still at your aunt's, Declan?'

'Yes, sir.' I don't tell him it's going to be for a month. I can just see Seaneen's ears flapping.

'Oh, while I remember – I need to have a word with you about your work experience placement. Come to my classroom at break.'

Bloody work experience. That's all I need. We shake him off when he sees a couple of Year Eights beating each other round the head with schoolbags.

'So, where's your work experience, then?' asks Seaneen. I shrug.

'Well, what did you put on your form? It's next week.'

'Can't remember. Sure it's a load of crap.'

'It's a week off school. I'm going to a nursery school. I can't wait.' Her tits and her curly pony-tail bounce.

'Seriously?'

'Yeah. I *love* wee kids. See our twins? I give them their bottles and all. They probably think I'm their ma.'

'My cousin has a baby sister. Half-sister, whatever.'

'Och, that's lovely,' she says in this soppy, girly voice. 'What's your cousin like, Declan?'

'Stuck-up bitch.'

'Is she pretty?'

'She's a dog.'

I wonder if I should forget about going to see Dermott at break but if I don't show he'll just pounce on me anyway. Probably haul me out of class in front of everyone. Easier to go.

Mr Dermott's marking books but he looks up and smiles at me. 'OK, Declan, sit down. Thanks for coming. I won't keep you long.' I think he hopes his politeness will rub off on us. God love him.

I pull out a chair with 'Liverpool FC' scribbled on its seat.

'OK. Well. Now.' He sounds a bit awkward. 'There's been a bit of a setback with your placement. You said you wanted to work with cars, didn't you?'

'That was your idea, sir. I didn't know what to put. You said cars because of the joyriding. People always think you must be interested in cars if you've nicked one.'

'Er, quite.' He tugs at his earlobe. Does he remember visiting me in there? He's never mentioned it. 'Well, it was just a thought. The problem is, we can't seem to get anyone to take you. And all our usual contacts … Anyway, time's getting short and I thought I would see if you have any ideas yourself. Any contacts.'

'Not those sort of contacts, sir.'

'This aunt of yours – does she have any contacts we could use?'

'Not that I know of.'

'Where does she work?'

I have to think for a moment. 'She's a librarian.'

'Oh.' He looks disappointed. 'Can't really see you in a library.'

'Me neither, sir.'

'And your uncle?'

'Solicitor.' I can't be bothered to explain that he isn't my uncle any more.

Mr Dermott looks surprised but not hopeful. 'Hmm. Any other ideas, Declan? Come on, help me out here.' He's trying to sound all jolly. I suppose he's getting a bollocking from Payne or someone for not getting me sorted out. 'What's your best subject?'

This is ridiculous. Mr Dermott's been my tutor since Year Eight. He knows what sort of marks I get.

'Well, last exams my highest mark was Religion.' I don't remind him it was 37%. 'So you reckon I should become a priest, then, sir?'

'Huh, a comedian, more like. Look, lad, time's getting short. It's really in your best interests to get something sorted and to do your best at it. If you get a good report – well, it all helps. You don't have to end up doing it for rest of your life. So will you go home and ask your aunt tonight if she knows *anyone* who would let you go there for a week?'

'Yes, sir.' I know I won't ask Colette this in a million years but it's the easiest thing to say. The bell rings for the end of break and I go to PE. I try to get interested in work experience. I try to make myself worry that it's next week and I haven't got anything sorted. But I can't make myself believe that any of it matters one bit.

Chapter 12

VICKY

The assembly hall looked so different from up on stage! Rows and rows of green uniforms, shiny hair and bored assembly-faces. At least being presented with showjumping rosettes was a bit different from hockey and tennis. I took my rosette from Miss Gowan, smiled and concentrated on getting safely to the other side of the stage without tripping. In front of me, Katie was strolling across the stage like she was on a catwalk. Behind me I could hear Aoife saying something intelligent to Miss Gowan.

Blue rosettes for second place. 'Let's hope it's red for first next time,' Katie said as she, Aoife, Jenny and I were on our way down the corridor after assembly.

'I'm having a jumping lesson every Wednesday night from now on,' I reassured her. 'I definitely want to stay on the team!' Then I crossed my fingers because although I *was* having a lesson this week, I hadn't asked Dad yet if he'd pay for one every week.

'Dublin, here we come!' said Aoife, flapping her rosette in the air.

'*Dublin?*' I didn't know what she was on about.

'Don't tempt fate, Aoife!' Katie warned.

'Hold on,' I begged. 'What's this about Dublin?'

'Whoever comes first and second in the provincial leagues goes down to a big all-Ireland final. At the RDS,' said Jenny.

'Oh my God!' My insides did a backflip. 'Are we in with a chance?'

Katie laughed. 'Keep up those lessons and we might be!'

I was at the door of my classroom now so I had to go. I told Fliss and Becca in History. Even though they thought it was weird to like horses, they still thought it would be cool to go to Dublin.

'So, what do you have to do?' Fliss asked. We were whispering behind our books. We had the student teacher on Mondays and she was really wet.

'Finish first or second. There's two more shows to go. We're second at the minute. But some of the others are *really* good.'

'Better than Flight?'

'Better than me,' I said honestly.

Three sentences about horses was about Fliss's limit. 'Are you all set for Niamh and Niall's party?'

'Yeah, you?'

She frowned. 'We're meant to be going to Donegal.'

'Oh, Fliss, no way!'

'I know. I'm trying to persuade Mum to wait and go on Saturday.'

'Niall's on the rugby team this year,' I reminded her slyly. 'Just think of all those lovely rugby players!'

'Yeah, like *Rory Marshall*, you mean?'

'Victoria and Felicity. Pay attention please.' The student was wet but she wasn't deaf.

'Sorry, miss,' we chanted.

The three of us got together at break on our special bit of wall. Fliss handed round a mini tub of Pringles.

'No, thanks,' said Becca. 'Got a new top for Niamh's party but at the minute I can't actually get all the buttons done. I'm not going to eat all week.'

Fliss could eat anything and stay thin as a pencil so she just shrugged and passed the tub to me. 'Come on, Vicky. You have to keep your strength up for this showjumping stuff,' she said, shaking the tub at me.

I took one and licked the salt off. 'Fliss, you *have* to tell your mum to wait until Saturday,' said Becca. 'I mean, it's not just any party. It's Niamh's.'

Fliss sighed. 'I know. But Mum won't see it like that. She's invited this new man of hers up to Donegal with us.'

My insides squirmed. I could never understand how Fliss could cope with her Mum having boyfriends.

'What's this one like?' asked Becca.

Fliss ran her finger round the salty scrapings in the bottom of the Pringles tub and sighed. 'Psychiatrist.'

'Weird!'

'He'll be analysing you all the time!'

'He's OK,' Fliss admitted. 'But what's the point in making an effort? She'll probably dump him next month.'

'Come on, girls. The bell has gone. Rebecca O'Reilly, is that nail varnish?'

Mrs Maxwell, head of Year Twelve and total fascist, loomed up behind us. We slid down from the wall, grabbed our bags and grumbled off to German. But it might as well have been Greek because all I could think about – through German, Physics, PE, everything – was Dublin.

Still, there was a lot to do first, I reminded myself as I walked home. Mustn't tempt fate, as Katie had said. Two more shows and I couldn't afford to make a mistake at either of them. At least I should have Dad and Fiona at the next one – and no Declan, of course. Last weekend – Mum getting involved in that side of my life – was a total one-off.

But walking up Sandringham Park, with all the houses cosy and solid behind thick hedges and lovely gardens, pictures of Declan's street kept barging into my head. That horrible estate with graffiti everywhere and old cars and some of the houses boarded up. No wonder Mum couldn't wait to get out of the place. No wonder she hardly ever went back. How weird that Theresa and Gerard *liked* it. Did Declan?

Mum was in the kitchen putting moussaka in the oven. The air was warm and garlicky. 'Hi love. I thought you might be Declan. He was getting the bus for the first time. I hope he managed it OK.'

'Mum! He's nearly sixteen. I'm sure he can get the bus to school on his own.' How ridiculous! He was supposed to be the streetwise one, and there was Mum worrying about him getting a couple of local buses.

It was lovely having Mum to myself. I told her about Dublin. 'So you see how important it is that I have regular lessons.'

'Yes, love.' She smiled. 'And you'll let Declan have a wee go on Flight on Wednesday?'

She never missed a trick! The thought of *anyone* riding Flight made my chest hurt – the thought of letting *him* anywhere near him –

'Mum! You're trying to get round me when I'm in a good mood!'

'Isn't that what you always do to me?'

'I suppose. Well, I *might*. But just a wee walk round the school. I mean, Flight's an inter-provincial show-jumper in training.'

She took off her oven gloves. 'Potentially. Don't tempt fate.'

Chapter 13

DECLAN

'Vicky says she'll give you a go on Flight this evening,' Colette says.

I shrug. 'OK.'

She looks up from peeling potatoes. 'Declan? Is anything wrong? Apart from your mum?'

I shake my head.

She doesn't give up, though. 'I know Theresa wasn't in great form last night.'

'Hmm.' What's the good of shoving things on top of a wardrobe when Colette keeps dragging them down?

'Maybe it would be easier if you go on your own next time?'

This would be a million times worse but right now all I want is for her to shut up so I just go, 'Maybe,' and it works.

I go up to the room I sleep in – Colette is always so careful to say 'your room' but it isn't – to change out of my uniform. For the first time what Colette said sinks in. *Vicky says she'll give you a wee go on Flight.* Christ! Do I want to? Part of me does, more than anything. Another part is shitting myself.

The stable yard is starting to look familiar now but something's different. There's a lot of rushing about and neighing and when Cam comes round the corner at the sound of Colette's car her short red hair is standing on end and she looks hassled. 'Oh gosh, Vicky, I forgot! I should have cancelled you.'

'What? Is something wrong with Flight?' Her voice is high-pitched.

'He's fine. But the young horse bucked Tony off this afternoon and he's pretty smashed up. I'm only back from the hospital and nothing's been done.'

Vicky gasps. 'Is Tony OK?'

'He's got concussion and a broken leg. I had to wait with him until we could get hold of his mum.'

'Oh, poor Tony. Well, I can help you now. I'm early.'

'I don't know if I can fit in – well, OK. You help for half an hour and then I'll give you a quick lesson *if* we get everything sorted out.'

She seems to see me for the first time. She looks me up and down like I'm a horse. 'You going to help?'

'Uh, OK.'

'*He* doesn't know anything about horses,' Vicky puts in.

'I'm sure he can stuff a few hay nets. Right, Vicky, the feeds are set out in the feed room. Now you, come with me. What's your name?'

'Declan.'

'You're Vicky's cousin, right?' She doesn't wait for an answer but leads me into a big, cold shed behind the stables. In one corner there's a huge round pile of hay stuff with all these string bag things heaped round it. 'Ever stuffed a hay net?'

I shake my head. 'I never even touched a horse till last week.'

She laughs. 'Well, it's not hard. Look, see the bale of haylage?'

'Yeah.' I can hardly miss it; it's nearly as big as me.

'Well, you want to put the haylage into the nets. Stuff it in as tight as you can. And when you can't stuff in another bit, pull the string tight – see, here, at the top of the net?'

'Yeah.'

'There's twelve nets. You probably won't get them all done, but do your best.'

'OK.'

She strides off and there's only me and the haylage and the nets. I pull off a big swathe of haylage with a pitch-fork the way Cam showed me. It's harder than it looks. The haylage is rough and damp and it smells funny – sweet and a bit sickly. I stuff and stuff and stuff until my hands sting. The nets are slippy to handle until they start to plump up with haylage. I get into a sort of rhythm. Vaguely I hear Cam and Vicky shouting across the yard to each other and the horses stamping their feet and neighing for their dinners, but it's quiet in the shed. I like the way the pile of fat hay nets is growing.

When Cam comes back I'm so involved in what I'm doing that I jump.

'Only one left? Good for you. We've done the feeds. Vicky's gone to tack up Flight. Look, you wouldn't mind doing something else for me, would you?'

'OK.'

She gives me a sort of plastic laundry basket thing and rubber gloves and tells me to go and lift the shit out of all the stables. 'You're happy enough about going into the stables? The horses won't touch you.'

'OK.'

Lifting shit is easier than stuffing hay nets. Horse shit isn't that bad, not like dog's dirt or anything. From behind the stables I hear Cam shouting instructions. 'Once more on that rein. Good. Now you need to put in a short one here.' It sounds like a foreign language.

The horses are all eating their dinners and most don't even look up when I open their doors. I suppose they're used to people. Some of them are huge but they have these gentle, interested faces. Not scary. One of them has a bandage on its leg. It leaves its bucket of food – looks like that muesli stuff Colette eats – and sniffs around me. It's brown. I talk nonsense to it and stroke its nose and it seems happy, biffing my chest with its head.

'Oh, that's our pet!'

I look up. Once again I haven't heard Cam and I feel stupid to be caught talking to the horse. She doesn't seem to think it's weird, though.

'She's been on box rest for three months. She cut her leg really badly on barbed wire. She may never be ridden again. She's a dote, isn't she?' She gives the brown horse a soft pat on the neck.

'What's her name?'

'Nudge.'

'That's a funny name.'

'I think it's because she loves to nudge people – see what I mean? So, how did you get on with the skipping out?'

'Just a couple left.'

'Good for you. You've done a great job. Vicky says you're going to have a ride on Flight.'

My stomach takes a nosedive. 'Um, OK. I'll just –' I wave my hand at the shit basket.

'Leave it. I'll finish up. Go on ahead – Vicky's in the school.'

I know now that she means the sandy field thing. Funny names, horsey things have. I don't know how I feel about riding Flight. Terrified of making a fool of myself in front of Princess Vicky. But when I see Flight walking round the edge of the school, foam flecking his mouth and his neck all curved, the floodlights gleaming on his shining red coat, I forget all that crap.

Vicky rides over to the gate and jumps off. She gives a sort of half smile. 'Here, my hat will have to do you,' she says. She pulls off her hat and her long blonde hair flies round her face.

'Do I have to?' The hat's dead gay.

'Number one rule. No hat, no riding. But if you don't want to –'

I hold out my hand for the hat and put it on. It feels funny, heavy and snug.

'OK, now put your left foot in the stirrup – here, I'll hold it for you. And then spring up.' She rattles off a list of instructions. I don't know about springing but next minute I'm sitting on Flight. I have to look down to find the other stirrup and the ground tilts at a strange angle. It's a long way down. Vicky puts the reins in my hands and manhandles them a bit until she says I'm holding them right. She pushes my leg into what she says is the right position. It's weird to have Vicky touching my leg.

'Look up,' she says. 'Yeah, that's it. Now squeeze with your heels – don't kick – and he'll walk on. I won't lead you if you don't want me to but I'll walk beside him. He should be pretty quiet – he's tired after jumping.'

'OK.'

And then we're off. You wouldn't think a horse just

walking would feel fast but it does. Powerful. I feel every step Flight takes. Every time his shoulder comes back I shift a bit in the saddle. I don't know if that's right or if you're meant to keep dead still. Vicky walks beside me for a bit, then she says, 'You're not nervous, are you?' She sounds surprised. 'I'll go and stand at the gate and you can go round on your own. Don't let him drift into the middle. Use your inside leg – this one – and sort of nudge him out with it. And your outside rein. Don't pull or kick, just a bit of pressure.'

I haven't a clue what all this means; I just try to keep going round the outside of the school. It's even better when Vicky isn't walking beside me. A bit scary but in a good way. Like driving – no, not like driving. Like nothing I've ever done before. This power, this strength – it's *alive*. Imagine having your own horse and being able to do this any time you wanted. Imagine being able to jump those jumps set up in the middle of the school. Flight's neck in front of my hands gleams with sweat. I take one hand off the reins and pat it – it's warm and damp.

'OK, better get off now,' says Vicky. 'Mum'll be back any minute.'

She comes over and shows me how to get off. Easier than getting on, but my legs buckle when they hit the ground. Vicky laughs – not nastily, I don't think. 'You'll be sore tomorrow,' she says. 'Riding uses muscles most people don't know they have.'

She does something to the stirrups, then takes hold of the reins and the three of us walk back up to the yard where she ties Flight up outside his stable and takes off his saddle. Steam clouds up from his back. 'Damn,' she says. 'I thought he'd have cooled down, walking round like that. I'll go and get his sweat rug. Keep an eye on him, would you?' She dashes off and I stroke Flight's nose and he nudges me, looking for food I suppose.

'You did a good job tonight.'

I look up. It's Cam. I shrug.

'Here.' She hands me a tenner.

I shake my head and step back. 'Sure I had to hang round anyway. It was better having something to do.'

'But you earned it.'

I rub Flight's nose and look at the ground.

'Look, I appreciate your help. We're seriously short-handed now. Tony works full time.' She pushes the tenner into my pocket. 'Take it.'

That's when I get the idea. But I can't say it out loud. I hate asking for things and if Cam knows anything about me then she won't want me on her yard. But the horses –

I make up my mind.

'I have to do work experience next week. I haven't sorted anything.' My voice sounds funny, like I've been practising the words. The next bit comes out in a rush. 'I could come here. If … if you wanted.'

'Work experience? For school?'

I nod. She looks uncertain. Shit. Should have just taken the bloody tenner and kept my mouth shut.

'I don't normally take people on work experience – but as you're Vicky's cousin…' She sounds like she's thinking out loud. I'm holding my breath, which is so stupid. As if it matters. It would just get Dermott off my back. She suddenly smiles and I realise she's not that old – like, twenty-five or something. 'Yes, Declan, OK. As long as you can get here.'

'Oh.' I hadn't thought of that. 'Is there a bus?'

'Not the whole way. But if you don't mind a bit of a

walk you can get a bus to the end of the next road and – look, here's Colette. Why don't we go and have a word with her?'

'Next *week*?' Colette looks at me like I'm not wise. 'What on earth would you have done if Cam hadn't been good enough to take you?'

'Dunno.'

'Well,' says Cam, 'looks like this will suit everyone. Give your teacher my number. Oh, hi Vicky. Meet my new stable hand.'

'Your *what*?' Vicky's arms are full of saddle and bridle. Luckily; she looks like she'd punch me if she'd a free hand.

Chapter 14

VICKY

I folded myself into the back of the car – Mum said we had to take turns in the front – and stared out at the dark road.

'So if you get off the bus here,' Mum was saying, 'and then walk up the main road a bit – look, just to that bungalow – and then –'

I tried to blank out her voice but it was no good. She was going on about bus timetables and packed lunches until I could have screamed. I stared at the dark, close-cropped back of Declan's head and hated him more than I ever had.

'So how come you do work experience in Year Twelve?' I asked.

'What d'you mean?'

'We don't do it until lower sixth.'

'We don't have a sixth form.'

'How *strange*.'

'Vicky.' Mum's voice came sharply from the front.

'What?'

But I knew I was being a cow. Every time I let Nasty Me out it was harder to keep her in. I slunk down in the seat and took out my phone. It had been on silent while I was riding but now I saw there was a text from Fliss: HOORAY, NO DONEGAL TIL SAT. WANNA SHOP 2MORO NITE? I thought about the party. I *so* needed a new top. Maybe I could get round Mum.

I tried when we got home.

She looked up from emptying the dishwasher. 'Vicky, you get fifteen pounds a week. *And* whatever your dad gives you. If you've no money left it's not my fault. What have you spent your pocket money on?'

'I had to buy that book, *The Complete Young Rider*. Katie recommended it. It's brilliant.'

'Is that the book that's been lying round the down-stairs cloakroom all week?'

'I'm consulting it when I go to the loo.'

'Looks a bit expensive to be lying around.'

'Oh, Mum, you're just trying to change the subject. It's only a book. But I've *nothing* to wear.'

'Oh come on, you're being silly. Do you want some supper?'

'No.' I stomped off to my room, pushing past Declan in the doorway.

* * *

I slid my back down the front of the lockers until I was squatting on the floor beside Becca.

'Hi Vicky. Want some?'

'Diet Coke? At half eight in the morning? No thanks. I've just had breakfast.'

'This *is* my breakfast,' said Becca and burped.

'Tut tut, Miss O'Reilly, that hardly constitutes a balanced meal. Don't you listen in Home Ec?' interrupted Fliss in Mad Max's voice, dumping her bag down.

'Never mind Home Ec. This really works. Diet Coke for breakfast, break and lunch, then a normal tea to keep my mum off my back. I've lost four pounds and I can get into my new top.'

'Yeah, talking of new tops, you coming into town tonight, Vic?' Fliss asked.

I sighed. 'I'm broke. I tried to get round Mum but she's being a total cow at the minute. Ever since –' I stopped. I still hadn't told them about Declan.

'Go on. Ever since what? I thought your mum was a pushover.'

'She is, usually.'

'So? Go on, tell us. Ever since what? Don't tell me *she's* got a new man at last.'

'*No.*' My insides turned to ice. 'Of course not. She's not *like* that.'

'Vicky, my love, everyone's like that,' Fliss said wisely.

I sighed. 'It's just we have this boy staying with us. My cousin. His mum's in hospital.' No way was I telling them the whole story.

'A *boy*? Since when?'

'Last week.'

'That boy I saw you with?' asked Fliss. 'The one you said your Mum was giving a lift to?'

I nodded.

'And you've kept it a secret?' Becca's eyes were wide with surprise. '*Why?*'

I shrugged. 'He's my cousin. He doesn't count. It's not like he's a *boy* boy.'

They looked at each other and back at me as if I was

crazy. The bell went for tutor group and we had to go, but they wouldn't leave the subject alone, hounding me the whole way up the corridor.

'Victoria Moore,' Fliss said slowly as if I were incredibly thick. 'He may be *your* cousin but he is not *our* cousin. As far as we are concerned he is indeed a *boy* boy. Very much a *boy* boy if I remember correctly.'

'Omigod!' Becca shrieked. 'I have had *the* most brilliant idea. Ask Niamh if you can bring him to the party!'

'No.' Something cold and sick washed over me. Imagine walking into Niamh's house with all my friends there, with *Rory* there –

'Vicky, you're being totally weird about this,' said Becca.

'And totally selfish,' added Fliss. 'You know we never know enough boys.'

'Yes, but he's not…' I tried to think how to put it without it sounding snobby. 'He's – he's a bit odd. Quiet. You know, with his mum being sick and that.'

'But a party would cheer him up!' Fliss beamed at me, all innocent.

'No,' I said. 'No way. Sorry, you'll just have to put up with me.'

Becca sighed. 'No wonder we can't get boyfriends.'

'Never mind,' I said. 'Maybe you'll pull on Friday, in your new top. Remember Niamh says the whole of the rugby team's been invited.'

'Well, bagsy me Niall,' put in Fliss quickly.

'And bagsy you Rory, I suppose, Vic? That leaves me with no one.'

'We'll find you a lovely big rugby player,' I promised. 'Come on, we're going to be late.'

Chapter 15

DECLAN

Mr Dermott nearly wets himself when I tell him.

'Anything?' he asks me as soon as I get in on Thursday. He's been pouncing on me like this every morning and I've just grunted and hurried off.

But not today. I stop by his desk. 'Yes, sir.'

'Really?' He doesn't even try to hide his surprise. 'Well, what's it to be?'

'An equestrian centre.' This is the proper name. I've been sneaking a look at this book of Vicky's in the downstairs loo.

'A – an *equestrian centre*?'

'Yeah. D'you not know what that is?'

'Yes, Declan, funnily enough I do know what it is. My daughter has riding lessons. It's just not the first thing that would have sprung to mind.' He looks at me. 'Well, well.'

'It's all sorted. Look.' I scramble round in my pocket. 'Here's the number.'

He takes the bit of paper and smiles at me. 'Good lad.'

Only two days of school and then a week off. I know it'll be hard work at Cam's – I hate to admit it but Vicky's right about my muscles – but it'll be a million times better than school. A whole week with no teachers on my back and no bloody Emmet giving me death looks.

Everybody's hyper because of being off next week. Seaneen says she can't wait. 'What if you have to change their nappies?' I ask her. It's English. Psycho Sykes is blethering on about some crap poem.

She shrugs. 'Sure I've changed our Tiarna and Saoirse's nappies hundreds of times.'

'Yuck.'

'Well, *you'll* be shovelling plenty of shite next week, Declan Kelly, from what you've told me.'

'Not wiping their arses. Anyway, horse shite's different. It's kind of –'

'Seaneen Brogan and Declan Kelly, would you like to share your conversation with the class?'

Seaneen giggles.

'No, you're alright,' I mutter.

'Please, I insist. Do tell the class what you were telling Seaneen.'

For a minute I'm *so* tempted to say we were talking about shite. But I don't want trouble. Even when Emmett said something the other day about loony bins, I just clenched my fists in my pocket and ignored him. So I go, 'It was about work experience, Miss.'

'Huh.' Psycho's about the only teacher who doesn't get all eager about the work experience. Probably thinks no one in this school could ever get a job anyway.

The bell saves me.

'Book logs tomorrow,' Psycho shrieks above the roar.

'And if you don't bring your own book you'll have to read one of mine. And write a report on it.'

Everyone groans. On Fridays you have to bring in a book and read it for the whole lesson. Only a few girls ever remember so the rest of us have to read Psycho's class library books. They're all ancient, falling to bits and crap. But there's books everywhere at Colette's house. I suppose she wouldn't mind if I borrowed one. Might nab that horsey one. *The Complete Young Rider*. Don't suppose anyone's that bothered about it or they wouldn't have left it in the loo. Wouldn't want anyone here to see it or they'd rip the piss out of me, though it'd be worth it not to have to read Psycho's books. *The Boy's Book of Spy Stories*. *The Goalkeeper's Revenge*. What century does Psycho think it is?

* * *

My chest squeezes tight as we drive through the gates of the mental. It doesn't call itself the mental, of course. 'Mountain View Healthcare Park', says the big, bright sign at the gates. Yeah, right. It doesn't seem like three whole days since we were here. I try to look at all the buildings as we drive round the one-way system. They're all called after mountains. I wonder how they decide on the names. Is Donard for madder people than Slemish because it's higher?

Colette slides the car into a spot right outside the building. Croob. I never heard of that.

'Is Croob high?' I ask Colette.

She gives me a weird look like she thinks I'm thick. 'It's where the River Lagan rises,' she says. 'It's only a bit of a hill really.'

'Oh. Good.' I sit back and undo my seatbelt. Slowly.
'Don't forget the magazines.'

I take them and look at the titles. *Good Housekeeping.*
Ulster Tatler. Both glossy. No way will Mum read those. I
suppose Colette's running out of magazines.

Why can't she see I don't want to go in alone?

'You don't want me around all the time,' is what she's
been saying. 'You and your mum need a bit of time to
yourselves.' How crap would it sound to say, 'Don't leave
me alone with my own mother'? So I just grip the handle
and pull and try not to drag my feet too much as I go
from the safety of the car to the door.

It's a small building, square and low. Not as scary as
the hospital in some ways. But at least the hospital just
looks like what it is. People in bed and stuff. Here you
have to ring a bell to get in. You could say that makes it
more like a normal house, or you could say they have to
lock the people in. I wipe my feet for ages on the stained
doormat even though they're already clean.

A nurse lets me in. She's the one I met on Tuesday and
she says, 'Hello, there. Your mammy's in the day room.'
Mammy. What age does she think I am? 'Do you want to
go on in?'

No, I think. The day room is huge. The TV's blaring
at one end. At first I look round in a panic because I
think Mum's not there and then I see her sitting beside
this grossly fat woman. They look weird together. They
aren't talking, just sitting. The fat woman is singing
under her breath. Mum's face is botchy and old. She
looks the worst I've ever seen her.

Worse than when the police came to the door for me.

Worse than when Barry dumped her.

Worse than when Gran died.

'Right, Mum?' I say.

She doesn't answer. She picks bits of skin off her hand. There's a red raw mark where she's been doing it.

'Here.' I push the magazines at her. My hand's sweaty. I rub it on my school trousers.

She looks at me for the first time. 'Colette get out of coming today, then?' It's a new voice, not the flat, dull one. More sour.

'She's outside.'

'Huh.'

She's jittery as hell. She lights a cigarette with a shivering hand. The hand that isn't holding the cigarette plays with her hair. There are cold sores round her mouth. She looks like shite. She doesn't even try to talk to me. Fatty keeps singing.

It's up to me. 'So – um, how are you?'

'How do you think?'

I don't answer. I mean, how the hell do I know? It's just something to say. I try to tell her about the work experience, but it doesn't spark anything. 'It'll be dead good,' I say. My voice sounds stupid because I'm trying too hard. 'I'm not scared of the horses or anything. They're wicked. And Mum, guess what?'

'What?'

'I rode Vicky's horse on Wednesday!' I can hear my voice getting stupider and stupider – all enthusiastic like some kid.

'Oh.' She sniffs. I think she has a cold.

'It was brilliant.'

'Huh. Well, you needn't be getting used to that sort of thing.'

It's like someone emptying ice cubes into your stomach.

She lights another cigarette. It smells lovely. I haven't smoked since that one Seaneen gave me. Mum doesn't even look at me. There's a clock on the wall. Only seven minutes have passed.

'Um, do you need anything? Next time I come?' That's what Colette always asks.

'Leaving already?'

I wish. 'I just meant –'

'You can bring me a bottle of vodka.' She isn't joking.

'Oh Mum, I know it must be dead hard –'

'You know damn all. All you know is how to wreck things.'

'*Mum.*'

'Och, just piss off, Declan.'

'But –'

'Look, just fuck off out of here. Go on.'

I go.

No one stops me. Walls. Fire extinguisher. Door. Stained rug. Outside. Rain.

Colette doesn't see me. For a second I watch her reading the paper, framed by the car window. Safe. I grab at the door handle. Locked. She starts. Looks up, frowns through the rain-streaked window. She clicks the central locking and I duck into the car.

'Did you forget something?'

'No.' I yank at my seatbelt.

She catches on. 'It didn't go well?'

I shrug.

She looks at me like she's trying to make her mind up about something and then she starts the engine. 'She probably has bad days. The withdrawal symptoms –'

'Yeah.' I scrunch down in the seat.

The whole way home I look out at the lights on the

wet roads. It takes forever. Rain streaks the windows but it's hot in the car. I pull off my blazer and throw it on the floor. I can feel the thump of my heart against my shirt. I think Colette must hear my breathing.

'Vicky's going to a party,' she says. I recognise her voice. It's the same trying-too-hard voice I was using to Mum. 'You could come with me to drop her off and then we could maybe stop and get a DVD on the way home. Your choice.'

I try to answer but the words are too far down to drag to the surface.

Vicky's putting on her make-up at the hall mirror when we get back. All I want to do is push past her and go up to my room but her stuff's all over the hall – powder and bits of cotton wool and a pink rucksack in the middle of the floor. I hang behind Colette.

'Vicky love, you know I don't like you doing that.'

'The light's better here.' She squints into the mirror. Her long blonde hair is all straight and shiny. She's wearing a tight white top. Her tits are crap. She licks the corners of her mouth. 'Is this lipstick a bit too red?'

'It's fine. You all packed for Dad's?'

'More or less.'

Vicky turns round to shove her make-up bag into the front pocket of her pink rucksack. 'OK, that's me, except, Mum, have you seen that book I was reading? The new one?'

'Which one? You're always leaving books all over the house.'

'*The Complete Young Rider*. I *really* need it. There's a chapter on jumping combinations; I need to –'

'The book that's been lying in the downstairs loo all week?'

'I suppose. Only it's not there now. Have you tidied it or something?'

Oh shit. I swallow and find my voice. 'Uh, Vicky, I borrowed it.'

Vicky swings round. '*You* took my new book?' Her voice is icy.

'Yeah.' I know I should say sorry but I'm not going to.

'Well, go and get it!'

'The thing is, I sort of left it at school.'

'What? You took *my* book to school? You didn't even ask me!' Her neck starts to turn pink.

'I didn't think you were reading it. It was just lying around.'

'Well, I need it!' She's shrieking.

I push my hands further down into my pockets. They're both balled into fists. I wish she would shut up.

Vicky's face is beetroot. So much for the make-up.

'Vicky, your book will be fine.' Colette's trying so hard. 'You have plenty of horsey books and Declan will get it for you on his first day back after work experience.'

'You just take his side!' She's nearly crying. Good.

'It's only a frigging book,' I mutter.

'You see?' Her voice is cracking. 'He doesn't even care. He just walks in here and takes what he likes.'

'Vic, that's not fair.'

'Yes it *is*!' She comes right up to me. Too close. I can see the tears in her eyes. The powder on her cheeks. 'No wonder your stupid mother couldn't stick you. No wonder she tried to kill herself to get away from –'

The first I know I've thumped her is when I feel her teeth graze my fist.

I take a step back. Then I'm out on the street, my fist still clenched.

Chapter 16

VICKY

Over my own sobs I heard the slam of the front door.

'Come on, let me see.' Mum pulled my hands away from my face. Blood flooded my mouth, hot and metallic and revolting. I dashed to the downstairs loo before I swallowed it.

The sight of the red swirling into the water of the toilet bowl made me retch. I spat again. Not so much blood. I turned on the cold tap and swooshed my mouth with water. It stung but it felt clean.

I stood up and looked into the mirror. Peeled down my bottom lip to see. It looked like nothing much. I thought my tooth must have gone through my lip for sure but there was only a red gash. Blood oozed to the surface but slowly. Mascara ran down my cheeks in dirty streams.

'Calmed down?' Mum's face appeared in the mirror beside mine.

'Did you see what he –?'

'Never mind what he did. I heard what you *said*.' I'd never heard her voice so cold.

'Well, I'm sorry, but he –'

'No.' She put up her hand. 'I don't want to hear. I'm ...' She seemed to be searching for a bad enough word – '*disgusted* with you. God knows, Vicky, you haven't exactly been welcoming – but that! That's about the worst thing you could have said.'

I stared at her in shock. 'He still shouldn't have hit me. He must think he's a real wee hard man. Hitting girls.' I sniffed and the snot running down the back of my throat made me feel sick again.

'Oh, grow up, Vicky! Of *course* he shouldn't have hit you. But I don't blame him.'

I looked down at my white top. It was spattered with red. 'Look! I can't go to the party in *this*!'

But Mum wasn't in the doorway any more. I snatched up a facecloth, pressed it to my mouth and followed her into the hall. She snatched up her car keys from the hall stand.

'Where are you –?'

'To find Declan, of course!'

'But the party...'

She swung round and for a split second I thought *she* was going to hit me. 'Do you honestly think I'm taking you to a *party* after that?'

'You mean I'm grounded?'

She hesitated. 'I don't care. Go to the party. Go to your dad's. Go wherever the hell you like. I have more important things to worry about.'

And she slammed the door behind her, just as Declan had done.

I sank down on the stairs and looked at the door. It looked very ... shut. Well, that proved it. She'd taken his side against me.

Then a cold feeling crept right over me and I heard my voice again – *No wonder she tried to kill herself* – and the cold melted to burning shame. Did I really say that? Why couldn't I just have lost my temper about the book and left it at that? I'd been in the right about the book. But now my breath shivered in my throat. What sort of creature *was* Nasty Me? Mum had looked at me like she hated me. No, that wasn't it – like she didn't know me. Like I wasn't someone she'd *want* to know.

No way could I go to the party now. Even if I cleaned my cut up and found a different top. But where *could* I go? Mum would be back in no time with Declan. I could phone Dad and ask him to come and get me. But then I'd have to explain. Dad might not be Declan's biggest fan but he'd still be horrified at me. I'd *have* to go to the party. I stood up slowly and peered at the facecloth which was only faintly spotted with blood now.

All my excitement about Niamh's party had evaporated. It was just somewhere to pass the time until midnight when Dad picked me up. I repaired my make-up, changed into a nice but old black top and swung my rucksack over my shoulder.

At the front door I paused. Should I leave Mum a note? Not that she'd be worried about me but I wanted her to know that I was ... well, sorry. I explored the inside of my lip. It still felt raw but it was almost welcome, like I deserved to feel it. In the end I sent her a text as I walked down the street, head down against the rain. My hair would get frizzy but it didn't seem as important as usual. I'M SORRY. I'VE GONE TO THE PARTY. I knew it wasn't enough.

It was a bit scary walking in the dark even though Niamh's house was only about a mile away. I ignored an old man who walked past me with his dog. My heart was thumping against my ribs and when a car slowed down behind me I nearly had a fit. I put my head down and kept on walking.

Then –

'Vicky? Are you going to Niamh's? D'you want a lift?'

It was Rory in a small blue car. I looked in. Sitting in the driver's seat, looking too big for the small space, his hands confident on the steering wheel, he looked even more gorgeous than usual. What was it about boys in cars? In the street light I could see that he was wearing a blue shirt which made his eyes look fantastically deep.

'Um, yeah, great, thanks,' I said. God, was I going to be so tongue-tied the whole way to Niamh's?

I could feel my cheeks burning, hotter than my sore mouth as I climbed in. Then I got my rucksack stuck at a weird angle and so I had to kind of rest my feet on it. I was all folded up and my legs looked huge. But I was in a car with Rory!

'So, um, you're at school with Niamh?' he asked.

'Yeah. Her parties are legendary. *Their* parties, I should say – I suppose it's Niall's too. I don't know if I'd like to be a twin and have to share everything, would you?' I was babbling like a moron but he acted like I was a normal person.

'I haven't really thought about it,' he said. 'There's five of us, so I suppose I'm used to sharing.' I remembered seeing his mum in the street with millions of kids. 'You're an only child, is that right?'

'Yes – well, no, I suppose. I have a baby sister. Half-sister.'

'Oh right.' He sounded a bit embarrassed. 'Do you mind?'

If I told him the truth he would think I was selfish and jealous. And I wanted to make a good impression, so I just laughed and said, 'Well, she's still at the puking and screaming stage. But I suppose she's quite cute. I like the car. Is it yours?'

'I just bought it.' He sounded really proud. 'That's what all those nights in the Rowan Tree were for. The car wasn't that dear – I mean, it's not exactly new, but the insurance is mad. If you're young and a guy they just assume you're a boy racer.'

That made me think about Declan again. I'd never exactly *liked* thinking about him being at my house, being at the yard, but now it made me feel guilty as well. I sighed. Don't spoil your night, Vicky, I told myself. You're with Rory! OK, not *with* him, but it's better than nothing. Better than you deserve, said a voice in my head – Mum's probably, and I wondered where she was now, if she had found Declan, if he had said sorry, what she had said about me –

'Vicky? I asked you if it was this one or the next one?'

'Oh, sorry! Um, next left.'

And then we were at Niamh's. I'd been to her house thousands of times and it was just an ordinary semi like ours, but there were fairy lights strung up in all the trees on the drive and it looked really pretty. Walking in with Rory was *amazing* but he got claimed by some rugby players more or less at once, though he did say, 'See you later,' and gave my arm a sort of pat.

'Vicky!' Niamh ran up to hug me. You look gorgeous!' she shrieked. 'I love your top.'

I looked down and shrugged. 'Go and get yourself a drink,' Niamh said. 'Fliss and Becs aren't here yet.'

I drifted into the kitchen. Niall was serving punch to

some girls but I didn't know anyone else there. I wondered where Rory had gone. I probably wouldn't see him again for the whole evening; I was probably just this boring girl who lived on his street who he'd felt obliged to give a lift to.

My mouth started to throb. I thought people were giving me funny looks. Had my lip swollen up? Was I grotesque? I went to the downstairs loo a couple of times to check that my camouflage make-up was surviving the action.

'Hi, Vicky, there you are.' It was Rory. Oh. My. God. Had he been looking for me? If only I hadn't been coming out of the loo when he met me. Had he noticed that it was the second time I'd gone in? Oh God, what if he thought I had the runs or something?

Then Fliss and Becca were there, screaming, 'Vicky!' like they hadn't just seen me in double Maths five hours ago.

Fliss was all jittery and kept looking round, to see if she could spy Niall, I guessed, and left Becca to do all the talking for once. And Becca, who was usually so shy with boys, was able to talk to Rory totally normally. I suppose because she didn't fancy him, incredible as that was. I wondered if he fancied *her*. Her Diet Coke diet had worked. Every button on her new top was done up except a few to show just the right amount of black bra and the impressive cleavage which Becca was apparently famous for at the boys' grammar. I looked at my own pathetic chest. Would Rory fancy me if I had boobs like Becca's? Somehow, despite Rory being here, I was depressed.

'So, Rory, have *you* seen Vicky's secret cousin?'

'What?'

I sighed. There was no getting away from the subject.

'It's just my cousin is staying with us while his mum's in hospital,' I muttered.

'She was keeping him secret till we, like, *forced* her to spill the beans the other day. She won't let us see him. Fliss got this fleeting glance of him and says he's *gorgeous*. So *I* reckon she wants to keep him to herself. You can marry your cousin, can't you? So, Rory, tell all! *Is* he gorgeous?'

'Oh, *I* couldn't possibly comment,' said Rory in a Graham Norton voice and we all laughed. Mine was pretty forced.

'You tried the punch yet?' Fliss asked.

'Yeah, let's go and get some,' Rory said. It was sort of an invitation and he must have meant it to *me* because they both had full glasses and he was drinking Coke as he was driving. Yes! I followed him into the kitchen and my depression lifted. 'So, um, yeah,' he said, handing me a glass, 'it looks like Mansfield are going to be our biggest rivals this season. They have two Ireland players, never mind a handful of Ulsters. And then you can never really rule out the country schools.' He took a swig of Coke and I watched the lovely smooth skin on his throat. He looked like he had just shaved. My fingers ached to touch his face. Or any part of him.

I fixed my mouth into what I hoped was an interested smile. *Rugby*.

'For us it's the country schools that have the edge,' I said. 'Though actually we came second to Mansfield in the last competition.'

'Hockey?'

'No!' I dismissed boring hockey. 'Showjumping.'

'*Showjumping*? That always looks pretty hard to me. On TV, I mean. I've never seen it in real life.' He smiled, showing straight, strong-looking white teeth. 'That big red wall thing – scary stuff.'

Scary. Good. That meant he would think I was brave.

I shrugged. 'I've been doing it for years now.' I didn't add that the puissance wall he was talking about was at least twice as high as any fences Flight and I would ever jump in our lives.

Fliss and Becca drifted in and Fliss raised her eyebrows when she saw us standing together.

'You should go and watch Vicky jumping some time, Rory,' she said. 'It's *really* good.'

'Yeah, we're going next Saturday, aren't we, Vic? You could come with us. It's great craic,' Becca said.

'Since when?' I couldn't help asking, but Fliss shot me a *trust me! I know what I'm doing!* look.

'I have a match in the morning,' Rory began and I rushed in, desperate to make up for my pushy, unsubtle friends.

'Yeah, you don't want to go standing around watching showjumping all afternoon in the cold.' I frowned at Fliss and Becca and they gave me identical *what sort of an ungrateful cow are you?* looks.

Rory went on, 'No, I *would* like to come. I was going to say, it's a home game so I'll be back around twelve.'

My stomach started doing a bit of showjumping of its own. What do I *really* look like in my white jodhs? What if I fall off? What if I get three refusals at the first jump?

'OK, we'll sort that out,' said Fliss. 'Hey, come on, Becs, Niamh is waiting for us.'

They left us alone again and somehow the conversation got easier, and even though people came and went, we kind of stuck together.

'Would you like a lift home?' he asked around eleven. I looked at him in surprise. 'I mean – whenever. Not now, obviously.'

'It's OK, my dad's picking me up.'

'Oh right.' He looked at his Coke. 'So – are you always at your dad's at weekends?'

I didn't catch on at first. 'Pretty much,' I said and then I thought that made me sound like I was never around or playing hard to get or something. 'I mean, it's only in Drumbo, not far.'

His face got a bit pink. 'I just wondered if you'd like to go out some time?'

'Oh!' I hadn't thought it would be so easy! 'Um – ye-yes, I would. Thanks.'

'Good. Maybe we can sort it out when I come to see you jumping?'

'Um, yes, that would be great.' OK, that meant we wouldn't even be making a date for another week. Still, things had moved faster tonight than I had ever dared to hope. I just wished I could get rid of that niggling voice that said, *you don't deserve this.*

He didn't kiss me goodnight but he did give my shoulder a sort of squeeze when I was going. I caught sight of myself in the cloakroom mirror as I lifted my rucksack. My mouth looked definitely swollen now. Not hideous, but definitely, well, enhanced, like I'd had collagen injections or something.

As I walked down the drive in the cold November midnight I noticed that the rain had stopped and the sky was pricked with stars. Dad's car was waiting, warm and welcoming, on the street. I felt a rush of joy. There was a whole weekend ahead and Fiona had said she might ride out with me on the farm tomorrow. And I was going to practise jumping in the school. And then on Sunday night when I had to see Declan again … I swallowed.

I would apologise.

I gave Dad as good a hug as I could manage in the car. It felt like much more than two weeks since I had seen him.

'Hello, darling,' he said. 'Good party?'

'Fantastic,' I said.

He gave me a funny look. 'Vicky, your mouth! What on earth have you done?'

For maybe half a second I considered the truth. Then, buckling up my seatbelt with my face half-turned away I said, 'Oh that. I got hit in the mouth in PE. It's no big deal.'

Chapter 17

DECLAN

Bitch. My feet pound it out on the wet footpath. *Bitch. Bitch. Bitch.*

By the end of the street I'm out of breath. Why bother to run? No one's after me. I glance over my shoulder just in case. Nope. The street's empty except for a wee old man walking a small dog in a tartan coat. He gives me a funny look. I look down at myself and see I'm only in my school shirt and it's soaked already, clinging and slapping against my body.

I slow to a jog, then a walk. My heart's hammering. Don't know if it's from running or anger.

It's dark. All the houses have their curtains shut tight. I get to the Lisburn Road. Cars. Lights. People. I stop. Where am I going? I put my hand into the pocket of my school trousers. Locker key, broken pencil, coins: fifty, ten, two. Great.

I cross the road and turn left. This is the way home. To my house I mean. I put my head down and trudge on. Try and stamp out those words. But the footsteps turn into the words and there's no getting away from them. *No. Wonder. She. Tried. To. Kill. Herself.* Like I need bloody Vicky to tell me.

I go under the bridge. There's this dead long, straight, boring road ahead. I start trying to think, forcing my mind to blot out those words. I imagine getting to my house, breaking in and just hiding out there. But it's a stupid idea. It's the first place she'll look. And when she finds me she'll get social services in. Colette is the kind of person who does things by the book. And there's no way they'll let me stay on my own. Maybe I'll get sent to a foster home or something. No more Princess Vicky. Good.

Yeah, but no more horses either. Shit. Like Mum said, all I do is wreck things. Why did I hit her? Because she deserved it. *No. Wonder. She. Tried. To. Kill. Herself.* I'm back where I started.

Getting over the roundabout's pretty hairy. I run for it. Cars blare. I don't care. Up the hill. My breathing's funny. Some bastard splashes my legs and a car slows. Stops. I keep going. Then I hear the swish of an electric window.

'Get in.' It's Colette.

I get in.

'Seatbelt,' she says. I don't look at her face. She pulls off and heads on up the hill. At the roundabout at the top she indicates right, goes all the way round, and straight down again towards home. Her home. I don't know I've been holding my breath till I feel it releasing.

'Where did you think we were going?' she says.

I shift in the seat. 'Thought you might –'

She turns to me for the first time. 'You're soaking.'

'Yeah.' My school shirt's sticking to me. Mostly rain

but as she turns the heating up I catch the sour reek of sweat.

'I'm sorry.' For a second I don't recognise my own voice. 'I didn't mean to hit her. But she –'

'I know. It was a terrible thing to say. But Declan, you can't go round hitting everyone who says something you don't like. Especially not girls.'

'I know.' My voice is small.

She won't let up, though. 'I mean, is that the sort of man you want to be? One who settles things with his fists?'

Like Barry. I can't answer.

'Come on, is it?'

'*No*,' I say. Something swells up and chokes me and next thing I'm crying.

Colette says something and I flinch away and try to look out the window. The lights of cars blur and dazzle. I scrunch my eyes shut but the tears force their way out anyway. I bite my lip and choke on a massive sob.

The car slides to a stop though we're not back at Colette's house yet. I feel her hand on the back of my neck. 'It's OK,' she says, dead soft and nice. I give up. I turn and sort of fall against her and she puts her arms round me and I know I'll never be able to stop.

A long time later I sit up, shivering, and blot my burning face with tissues. My breath shudders but I've got hold of myself. My face feels swollen and raw. There's a banging in my head and I feel sort of outside myself. Spaced out and knackered, like I've been awake for days.

Colette hands me another tissue. 'Better?' The front of her jumper is all soggy with tears. I hope there isn't any snot.

'Yeah. Sorry.'

'*I'm* sorry. Your mum upset you, didn't she? That's what started this?'

I suppose it is in a way. I nod.

'Come on, let's get you home.'

'What about Vicky?'

'She went to the party. You won't have to see her until Sunday. When *naturally* she will apologise, and –'

I swallow. 'Me too.'

'That's OK then.' She says it like it's not a big deal. She starts the engine. When the dashboard clock lights up it says twenty to nine but it feels like the middle of the night.

We're at her house in a few minutes. Half an hour ago I thought I'd never be back here again. The light's on in the hall. No Vicky for two days. I can hardly drag myself out of the car.

Colette seems to know how I feel. 'Go on,' she says. 'Get those wet clothes off and I'll run you a bath. Are you hungry? You haven't had any tea.'

I shake my head.

'Well, I'll heat up some soup anyway. You'll probably feel like it in a bit.'

I move in a blur of tiredness and relief. Let her take control. Have a bath. Eat soup. She hands me two paracetemol and a glass of water. 'Go on, take those and go on up to bed. You look exhausted.'

There's a hot water bottle in my bed. I hug it. Don't think. Sleep.

* * *

I wander into the living-room with my cornflakes, flick through the TV channels. Saturday morning crap. Then

I hear Colette getting out of the shower upstairs and my stomach dips. Oh God. Last night. My face burns at the memory. I decide to make her a cup of tea and hope she won't mention it.

'So what do you normally do on Saturdays, Declan?' she asks when we're both drinking our tea.

I shrug. 'Just hang around and that.'

'D'you miss your friends?'

'Not really.'

'Look, it's a lovely day. What do you say to going out somewhere?' She has this sort of hopeful look on her face and I suddenly wonder what *she* normally does on Saturdays – is she glad to get Princess Vicky out of the way or does she miss her?

'I don't mind.'

'Any ideas where you'd like to go?'

'I dunno.' Then for some reason I remember the houses at the loony bin. 'Mountains?'

'Oh.' She sounds a bit uncertain. 'I suppose – yes, we could go down to the Mournes.' She grins at me. 'OK, why not?'

So an hour later we're back in the car.

'Look over there,' says Colette, when the dark shadow of the mountains first hunches up ahead. 'That's where we're going. We'll be there in half an hour.'

'I never knew they were so near.'

'About thirty miles away. Have you really never been there?'

I shake my head.

Half an hour later we're driving into a big forest. The mountains are so close you feel you could reach out and touch them. It's like that *Lord of the Rings* film.

At first it's weird walking on my own with Colette

because I keep thinking she's going to start on about … well, any one of the long list of things I don't want to talk about. Mum. Vicky. Last night. But she doesn't. She just keeps looking round and saying how lovely it is and how long it is since she's been out in the country. I only half-listen. The lower paths are busy with people. Lots of dogs splashing in the river. But soon it starts to get steeper and lonelier. Then we need all our breath just for getting up the path and I stop worrying about what Colette might say. The paths are covered in mushy leaves and the air has a damp leafy smell I never smelled before. Even though I'm sweating getting up the hill, I feel sort of clean.

'Let's stop for a rest at the end of this path,' pants Colette. 'Have some lunch.'

I rush to get to the end of the path first. And gasp. 'Jesus!'

All the way up through the forest you could only catch the odd glimpse of the mountains. But suddenly here they are, huge and bare and grey-green. Nowhere to hide – sort of scary. Sheep turn their woolly heads and stare at me, then go back to eating the grass.

I jump onto the low stone wall and wait for Colette. I try to imagine Mum here. Or anyone I know. Imagine Barry pushing his big belly up that hill.

'Sandwiches and stuff in there,' says Colette, dumping her wee rucksack on the ground. 'It's lovely, isn't it?'

'Yeah.' I struggle to say more. I mean, she's driven all the way here. 'I've never seen anywhere as … as wild as this. I mean, you can see mountains from Belfast, can't you, but it's not like this.'

She smiles and hands me an apple. 'Vicky's dad and I used to come here before we were married. It's nice having someone to come with.'

I turn and rummage in the rucksack for a drink when the wall seems to shake.

Thundering towards us are three horses, manes and tails flying, hooves ringing on the hard forest path. For a second it looks like they're going to run over the top of us but they slow into what I now know is a trot and turn left up the stony path beside our wall. Their riders laugh and call to each other.

I follow them with my eyes as far as I can.

Colette sees me looking. 'That'll be you this time next week,' she says.

'Nah. I'll just be shovelling the shit.'

'Would you like to learn to ride?'

I feel the slow burn of my cheeks. Is it so obvious? I shrug. 'Not much point.'

'Why not?'

'Well, you know –' I wave the Coke bottle to show it's no big deal. 'I'll be going home soon.'

'So?'

'Not much riding round our way. 'Cept joyriding.' I laugh but it comes out wrong – a hard sort of sound.

'You don't have to stay there forever, Declan.' She brushes crumbs off her jeans. 'You're leaving school this year, aren't you?'

'Yeah, but – where else would I go?'

'What do you want to do?'

I shrug again. 'Haven't thought about it.' And definitely don't want to talk about it.

She doesn't start into the usual stuff, though. Instead she starts going on about herself. Which is way better than me having to say anything.

'God, I remember fifth year. Swotting every night for months to get good grades.'

'Like Vicky?'

Vicky's always doing her homework. Every night.

Colette laughs. 'Vicky does *nothing*! Well, she does what she has to and nothing more. She's not as ... as *hungry* as I was. I was obsessed. Your mum thought I was mad.'

It *sounds* mad. But then look at Colette now, in her nice house and all, and look at Mum. Not that I could start all that homework and stuff.

'Vicky keeps changing her mind about what she wants to do,' Colette goes on. 'She used to say she wanted to be a vet but she's not good enough at science. I think she might end up doing law like her dad.'

'Oh.'

'Declan?' She smiles. 'People don't *have* to end up doing the same as their parents, you know.'

'Yeah. Can we go on up to the top of that hill?'

* * *

We end the day with fish suppers in a dead old-fashioned café in Newcastle, facing each other across one of those shiny old tables. Every time the door opens, a whip of cold, mountainy air lashes into the warm greasy café fug. Locals queue up for takeaway but we're the only ones sitting in.

'God, these are lovely,' says Colette, dipping a big fat salty chip into tomato ketchup. 'I haven't had fish and chips for years. We used to get them every Friday night for a treat when I was wee. From the chippie round the corner.'

'The Golden Fry?'

'Yes! Don't tell me it's still there?'

'Yeah.' I make a chip buttie and squash the two halves together. Butter oozes out and I lick it off my fingers.

'Can you still get mushy pea fritters?'

'Yuck, I don't think so! That sounds gross.' I look at Colette, all neat and clean, though her short hair's a bit ruffled by the wind, and try to link her with something as minging as a mushy pea fritter.

She laughs. 'Frankie never needed to ask me what I wanted; it was always the same.'

'Fat Frankie? Was *he* there in those days?'

'It wasn't that long ago. Is he any slimmer these days?'

'He's huge. No-one knows how he fits his belly behind the counter.'

'That's what we always used to say!'

'Too many sausage suppers!' I spear a chip and we both laugh.

'I'd forgotten all about Fat Frankie till now,' says Colette. 'Me and your mum and dad used to go there. When we were too young to get into the pubs and didn't have anywhere to go, there was always the chippie. We used to put our money together and share a chip. That's when we were about fourteen or so. After your mum and dad started going out together I didn't really hang round with them.'

'Did they not want you?'

'Partly.' She takes a sip of tea. 'Mainly it was because I was always studying. All I thought about was exams and doing well and getting away from home. I was the odd one out.'

I try to imagine Mum being fourteen and sharing a chip in Fat Frankie's with her boyfriend. 'I don't remember my dad,' I hear myself saying.

'No. Well.' Colette looks as if she doesn't want to talk

about my dad. Then her face kind of softens. 'You're very like him, Declan. I don't just mean to look at – though you do look like him. I mean – you know.'

I don't know. Not really. Just a few stupid facts. He played the guitar. He never had a job. He got killed in a car crash when I was one. How had having a laugh about Fat Frankie led us here?

Colette says, 'OK, I'll go up and pay.' Just as she stands up her mobile rings, making me jump. It's sitting on the table and I see the display flashing: VICKY CALLING. She grabs it and I hear half a conversation – pretty quiet, because Colette's the kind of person who thinks it's rude to yell into your phone in public.

'Oh right. Yes, that should be fine.' She sounds a bit cold. Normally she talks to Vicky like she really loves her. Thinking about Vicky coming back home tomorrow night is enough to make my last couple of chips turn to cold rubber in my mouth.

Tomorrow I have to apologise.

Dear Vicky. I am sorry that I hit you. Declan Kelly.

Only this time, that won't be enough.

Chapter 18

VICKY

The horses arched their necks and pranced at the entrance to the farm trail. Even Joy, normally quiet and sweet, was all bizz, ears pricked and nostrils flared. It was that kind of afternoon that made you feel you could run up a mountain or gallop for miles – all gold and blue and sharp. The cold air scratched my eyes – I'd hardly slept last night. One minute I was over the moon about Rory; the next I'd remember what I'd said to Declan.

'God, I've missed this,' Fiona said, stroking Joy's grey freckled neck. 'I hadn't realised how much.'

'I'm never having babies,' I stated. 'Not if it means not being able to ride for months.'

Fiona laughed. 'I used to say that. But things change – mind you, I hope you won't even think about it for at least another ten years. Fifteen would be better.'

'Mum was only nineteen when she had me.'

'Well, yes.' You could tell she didn't want to say anything nasty about Mum. She changed the subject. 'Mossbrook again next Saturday?'

'Yes. Can't wait. We *so* want to qualify for Dublin.'

A bird flew out of the hedge and Flight skittered sideways, bumping into Joy who laid back her ears and made a face at him. Fiona laughed. 'Lucky for me Sally's been riding her. She'd have been too fresh for me today otherwise.'

'Flight's a bit full of himself,' I admitted, as he nearly pulled my arms out of their sockets. 'He could do with more exercise during the week. 'Specially if I'm going to keep him fit enough for showjumping.' I had a horrible image of myself next week at Mossbrook, storming round the arena, out of control, letting the team down. In front of Rory. 'D'you think Dad would pay for a few extra lessons? Like, one a week?'

I'd meant to ask him last night but as soon as we'd got home he and Fiona had given me this gorgeous French perfume so it didn't seem the moment to ask for more.

Fiona considered. 'What does Cam charge for private lessons?'

'Twenty-five.'

'Hmm. That's a fair bit on top of what he pays for your livery.'

'Oh Fiona!' I couldn't believe she was being so negative. 'It's only for a few weeks, till the league's over. He can afford it.'

'It's not that. But he might think you should pay half or something.'

'But that'd be half my pocket money!' I bet if Molly needed an extra twenty-five pounds' worth of nappies every week he wouldn't think twice, I gloomed, biting at my glove. 'What's the point in buying me a showjumper and not letting me have proper lessons?'

Fiona laughed. 'Vicky, he hasn't said no yet! Look,

sweetheart, it's nothing to do with me.' She could always cop out of things by saying they weren't her business. 'I tell you what,' she said, 'I'll put in a word for you.'

'OK.' I smiled at her. She looked easy and relaxed on Joy, even if it was a year since she'd been in the saddle. But then Fiona had been riding since she was four. We turned on to a grassy path and Flight gave a high-spirited buck and snatched at the bit.

'Soon,' I told him, looking round for logs to jump.

'Oh yes, Cam said your cousin was coming up to help next week,' said Fiona, as if she had just remembered. 'Work experience or something?'

'Hmm.' I felt my good mood evaporate. I twisted a bit of Flight's red mane. I licked the inside of my mouth, feeling again the raw, sore flesh. Imagining it red and open. You cow. You nasty, vindictive cow. 'Are you up for a canter? Race you to the top of that hill.'

* * *

Dad lounged in his favourite armchair, rugby on the TV, Molly at his feet on her activity mat. She kept rolling onto her side and grabbing Dad's feet and gurgling.

'Aww,' said Fiona. 'Are you playing rugby with your daddy's foot? Are you? Are you?'

Puke, I thought. Talking of which, there was a distinct whiff of shit in the air. Had everyone else lost their sense of smell?

'I don't know why you say she's so exhausting to look after all day, Fi,' said Dad with a smug air. 'We've had a great time together. She's been as happy as Larry all after-noon. Who *was* Larry, anyway?'

'No idea. But I bet whoever he was he wouldn't have

been so happy if *he'd* had a dirty nappy,' said Fiona, swooping down and bearing Molly off to change her.

I plonked myself down on the sofa, shifting Tigger from down the side of the cushion. Molly was obsessed with him. I hardly ever let her touch him but that morning I'd let her have him for a while. I wriggled my toes. We'd ended up riding round the farm trail for two hours and my legs were aching.

On screen the rugby looked muddy and primeval. There was a clique of girls at school whose boyfriends played on various teams. They were always getting up early on Saturdays and watching them in the rain. If if *if* anything happened with Rory would I be one of them? I imagined him coming off the pitch, sweaty and muddy, hugging me. I found the idea strangely exciting. And he was coming to watch me jump! This time next week! I imagined myself trotting out of the arena, bending down and kissing him on the way past. What would he think of my legs in white jodhpurs? I stretched them out on the sofa. There was no getting away from it – they were pretty sturdy.

'Here, darling, go to your big sister.' I started out of my Rory-dream as Fiona plopped Molly – now thankfully smelling of baby powder – in my lap. 'Keep her occupied while I make dinner?'

'OK,' I mumbled. I joggled her about a bit.

'Dah!' she said, grabbing at my pony-tail. I prised her hands away. Delighted at this game, she shrieked, 'Dah!' again and yanked harder.

'Ouch! That hurt!' I released my hair. 'Bad girl, Molly.'

She roared with laughter. Her cheeks were big red balloons.

Dad turned round. 'Vicky! Can you not keep her a bit quieter? This is the last ten minutes. Honestly, you girls. You just get her all excited. She was as good as gold for me.'

I laid her down on her activity mat but she grizzled and arched her back.

'I know.' I pulled out Tigger. She crowed and made a grab for him. Seconds later all was peaceful. Dad beamed at the screen – Ireland was winning; Molly beamed at Tigger and stuck his ear in her mouth. She did look quite cute. I sighed and picked up *Macbeth*. We had a test on Monday. I tried not to mind Molly slobbering all over Tigger's ears and wondered if he would survive going into the washing machine.

* * *

'Hey, Mum, where are you?' I could hear cutlery and talking in the background.

Mum laughed. 'In a chip shop in Newcastle.' She said it as if this was a perfectly normal place for her to be on a Saturday evening in November.

'Why?'

'You're always telling me to get out more.'

'Yes, but…'

So he was getting a reward for hitting me! Suddenly I felt really confused. Mum's voice was low and furtive. 'Look, Vic, when you get back tomorrow night Declan will apologise to you. Naturally.'

'Hmm.' I picked at a loose thread on my jodhpurs.

'And you, *naturally*, will apologise to him.'

I sighed. 'I know.' I pulled the thread out.

'OK, just wanted to make that clear.'

I ended the call and pushed open the living-room door. Fiona was leaning over Dad's chair.

'So you see, Peter darling, she really does need those lessons. I mean, this could be her big chance.' She sounded very earnest. They both turned and smiled when they heard me.

Dad stretched out his hand to me. 'What's all this, princess? Letting your wicked stepmother get round me? You'll have me ruined between the pair of you.'

I shot Fiona a grateful glance. 'So I can have the lessons?'

'You can have the lessons. On one condition.'

'What?'

'You make sure you qualify for Dublin!'

I hugged them both. 'I'll do my best!'

* * *

A low drone of conversation came from behind the kitchen door. When I pushed it open the talking died. There was Declan at the table just as he'd been that first night – was it only two weeks ago? Mum was ironing. The air was steamy and linen-scented. My school uniform hung over the back of a chair.

'Hello, love.' She folded the T-shirt she was ironing and added it to a pile of clothes. I saw at once that it was *his* T-shirt; *his* clothes. My chest contracted.

'OK.' Mum switched off the iron at the wall. 'Just going to take these upstairs.' She closed the door on her way out. Nought out of ten for subtlety, Mum.

I picked some grapes out of the fruit bowl.

Declan picked at a rough bit on the table.

He stared at me, his eyes like burnt matches. I stared

back. He was looking at my mouth. There was nothing to see now, from the outside. He slid his eyes away first. 'Vicky.' He'd hardly ever said my name before. 'I'm sorry I hit you.'

I seemed to see everything with hyper-clarity. A muscle twitched in his jaw. There was a tiny mole I'd never noticed before on his left cheek. He bit the side of his finger and I saw for the first time a strange round scar on the back of his hand.

Something tight and hard uncurled inside me. '*I'm* sorry,' I said. It was easier than I thought. 'I mean, *really* sorry.'

His dark eyes widened. 'Oh,' he said. 'Thanks. And,' in a rush, 'your book –'

I'd almost forgotten. 'Oh yeah. Well, you can just get it next week. Whatever.'

He nodded. The room was heavy with that awful mixture of embarrassment and goodwill that follows an apology. Fliss and Becca and I used to fall out all the time when we were younger. But we'd cry and hug each other. It's easier when you're girls. It's easier when you actually *like* each other.

Chapter 19

DECLAN

Cam looks in the wheelbarrow. 'Hmm.' She grins at me. 'Don't worry, it gets easier.'

It'd need to. Seaneen was right about the shit. I'm up to my eyes in it. I've been here for two hours and already I've seen, shovelled and smelled more horse shit than I knew existed.

Mucking out is backbreaking. It's also dead tricky. You have to sort of persuade the stuff onto a fork and make sure you aren't lifting up half the bed with it. Then you have to make the bed all neat again. I'm sweating like a boxer and my shoulders are killing me. What have I got myself into? This is only shit-shovelling and I can't even get it right. I straighten up and wipe the sweat out of my eyes. My hands stink of piss and shit. This is only my second bed.

Jim's about a hundred but he has six beds finished before I get to my third. He doesn't say much, but every so often he looks at what I've done and gives his verdict. Usually a sniff. The best I get is 'not bad'.

It takes most of the morning to get the beds finished. Then Cam gets me stuffing hay nets again. At least I know how to do that. It's cold in the big, open-sided hayshed and the sweat running down my back chills and dries. Cam takes horses out one at a time and works them in the school. She stands in the middle and they run round her on a rope. I recognise Flight. He dances, lifting his legs high. He looks amazing but a bit mad. When she cracks her whip he shoots his back legs out behind him before going dead fast. His hooves pound the hard sand and his neck arches like a charger. I have to make myself look away and concentrate on my hay nets.

'This one needs more than the odd lunge,' Cam calls to Jim when she brings Flight in, sweating. 'If Vicky expects to jump him properly she should be exercising him every day. A lesson a week and a quick lunge when I've time – which, let's face it, isn't very often at the minute – isn't enough.'

'More money than sense,' growls Jim. 'I could have bought ten horses for what they paid for that.'

I get on with stuffing the nets. It's like they've forgotten Vicky's anything to do with me, which suits me.

'Here,' says Cam. 'You want to know how to put a rug on?'

'OK.' I might as well. Even though I am going to walk out of this yard at the end of the week and never see another horse. Vicky probably thinks I can't do it. Mum doesn't care. Seaneen thinks it's just shovelling shit. So I learn how to put a rug on Flight. It's like putting on a coat with loads of straps. Flight looks bored and stamps his feet a bit, but even when I do up one of the straps wrong Cam's dead patient. 'It's OK,' she says. 'Just try again.'

I don't have many minutes to stop all day. This place is all go. Horses out to the field. Horses in from the field. Nudge's owner comes and leads her to the edge of the school to eat grass. She spends ages with Nudge, grooming her and talking to her and hosing her bad leg with cold water. If I had a horse I would do all that.

Me and Jim eat our lunch in the tack room. That's where they keep the saddles and that. Colette gave me sandwiches this morning and by the time I get to eat them I'm starving. Normally at this time on a Monday I'd be in Psycho's class getting the bollocks bored off me.

'You'll be tired the night,' says Jim. 'Weekends are enough for me these days. It's as much as I can do to see to my own horses. But I wouldn't see Cam stuck.'

'How long have you worked for her?' Jim's easier to talk to than most people.

He chews a bit of bread. 'It'd be a right few years now. I worked for her da and then when he was killed and she opened up the yard I just stayed on.'

'Her dad was killed?'

'Oh aye, and her ma. In a car crash. She was only nineteen. She inherited the farm and started up the horses all by herself. There's not many could do that.'

'No.' It's weird to think Cam's family died the same way my dad did.

Jim is skinny with tattoos and gaps in his teeth. He wears one of those old-man caps and a waxed jacket that's so faded you could only guess what colour it started off as. He doesn't look like a man who would have his own horses. I thought only snobs could afford horses.

Talking of snobs, after lunch I have to lead this wee kid round on Hero, a tiny pony, while Cam gives him a lesson. He's so small his legs don't even reach to the bottom of the saddle, but he has all the gear. Hat and boots and those jodhpur things Vicky has. And a wicked-looking whip. All matching. His mum hangs over the fence watching every move. 'Oh, well *done*, Casper, darling!' Casper! No wonder he's a prat. When it's time to get down he doesn't even pat Hero or anything. Just runs to his mum on his fat legs shrieking, 'I want a *fast* pony next time, Mummy. That stupid pony's too *slow*.'

By the time I take Hero to his stable and take off his tack – Cam shows me what to do – it's getting dark. I stand in the yard with Hero's saddle over my arm and sense the dim, quiet fields all round. The clean, cold air burns my nostrils. It's weird to be somewhere without streets and lights and cars. I can't believe how fast the day's gone. I've mucked out six stables, put on three rugs, filled twelve hay nets, pushed a million wheelbarrows to the muck heap and brought five horses in from the field. That was the best bit, handling the horses. I know some of the names. Flight is my favourite. I sort of wish he wasn't. Then there's Nudge, of course, and a hairy black one called Kizzy.

The last thing I do is make up feeds. Or rather, watch Jim do it. You'd think it'd be easy but it isn't. The horses all get different stuff: food to make them put on weight, food to make them lose weight, food to make them calm, food to make them lively. Garlic. Herbs. Vitamins. There's a chart on the wall with it all written down. Jim sends me round the stables with the food. The horses don't even look at me. They tear straight in and then there's just the sound of munching. I'm starving too. Lunch feels like ages ago.

'You'd better hurry if you're going to get that bus,' Cam says as I'm coming out of Nudge's stable. It feels like years since I got the bus this morning yet today's gone a million times faster than a normal day. School gives you too much time to think. As I pick up my bag from the tack room I realise I'm looking forward to tomorrow.

'I'll take him to the bus stop,' says Jim. 'Sure it's only a minute out of my way and it's raining again. Come on, son.'

Jim's car is this ancient old Land Rover you have to really climb into. It smells of damp and dogs and smoke. He lights a cigarette and turns the key in the ignition. Country and western jangles out. Jim parks the car in a gateway and waits until we see the lights of the bus coming round the corner.

'See you tomorrow,' he says as I climb down. 'You done well the day, son,' he adds. 'Fair play to you.'

* * *

A blonde woman swings her leg over Joy's saddle and dismounts right beside where I'm filling the hay nets.

'Hello there,' she says. 'You're Declan?'

I nod. She must be Fiona, Vicky's da's wife. I wonder what Vicky's told her about me. Nothing, or she wouldn't be so nice. She smiles and says, 'Getting on OK?'

'I think so.'

'Would you like a ride on Joy? She's very quiet, and I've just had her out for an hour so she's pretty tired. Why don't you ride her round the school for ten minutes? You can cool her down for me.' She has a posh voice but she's smiley.

'I can't ride.' It's stupid how much I hate admitting this.

'Time you learned.' She shoves her hat at me.

I scramble up. Joy's smaller than Flight and not as bouncy. As we walk across the yard to the school I try to remember the stuff Vicky taught me.

'Hey,' Fiona says, 'thought you couldn't ride?'

'I can't. This is my second time. Vicky let me have a go on Flight last week.'

Her blue eyes widen at this. 'Gosh, you're privileged! Now, heels down.'

She stands in the middle of the school and I walk round her. Joy is sort of lollopy. It doesn't feel as amazing as it did on Flight but I can feel myself relaxing more.

Cam pauses at the gate of the school, a tangle of head-collars in her arms. 'Hi Fiona! You pinching my new worker?'

Fiona laughs. 'You don't mind?'

'Course not. He deserves it. He's learned more in three days than most people do in a month.'

She can't mean this – I have to ask Jim about a thousand questions an hour – but it's a nice thing to say.

'Remember you're staying here until Vicky comes up later,' Cam reminds me, when the three of us are walking back to the yard with Joy.

I haven't forgotten. Hanging round here will be loads better than getting the bus back to Belfast. When I sit down to eat my lunch I see that Colette's packed twice as much as usual so I can have some later, but I'm so hungry I eat most of the extra sandwiches as well. I go out to put the papers in the bin and Cam says, 'If you clean all the tack this afternoon – I'll show you what to do – I'll give you a lesson at teatime. You can ride Kizzy. Fiona reckons you're a natural, so let's see if she's right.'

* * *

I don't know about being a natural. It doesn't feel like it when I bounce and bump all over Kizzy's broad back as Cam stands in the middle of the school hollering, 'Up down, up down, up down, oh you nearly had it there. OK, bring her back to walk and get your breath back.'

My legs scream with pain and Kizzy sighs – she's probably pissed off with me by now. Cam's trying to teach me that rising trot thing. It looks easy when you see other people do it but getting your own legs to respond to the up and down beat of the horse is a different story. And every time your arse hits the hard leather of the saddle with a bump it *wrecks* you.

Thank God Jim's gone home and there's no one around. I must look even stupider than I feel. Please don't let Vicky arrive yet. Every time I hit the saddle I think, that's it, my legs are going to give up now, they can't lift me up this time, but every time I grit my teeth and they do.

'Don't *try* so hard! Relax and it'll come!'

Relax! If I had enough breath I would tell Cam where to go. Then suddenly – I can do it! Not every time, but for about ten strides I get it right. Then bump, bump, bump and yes, I get it again. Up – down – up – down. I laugh. 'I can do it!'

Cam laughs too. 'Well done. OK, walk for a bit and get a rest.'

'No way. I don't want to forget how to do it.'

She's suddenly severe. 'Declan. When I say walk you walk. And you need to think of your horse. D'you think Kizzy enjoys trotting round in circles non-stop?'

I slow to a walk. 'Sorry.'

'Most important thing – always put your horse first. If you want a machine, get a bike.' But she's smiling. For half an hour she keeps me working, sometimes walking, sometimes trotting, and every time it gets easier.

'When can I canter?'

'Typical boy. I suppose you think you'll be jumping round these jumps by the end of the week!'

When she says 'the end of the week' my legs betray me and for a few strides I'm bumping and sliding again like an eejit. Only two more days. Next week it'll be back to school and this will seem like a dream. A busy, exciting, unreal step sideways from my real life. I know I won't be jumping by the end of the week. Or any time.

'Well done,' says Cam. 'OK, you can put her to bed and get Flight out for Vicky.'

As I'm tacking up Flight – I can do it properly as long as I concentrate – Cam comes into the stable. 'Just got a text from Vicky. They're running a bit late. Can you take him out and warm him up? Just walk him round the school, get him loosened up a bit. I've another lesson at eight and if he isn't loosened up there won't be time for her to jump him.'

'Me? Take *Flight*?'

'It's only to walk him round the school for fifteen minutes. He won't do anything. Just keep him on a loose rein and be gentle but firm.'

'But –'

'Go on, Declan. I need to go and grab a sandwich. I'll be right back. I promise you'll be fine. I wouldn't let you do it if I didn't think you were perfectly competent.'

Riding round the floodlit school on Flight, all my own, is – magic. At first I think he'll play me up but Cam's right – he just walks round the school. Beyond the fence everything is dark, but in here is our own lit-up world. Just me and Flight. Our breath snakes into the night like the aftermath of a firework. I reach down and clap his warm neck.

A brisk thud of riding boot on concrete replaces the muffled skim of Flight's hoof beats in the sand. I look up to see Vicky pulling up at the gate. 'Oh!' she says. 'I didn't know that was *you*.'

At her words the spell holding me and Flight splinters.

'Yeah. Cam said if he wasn't warmed up there wouldn't be enough time for you to jump.' I try not to sound apologetic – after all Cam did *tell* me. I bring him to the gate, kick my feet out of the stirrups like she taught me, and try to jump off. I brace my legs for landing, willing them not to buckle like they've done the other two times. Not a chance, though: all that trotting has wrecked them and my knees give way before I can stop them. Please let her not have seen. It's like a test and for some reason I have to pass. She's been a lot nicer since I gave her that thump on the mouth but as she grabs the reins from me her eyes are cold as pebbles.

Chapter 20

VICKY

'Don't forget I'm out tonight, Vic,' Mum said, coming into my room with some clean laundry on Thursday afternoon.

I turned round from my desk. 'Oh yeah. Poetry reading, isn't it?' At least she wasn't trying to drag me along.

'Yes, I won't be late. Be –'

'Were you going to say *be good*?'

She laughed but kind of seriously. 'I suppose I'm a bit anxious after Friday. I don't want to leave you together if there's a bad atmosphere.'

'There isn't.'

'Sure?'

I sighed and clicked the top of my pen. 'Mum, we might just manage to spend an evening in the same house without violence.'

'Hmm,' she said, as if she wasn't so sure. 'You were very quiet last night. You didn't fall out again, did you?'

I sighed. 'I was just tired after my lesson.'

'Cam said Declan was doing amazingly well,' Mum

went on. 'She couldn't believe he'd had nothing to do with horses before. Says he's a natural.'

'Mum, I need to get this English done.'

'Stop changing the subject, Vic. You don't ... you don't *mind* him being at the yard, do you?'

'No.'

'Because it would be very selfish of you.'

'I *don't* mind. I'm even letting him come to watch me jump on Saturday.'

'With Rory?'

'Yeah, Fliss and Becca *said* they would come but they're not. I think it was just a trick to get Rory along.'

When she left I doodled in the margin of my *Macbeth* and when she called me down for tea I still hadn't finished. I decided to work in the living-room when she went out – see if a change of scene would help me concentrate.

Declan was there, watching *Top Gear*. He was just out of the shower. Every day he came home filthy and stinking of horse piss. I never got like that at the yard, but then I only ever rode and went home.

I pulled books out of my bag and piled them round me on the sofa. 'Mum hates me doing homework in here,' I said. 'She's got this thing about working *in* your room, *at* your desk. Is yours like that?'

He looked up as if he was surprised to hear me talking to him. 'Nah,' he said. 'She's not bothered.'

'Lucky you.' I sighed and started twisting a bit of hair to look for split ends. I really wasn't in the mood for homework.

'D'you want me to turn the TV off?' He waved the remote.

I glanced up from my book. 'What? Oh no, you're

OK. I quite like background noise. Of course *Mum* says you can't concentrate that way. Year Twelve's crap, isn't it? We just get all the teachers stressing at us all the time. Are yours like that?'

He shrugged. I'd thought *I* was a good shrugger until Declan came to stay.

I tried to imagine his school. I supposed it must be pretty rough. Maybe they didn't really bother about exams and things. He certainly never did any homework. Not like Rory: I knew he wanted to go to Cambridge to study medicine like his dad. I wanted to do law like *my* dad. Maybe that's what everyone ended up doing. Declan's dad was killed in a car crash, only there was some mystery about it – like it was a stolen car or something. Because when Gran died I remembered the neighbours whispering at the wake. *Poor Kathleen … it was the shock done it … the police at the door … she couldn't go through it again*. Declan must have heard them too.

I looked at him now, watching *Top Gear*, his dark hair damp from the shower. It had grown a bit, so he didn't look quite so much of a wee hard man. I wondered what he would say if I suddenly asked him about Gran. I would kind of like to know what he thought – did *he* blame himself for Gran's heart attack? It *was* the day after he was caught joyriding. Then my tongue slid across the roughness inside my lip, and I knew I would never dare ask.

I looked down at *Macbeth* again. 'Like our English teacher, Mrs Brennan – she gave us a test yesterday *and* we've got these stupid questions to do tonight. Lady Macbeth. She's sleepwalking. She's mad as a rat and we're meant to analyse all this meaningless rambling.'

'It's *not* meaningless.' It took me a second to realise he

had spoken. 'She's only mad with guilt. And bottling it up. *What's done cannot be undone.*'

I felt my mouth drop open so far that he could probably see the red mark where he thumped me. '*You* do *Macbeth*?'

'Yeah. Why not? Cause I'm at a thick school?' His dark eyes narrowed.

I bit my pencil. 'No, of course not.' I bent over the book again, letting a curtain of hair hide my burning face. I tried to think of something to say to change the subject. Because he was right – I never imagined people at that sort of school doing the same as us. Not *Shakespeare*. I thought of Mum being so desperate for me to be nice to him, so I said, 'How's your mum?' before I realised how that must sound – like, 'Oh yes, talking of people who are mad as rats, how's your mum?'

He looked at me closely. 'D'you *really* want to know?'

Did I? 'If you want to tell me.'

Another shrug. 'Colette says up and down, but I think it's more like just down.' His voice was uncertain. 'Friday night,' he bit his lip, 'she was really, like, angry. Nasty. Then on Tuesday she just cried.'

'She phoned my mum last night. Did she tell you? That's why we were late for my lesson.' Mum hadn't told me what Theresa had said but she'd talked to her for ages even though she knew I needed to get to the yard.

'Yeah. She wants to go home.'

'Oh. I suppose that's – well, natural.'

Suddenly he said, 'Is your mum away out with a man?'

'Of course not!' I snapped. Suddenly I didn't feel so sympathetic. 'She's at a poetry reading. What on *earth* made you think she was on a date?'

I saw his lips twitch at the word 'date'. 'Well, I dunno, just – does she not have boyfriends?'

'*No.*'

'What, never?'

'Never. Unless,' I tried to make a joke of it, 'unless she has a secret life when I'm at Dad's. Why, does yours?'

'Have a secret life?'

'Boyfriends?' I sucked the end of a strand of hair.

'Sometimes.'

'God, I'm *so* glad mine doesn't. My friend Fliss – her mum's had a few. Do you not hate it?'

'Depends. She's sort of happier when she has a man. Trouble is, she has crap taste.'

'Oh.' I wrinkled my nose. 'You mean they're prats?'

'*Prats*? No, I could handle prats. It's psychopaths I don't like.' He was obviously trying to impress me.

'I'd hate Mum to have a boyfriend,' I admitted. 'I know Dad has Fiona and that's fine. I mean, she's lovely. But it's different with Mum. Does that sound really selfish?'

'Well … I dunno.'

It did. But I didn't know how to feel any other way about it.

Chapter 21

DECLAN

'OK to trot here?' Cam half turns in Flight's saddle.

'Yep.' I gather up the reins. Out here on the farm trail, surrounded by open country, Kizzy feels a lot livelier. Her black ears are pricked. The rising thing is easy now; I don't have to think about it.

In front of me Flight's ginger bum swings powerfully, muscles rippling like an athlete's. I push Kizzy up beside him. 'Does Vicky mind you riding Flight?' I ask.

'She wants him kept fit for jumping. She can't have it both ways. I don't have time to lunge him today.'

'Does riding not take longer, but?'

She laughs. 'Ah, this isn't *work*. This is me thanking you for working so hard all week. A treat for your last day, if you like.'

Your last day. I push the thought away and look round at the fields instead. Riding in the school is great – yesterday I got a whole hour's lesson when someone didn't turn up – but being out here is magic. It's a clear day with just a few wisps of cloud. Cold air itches my hands and the leaves crunch under the horses' hooves, even though it's December tomorrow.

My legs ache with trotting but Kizzy feels like she could go on for ever. When Cam asks, 'Are your legs not getting tired?' I just go, 'No,' and grit my teeth, but she looks at me and laughs. 'I keep forgetting you've only been on a few times. Come on, we'll walk.'

As Kizzy slows to a swinging walk I look round. Fields as far as you can see. Mostly empty, some with jumps in them – solid-looking things made out of logs and bits of hedge, way more scary than the brightly-coloured poles in the school or at Mossbrook. More like something you would see on the racing on the TV. The trail goes round the edges of the fields and then up through a wood.

'Is this *all* yours?'

'Yes. It used to be my parents' farm. I'm sure Jim's told you.'

Despite the cold my cheeks burn. Jim *did* tell me. I feel crap for forgetting and worse for mentioning it. 'Oh. Um, yeah.'

Please don't let her say any more, I think, but she goes on, as if it's a normal thing to talk about. 'I wanted to keep the land, but I didn't want to farm.' I wish I hadn't asked. 'I sold half the land to finance the stables and the farm trail,' she goes on. 'I always wanted to work with horses and I'd just finished training when it happened. Anyway, I've been running the yard ever since.'

'It's hard work, isn't it?'

For some reason it's easier to talk to someone when you're riding along side by side. Maybe because you can't see their face.

She laughs. 'It would have been a jolly sight harder this week without you.'

Happiness floods me like hot tea. I try to sound casual. 'Well, I still don't know *much*.'

'True,' she says and the tea cools a bit. 'Oh, don't look like that! I mean you know hardly anything compared to everything there is to know. Gosh, *I* know hardly anything. But you've certainly picked up the basics really quickly.'

'Jim says my beds are still crap,' I admit.

'You'd need to be mucking out for fifty years before you would please Jim.'

'I wish –'

I wish I could stay.

I wish this was my real life.

But I don't say it. All week I've dreaded this ending. I just didn't think it would be this *bad*. I twirl a piece of Kizzy's springy black mane. I twist it until my finger throbs. Bloody horses. Why did I ever go near them in the first place?

Ask her. She can only say no. But weekends – Vicky at the yard, hanging about, giving orders and dirty looks. Remember Wednesday night? She was nice to me all week at home, and then as soon as she got to the yard on Wednesday she was back to being a snotty bitch.

'When does Tony get back?' is what I finally ask.

Cam gives a huge sigh and Flight jumps sideways in alarm, skittering leaves with his dancing hooves. Cam doesn't even move in the saddle. 'Not for ages,' she says. 'I went to see him last night. He's got a pin in his leg.'

'Yuck.'

'Yes. It'll be spring at the earliest. You see – dangerous old brutes, horses. You stay away from them if you want to stay in one piece.' She strokes Flight's neck.

Ask her. 'Could I keep coming? At weekends I mean?'

'Yes, if you like.' She sounds like it's no big deal. 'Always glad of the help. Though I have to warn you, it won't be like this.'

'Like what?'

'No sloping off in the middle of the day for a jolly round the farm trail. I've lessons nearly all day on Saturdays. You going to want to lead kids round the school for hours?'

'I don't mind.' It'd be the horses I'd be leading, not the kids, I think.

She laughs. 'Even Casper?'

'Well –'

'Look, you're *great* with the horses. But you'll have to work on your people skills.'

'OK.' If a teacher said this I'd be raging.

'So you'll be up tomorrow?'

'Oh!' I suddenly realise. 'I told Vicky I'd go and watch her jumping at Mossbrook.' I look at Flight jingling his bit, arching his neck and dancing on the spot. I really, *really* want to see him jump tomorrow.

'That's OK. We'll give you a day off for good behaviour. Come on Sunday. There'll be plenty of tack cleaning. Something else you could improve on. Now,' her tone changes, 'what about your first canter?'

'Seriously?'

'I don't see why not.' She looks me up and down. 'You've got fantastic balance and you're not nervous, are you?'

'No.'

'OK, then. See that hill? We'll canter up it. Just relax. Lean forward a bit; grab her mane if you need to. The main thing is – enjoy it!'

I start to say 'OK' but Flight takes off like a bullet and

Kizzy plunges after him. For a moment the earth tilts, then I settle down into the power and speed. It's the best thing ever. Fast cars, motorbikes – nothing could beat this rush of trees past me and the drum of hooves up the hill. The wind whips tears from my eyes and Flight's hooves in front of me catapult tiny stinging stones into my hands and face.

It seems only seconds before Kizzy slows into a raggedy trot, then a walk. At the top of the hill both horses are huffing, nostrils flaring like Grand National winners. I try to speak and find I'm out of breath too.

'OK?' says Cam. 'Your face is all muddy!'

'That was –' I search for a word but nothing's good enough. I shake my head. 'I didn't think it'd be so fast!'

She laughs. 'It wasn't meant to be. This guy's just a bit full of himself and Kizzy didn't want to get left behind. But you stuck on brilliantly.'

We head back at a walk. Even Flight is tired, steam rising off his red shoulders. My legs are like chewed string and my cheeks smart and sting, but even so, the back of a horse feels like the best place in the world to be.

* * *

'Declan! Rory's here! Don't forget your gloves.'

I grab the gloves Colette dug out for me last night after seeing how raw my hands were, and the fleece I've been wearing to the yard all week. It smells of horses.

'Have a good time, love,' Colette says.

I get in and fasten the seatbelt. The car's small but very clean. I bet Rory's the kind of guy who's always cleaning his car. The radio's on, not a blaring techno beat like Emmet would have had; sounds like the sports news. I wonder what we're going to talk about the whole way to Mossbrook.

Nothing, at first. It takes a while to get out of the city and on to the motorway. Rory's driving is careful but confident. I feel safe with him. The only other guy I've been driven by was Emmet – and you never felt safe with Emmet. But Rory's the total opposite. I know he's eighteen but he seems older in some ways. Buying his own car and that. But in other ways he's younger than the guys round my way. Like, still being at school at eighteen. He's a big guy, around six feet tall and pretty broad. His brown hair's still damp. He must really fancy Vicky to be driving all this way to see her.

'Did you win your match?' Vicky told me he was playing rugby this morning. I don't know anyone who plays rugby.

'Yes, 15–3. Which was brilliant, because Mansfield usually beat us.'

'Great,' I say and there's another silence.

'D'you play?'

'Rugby? Nah. Football. Bit of Gaelic.'

'I've never tried Gaelic.'

Is he a Catholic or a Prod? Nobody seems to bother much round their way. Rory indicates and pulls out to pass a horsebox. I wonder if it's going to Mossbrook. I wonder if Flight went into the horsebox OK today.

'Have you been to this place before?' Rory asks.

'Two weeks ago. Don't ask me how to get there, though.'

'It's OK. I've got directions from Vicky. She said it's about an hour away. Good for the car to get a proper run. An old man had it before me. I don't think it's ever done more than thirty miles an hour in its life.'

'You must have saved for a long time. I'm a terrible saver.'

'Well, I've always wanted a car. I suppose if you want something badly enough you make sure you get it somehow.'

Yeah, I thought, in your world, mate.

We turn off the motorway and the little car swishes through puddly, bendy roads. We get stuck behind a tractor and trailer. Rory keeps cool – Emmet would have been tearing past it, honking like mad, not that there were ever any tractors round our way – but after a few minutes he starts to look a bit agitated. 'No chance of getting past on this road,' he says.

'Well, it'll have to turn off some time.'

'It's just … ' He glances at the dashboard clock. 'Vicky texted to say her team was jumping at two. It's after half one now. I wouldn't want to come all this way and miss her.'

Christ, I think, he really likes her! But then I don't want to miss Flight either.

'They jump two rounds,' I say, feeling like an expert. 'So even if you miss the first one –'

Just then the tractor indicates right and lumbers into a field. We're going to make it after all.

The car park is just like last time – all mud and neighs and shouts – but parking a Clio is a lot easier than parking a horsebox.

Rory looks round. 'So where d'you think Vicky will be?'

'Well, if they're jumping at two she's probably outside the ring, waiting to go in.' I love this feeling of knowing more about it than Rory.

'So where's that?' He pulls a woolly hat down over his hair and frowns into the rain.

'Inside. Look, you go past the practice arena and down that path. See?'

The practice arena is deserted apart from a black horse cantering down the far end towards a big fence. I recognise Patrick Scott and Dan. They're flying. I slow down beside the open gate to watch them for a second.

What happens next is so fast that I hardly know it's happened until it's over. The horse skids before the jump; there's a splintering crack of wood, then he's on the ground, all mixed up with bits of pole and Patrick. He struggles up with a grunt and charges away from the carnage, leaving Patrick under the broken bits of fence.

'Bloody hell!' I don't know if it's me or Rory who says it.

Then Dan hurtles towards us, reins and stirrups flying. No time for fear. I throw myself into the gateway, blocking his path. For a second I think he's going to mow me down but his hot breath fans my face, a stirrup bangs my shoulder and next thing I know I've grabbed his reins and he judders to a halt.

When I look up I see Rory in the arena, bending down beside Patrick. His voice travels through the rain. 'Don't try to move, mate. No, just keep still. That's right.' He turns and shouts over to me, 'Go and get someone quick! We need an ambulance!'

* * *

'So we missed Vicky jumping after all.' Rory slides into the driver's seat and hands me a packet of chips. A friendly smell of vinegar fills the car. We're parked outside a chip shop in some wee village in the arse-end of nowhere.

'It was all for a good cause.'

Rory opens his chips. 'I don't know how you just jumped in front of that mad horse. I thought he was going to run you over.'

'So did I,' I admit. 'He wasn't mad, but. Just scared.'

'I couldn't have done it for a million pounds. Anyway, the main thing is the guy's going to be OK. I thought he was a goner. You should have seen the hoof prints all over his back.' Rory shudders. 'And I thought rugby was rough.'

'Yeah.'

'Lucky we were there.'

Turned out the first aid volunteers were in the indoor arena getting a cup of tea. *And* there was some rule saying you weren't allowed to ride in the practice arena without someone in attendance. So a few people were going to be in trouble. Not me and Rory, though – we were heroes.

'So how come you knew exactly what to do? Not letting him move and all?'

Rory shrugs. 'I've done first aid. I'm going to be a doctor.'

'I suppose your da's a doctor, is he?

He looks surprised. 'He is, actually. I've got an interview at Cambridge next week.' He wrinkles his face as if that's a scary thought.

'Well, tell them what you just did and they'll let you in, no bother.'

'I wish!' He mops up some tomato ketchup and looks thoughtful. 'So what about you?'

'What about me?'

'You going to work with horses?'

'Nah.'

He looks surprised. 'Didn't you just do your work experience at the stables? What was that about if you don't want to work with horses?'

'Just something to do for a week.' I don't want to tell him I'm staying on at weekends. He might tell Vicky and I don't want her to know. Not yet.

'But you liked it, didn't you?'

'It was OK.'

'So why not do it for a career?'

'Because ...' I don't know how to explain it in any way that he'll understand. He's going to frigging Cambridge, for God's sake. To be a doctor. How can he understand that shovelling horse shit is out of my league? Then I get annoyed at myself, because one thing I've learned this week is that there's a hell of a lot more to it than shovelling shit.

But he's talking again. 'Surely there must be a course you can do at the tech?'

'For horses?'

'My friend's sister went off to do something like that. Racehorses, I think she works with. She went to college. Where was it? Enniskillen, I think.'

'I couldn't go to Enniskillen.' I'm not even sure where it is.

'Why not?'

I'm about to say I couldn't leave my mum, but I catch myself on. I remember last Friday night. *Just piss off, Declan.* So what if I did? What if I pissed off to Enniskillen? Or anywhere? It's such a big thought that I nearly choke on my chips.

Rory wraps his empty chip packet up tidily. 'You should at least find out about it. Seriously. Though the way you handled that horse today, maybe you should go into the circus.'

'Yeah, maybe.' I can see myself telling Mr Dermott that.

But I suppose it wouldn't do any harm to look it up.

Chapter 22

VICKY

I leaned over Dad's chair as he squinted at the label on the bottle. He was too vain to wear his glasses except for work.

'I don't know if we should have champagne,' I said. 'I feel a bit mean.'

'You won fair and square, darling.'

'Yes, you were brilliant, Vicky.' Fiona set three glasses on the table. 'Two fantastic rounds. Those lessons are obviously paying off, Peter.'

'I should hope so, at twenty-five quid a go,' said Dad, but he smiled as he twisted the bottle to uncork it.

'Flight was *amazing*.' I couldn't keep my mouth from stretching into a grin at the memory of Flight, confident and clever underneath me, launching at every jump without hesitation. 'It's just that we probably wouldn't have won if Patrick had been jumping.'

'You don't *know* that,' Dad put in. 'Anyway, it's put you at the top of the league.'

'For now.' I crossed my fingers.

'Well, there's only the Ulster final to go now, isn't there?' asked Fiona.

'Yeah, but it's not for three weeks – the Saturday before Christmas.'

'Here – don't let it overflow.' Dad sloshed the champagne into the glasses. We always seemed to be drinking champagne these days. Not that I was complaining. 'I hear your chap was the hero of the hour.'

'*Chap*? Wise up, Dad!' I took a glug of champagne and the fizz went up my nose. 'But yes, he knew exactly what to do,' I went on, mainly for the pleasure of talking about Rory. I'd been *so* gutted when he hadn't turned up to see my two perfect rounds, but when I realised he'd been at the centre of the drama outside, that made it all OK. And he *had* been in time to see our lap of honour, galloping round the arena with our red rosettes flying, the four of us. Magic. And Rory clapping and smiling from the side, fresh from his heroics. I was so proud of him.

'*And* Declan,' Fiona reminded me, as if she could read my thoughts.

I had to be generous. 'Yeah, they were both pretty good.'

Rory had told me all about it afterwards. I'd been putting Flight back onto the trailer and he'd come to talk to me. 'You should have seen that horse, Vicky,' he said, looking sick at the memory. 'I thought he was going to flatten Declan. I ducked! But he just grabbed and held on. Honestly, if he hadn't been so brave, God knows what that horse would have done!'

'Probably just stood around the car park eating grass,' I said. 'Can you pass me that tail bandage?'

'Um, this?'

'No, that's a travelling boot. That blue thing.'

'Oh.' He handed it to me. 'You're the one who knows about horses. But to me that horse looked pretty het up. He might have run onto the road or anything.'

'Well, he didn't.'

As if he'd just noticed, Rory glanced up and down at me. Under my warm, quilted coat I was still wearing my black jacket, white breeches and black leather boots. Despite the cold, damp air I felt my cheeks burn. 'You look very ...' He paused. 'I was going to say very sexy but you might think that's a bit forward.'

I'd never been called sexy before in my life! 'Thanks,' I said, and bent down to fix Flight's boots so he couldn't see how much I was blushing.

'So you're heading back to your dad's?'

'Soon as we drop this champion showjumper home.' I scratched Flight's damp neck.

'For the whole weekend?'

'Yeah. But it's only at Drumbo.'

'I'm away next week,' he said. 'Got my Cambridge interview. I'll be back on Thursday. Maybe we could go out on Friday for a pizza or something? I could take you to your dad's afterwards.'

'Oh, that's OK. He could pick me up on Saturday morning.' My heart thumped.

'Would you wear those jodhpur things?' He grinned.

'Ha ha!' I threw a dandy brush at him, he grabbed at my coat and next minute he was kissing me. I touched his face. It was damp but his cheeks were warm. Like mine. I never thought my first kiss would be on the ramp of a horsebox in the rain.

Remembering it now made me fizzy inside – it wasn't just the champagne.

* * *

'Homework all done?'

'Mum, you ask me that every Sunday night.' I shrugged my rucksack off my shoulders.

'Well, it's not long until your mocks.'

'I did Geography coursework all afternoon.'

'What about the yard? Declan said he didn't see you.'

'Well, it was too wet to ride. Not much point.'

'You used to hang around there for hours in all weathers.'

'Well, yes, when I was a *kid*. But you grow out of that stage.' I remembered myself with fat, short plaits and pink little-girl jodhpurs, buzzing round Cam begging to be allowed to help. That's the stage Declan's at, I thought patronisingly. Then I remembered what Cam was always saying. 'It doesn't matter how much you ride a horse, you need to build up the relationship on the ground as well.' I supposed I could have gone up and just groomed him or something. But there was always next week, I thought, rummaging round in my rucksack for my memory stick. 'Just going to print this out,' I told Mum. 'Dad's printer's out of ink.' I bounded upstairs, threw my bag into my room and went next door to the tiny box room where the computer lived.

'Oh.' I stopped. No one was *ever* on the computer. Officially mum and I shared it but it was basically mine. And there was Declan, so intent on what he was doing that he obviously hadn't heard me come in.

'Hi.'

'Oh, hiya.' He swung round. But not before I'd seen him hit 'minimise'. 'Um, do you want on?'

I waved my memory stick. 'I need to print something.'

'I'll just –' He nodded at the screen and I realised he was waiting for me to leave. This was *my* house and *my* computer!

I walked on into the room. 'What are you doing?'

'Something for school.' He looked even more furtive than usual.

Yeah right. I had never seen him do *anything* for school.

'So why've you minimised it?' A thought struck me. 'Are you looking up *porn*?'

He didn't miss a beat. 'Yeah,' he said. 'Rory showed me some really good sites. Want to see?'

'Very funny.'

He hit a few keys too quickly for me to see what he was doing and stood up. 'All yours.'

I had to step aside to let him out. And as he squeezed past me the sudden sweet whiff of haylage and horse sweat reminded me he'd been at the yard all day. It was true that I hadn't gone up because of the weather but I knew it was partly because he was there. Another two weeks at the most, I thought, plugging in my memory stick. Then he'll be gone. Out of this house and out of the yard.

I clicked on my Geography coursework and checked through it before printing. I'll just check my emails, I thought, going online. The 'history' icon seemed to flash at me. Of course! I clicked it. Sites visited today.

That's when I found out what he'd been up to.

It wasn't porn.

I wish it had been.

* * *

Becca pulled her History textbook further up to hide her face. A group at the front were doing a presentation about the Nazis and the wet dweeb of a student teacher could only focus on one thing at a time so we were pretty safe as long as we whispered. 'I can't see what the problem is,' she mouthed. 'So he was looking up courses at agricultural college. Big deal. It's a free country.'

'Yes but –'

'Vic, what odds is it to you if he goes and trains to be a … a groom or whatever it's called?'

'Well, it's …' I shrugged. I knew it sounded stupid. *My* thing. *My* mum. *My* house. *My* yard. *My* horse. 'Anyway,' I went on, partly to convince myself. 'He hasn't got a mission. He knows nothing. He needn't think a few days shovelling shit in a small yard is proper experience.'

'Do they not train you on the course, though?'

'They don't just take anyone!' The teacher raised anxious eyes in our direction and frowned. I sighed and scribbled in the corner of my exercise book: *You have to be a competent rider*. I remembered finding him riding round the school on Flight like he had a right to.

Becca scrawled back: *Tell me at break*!

At break we sat on our wall. 'Vicky, I can't believe you're being so unfair,' Fliss said, unwrapping a Mars bar. 'You just said this place was miles away. How is it going to have *any* impact on you?'

'It's just – it's a bit cheeky, isn't it? Anyway, I told you. He won't get in. They'll laugh at him if he even gets as far as applying. I mean, he hasn't exactly become a competent rider in a *week*, has he? And,' I went on before she could answer, 'you have to have four GCSEs.'

'*Four*? Surely anyone could get four GCSEs?' said Becca.

'Yeah, Becs, anyone normal, at a normal school. But he goes to a thick school. Half of them don't get any exams at all. They're just hoods. Anyway, can we please talk about something else?'

Becca's round face looked hurt. 'You're the one who's obsessing about this!'

'Indeed you are, Miss Moore,' agreed Fliss. '*And* we're getting fed up with it.'

'*What?*' I felt like something had stung me. 'What d'you mean?'

'What I said,' said Fliss. 'No, I mean it, Becs,' as Becca opened her mouth, 'we agreed we should say something.'

'You *agreed?*'

'It's just…' Becca chewed her lip. 'Every time you talk about Declan you're so … like, so *poisonous*. Honestly, Vic – you should listen to yourself.'

'But I've hardly even mentioned him!'

'But when you *do*,' Becca persisted. It was so unlike her to criticise anyone.

I looked at Fliss. 'So you guys have been *talking* about me?'

'We just don't like to hear you being so bitchy,' said Fliss. 'You've really changed since he came to your house.'

'Look, you don't know what you're talking about. You're just annoyed because I wouldn't let you meet him. You're not missing much, take my word for it.' It was like they'd punched me. I wondered when they'd had this little tête-à-tête about me. When I was at the show? The show they *said* they'd come to? Something struck me. 'This has nothing to do with Declan. You're just jealous, aren't you?' I jumped off the wall and faced them both.

'Jealous?' Becca wrinkled her forehead.

'Of Rory.'

Fliss sucked in her breath. 'No, Vic. If you think about it, we're the ones who *helped* you get Rory. Getting him to go to your show and everything. *You're* the jealous one – not us!'

And they stalked off and left me.

Chapter 23

DECLAN

Mr Dermott sounds fed up already. He must have had a nice week without us lot. 'Five minutes left. And remember to do the last question *properly*. At least fifty words.'

There's a groan. A shuffling and scuffling of papers.

'Sir, fifty *different* words?'

'Sir, what about Cathal? He doesn't know fifty words.'

'He can't count to fifty anyway!'

'Sir, this is *gay*.'

'*Four* minutes,' says Mr Dermott. 'Anyone who can't manage to finish it now is very welcome to come back at breaktime.'

Louder sighing and groaning and 'Sir, that's not fair!'

I look again at the green form. No one said we'd have to do all this. *What was the most valuable thing you learned on your work experience? Which of the following best describes the skills you have learned? Tick as many as apply.* I sigh. It's not that I can't do it. But it spoils it to have to put it all into words and ticks.

In front of me Seaneen Brogan's curly pony-tail bobs

up and down as she covers her green form in her huge, loopy, girly writing.

'OK, time up. Who's coming back at break?' Mr Dermott glances at the green forms as he does the rounds. 'Natalie – well, maybe we'll leave it.' Natalie Doyle is five months pregnant so I suppose Dermott thinks her career is sorted for a while. Natalie smirks and clutches her schoolbag to her swollen middle. Dermott flicks through more forms. 'Cathal Gurney – see you at break.' Cathal sniffs. 'And who's this without a name? Declan Kelly?' He sounds surprised.

'Yes, sir.'

'Right. Breaktime in here, then, lads. Off you go.'

Seaneen grabs my arm on the way out of the class-room. I wonder if it feels muscly after all that mucking out. 'Well, how was it?'

I shrug. 'OK.'

She glares at me. 'Is that all you can say?'

'What is there to say?'

Plenty, as far as Seaneen's concerned. 'And I just can't wait to go to the tech and do childcare,' she's still jabbering when we get to Psycho's classroom. 'And Sandra – she's the boss – said she was going to give me a dead good report.'

'Miss Brogan, Mr Kelly, you are *late*.' Psycho blocks the doorway, vicious as ever. She was grumpy about us going on work experience but she's even grumpier to have us back.

* * *

Mr Dermott looks at my green form. Then at me. Like something doesn't add up

'What's wrong, sir? I filled it in right.' Not like Cathal

Gurney. Mr Dermott had to let him take his form home, though I don't think anyone in Cathal's house could do much better.

Mr Dermott runs a hand through his thin ginger hair. 'Well, yes, technically; I mean, you've ticked all the boxes. But it's not really what I expected.'

'What d'you mean?'

He takes out a blue form, covered in neat black writing, from a folder on his desk. 'This came this morning. From Ms Brooke.'

Cam.

'Ms Brooke has a great deal more to say than you.' His face breaks into a big dopy smile. 'Declan, this is one of the best reports I've ever seen.'

'What?'

He shakes out the blue form and makes a big deal out of putting on his glasses. '*Outstanding. Natural affinity with horses. Valuable member of the team. Eminently suited to this type of work. Trustworthy. Fast learner...*' Close your mouth, Declan. She wouldn't call you a fast learner if she saw you looking like that.'

I snap it shut, feeling my lips stretch into a grin wider than Mr Dermott's as I do.

'So? What do you have to say?'

'Well, I knew I did OK,' I begin.

He snorts. 'OK! This is more than OK. So why,' he picks up my green form again, 'do you have so little to say for yourself?'

'Don't know sir. Didn't know what to put.'

'"Don't know sir. Didn't know what to put!"' He shakes his head, takes off his glasses, and looks at me. 'What do you intend to do with your life, lad?'

Suddenly I can say it. 'I want to work with horses.'

'Great!' He sounds like he means it. 'And what will that involve? I'm afraid I don't know anything about it. We've never had anyone –'

'There's this thing you can do.' Suddenly the words are rushing out. 'A course. At a college in Enniskillen. The whole place is to do with animals and stuff.'

'Agricultural college.'

'Yeah, I looked it up on the internet.'

'Well well. Good for you.'

'But –' Then reality kicks in. 'I don't know if someone like me – I mean, I probably wouldn't get in.'

'I don't see why not.' The bell clangs for the end of break but Mr Dermott ignores it. 'Ms Brooke would obviously give you an excellent reference.'

'Yeah but – it's miles away. *And* you have to have four GCSEs.'

'So?' He raises his shoulders as if anyone could get four GCSEs.

'Sir! I haven't a hope.'

'Not with that attitude,' he agrees. 'And maybe not on previous form. But if you started applying yourself – well, you're not stupid. There's six months before the exams. Who knows what you could do if you tried?'

'*Applying* myself?' It doesn't sound much like me. I think of something else. Maybe the biggest thing. 'It says you have to be a competent rider.'

'But Ms Brooke says, eh, let me see…' He scans the blue form again. 'Oh yes. *Considering he has never ridden before he has made unusually swift progress.* That sounds good. Now it's only December. Surely you'd have time to get more competent before you applied for the course. Especially as she says she's happy to offer you weekend employment. So what's your problem?'

This is all going too fast. Mr Dermott's acting like all I have to do is want it and I can get it.

'I don't know.'

'Come on, lad! This could be your big chance.' His voice changes. 'When I think of this time last year …'

'Sir, don't.' People like Payne cast it up all the time, but not old Dermie.

'Yes.' Mr Dermott scratches his cheek. 'I don't mind telling you, I've had my worries about you. But you've kept out of trouble, more or less, haven't you? Parted company with Emmet?' He doesn't wait for an answer. Gets suddenly businesslike. 'Right. Here's what we'll do. *You* need to start knuckling down if you're going to get those GCSEs. *I* will get all the information about the course and applying for grants – all that sort of thing. And,' he adds, 'I'll be keeping an eye on you, make sure you're working. Is that a deal?'

I nod. Speechless. Cam's words are singing in my ears. *Outstanding. Valuable.* Walking to Technology my head's full of plans. Should I start working hard in every subject and hope for the best? Or should I target the ones I might have a chance in and give up on the hard ones? The sludge-coloured school walls melt away into a green path in the farm trail and I'm trotting up it on a chestnut horse. Its ears are pricked and it feels powerful and confident beneath me.

'Oi, Kelly. Watch where you're going.' Emmet McCann shoves me into the wall. For once he's on his own.

'Piss off, McCann.' I shove him back. 'Oh dear. Is that the best they could do for your nose?'

He sniffs. 'I can still smell *you*, anyway. How's your ma? Still up in the loony bin? Or is it the drying out clinic?'

'I think it was casualty *you* ended up in the last time you insulted my ma, McCann?'

I'm only going through the motions. The swelling

hatred I felt the day I broke his nose, the red rage that made me thump Vicky – there's nothing like that now. I just elbow past him, laughing. Emmet McCann can't spoil this.

* * *

'So I'll be home by the weekend,' Mum says. She pulls her cardigan tighter round her and smiles at me. 'Don't look so worried! I thought you'd be pleased.'

'I am. It's just, I thought you'd be in here for another few weeks.' I look around the day room. Some of the women are familiar to me now – the fat one that sings, the really skinny one with the huge eyes who only looks about my age.

'No need,' she says. She's in a totally different mood from last week. Her eyes are clear and bright and she's lost that yellowy look she had when she first went in.

'So you're … you're better?'

'Haven't touched a drop.' She sounds dead proud.

'But sure, in here, you wouldn't be able to …' I can't keep the doubt out of my voice.

She laughs. 'Och, son, I haven't even felt the need for it. Honestly. I'm fine. I just want to get home and get things back to normal.'

'And the doctors and all – they don't mind?'

'Declan, anybody'd think you didn't *want* me home!' Her voice falters a bit and I rush in.

'Course I do! It's brilliant! It's just a surprise.'

I wonder if Colette'll be as surprised as me, I wonder, walking out to the car. This is the first time I've gone in on my own since that Friday. And now – well, I suppose this is the last time I'll be in here. I turn round and look at Croob before heading over to the car.

'I thought things were heading that way,' Colette says, starting up the engine. 'She's been phoning me a lot, saying how well she's doing, how she wants home for Christmas.'

'You don't think she's ready.' I can tell by her voice.

She sighs. 'Declan, love, I hope she is. I'd just feel happier if she'd completed the programme.'

Panic surges up in me. It's too quick. I don't want to go home yet. But how can you say that? 'She'll be fine,' I hear myself say instead. 'I'll look after her.'

'I know you will.' She pats my knee. 'And you know where I am if you need me.'

We get home around eight and Colette says she's got to be out again by half past. 'So I'll leave you to tell Vicky the good news,' she says. 'I'm off for a shower.'

I plonk myself down at the kitchen table and pick up the English books I left there before Colette and I went up to the hospital. Vicky's making a cup of tea but she's been revising. Her books are spread out all over the table.

'What good news?' She swings round from where she's waiting for the kettle to boil.

'Mum's getting home. I'll be going at the weekend.'

She's probably delighted but she doesn't let it show. She pours hot water into the teapot.

What'll Mum think about me going to the yard all day Saturday and Sunday? It'll be harder to keep an eye on her. My stomach squeezes with nerves the way it always does when I let myself think about The Plan. All week Mr Dermott's been hounding me about getting the work done and he keeps giving me stuff he's downloaded about grants and career prospects. You'd think he was the one wanting to apply for the course.

Seaneen's noticed something's going on. 'You're acting

weird,' she complained this afternoon. 'I mean, more than usual. That's the second time this week you've done your Maths homework. And why are you redrafting that *Macbeth* essay? Sykes said you only had to do it if you wanted to try and get a better mark for your coursework. You don't have to.'

I'd just shrugged. Now, looking at the essay, I think she had a point. Maybe I won't bother after all. Then the picture from the prospectus Mr Dermott downloaded for me pops into my head – a boy and girl holding a bright chestnut racehorse – and I grit my teeth and get down to it.

Opposite me, Vicky sighs and cups her hands round her mug. 'What are you doing?'

'*Macbeth* coursework. Still.'

'I'm doing History – the Nazis.'

'We do them.'

'Would you ask me this when I've learned it? Mum usually does but she's going to see a film.'

'OK. Then,' I hate asking her for anything and she was a bit weird when she caught me on the computer the other night, 'could I use your computer to type it up on?'

'OK.' She smiles. She's been far nicer since she started hanging round with Rory.

I look at the scribbled rubbish I handed in a couple of weeks ago. 'Discuss the theme of guilt in *Macbeth*.' I can think of far more to write now. Like your man Macduff – he feels crap about leaving his family to get murdered. I never thought of him before. I never usually bother to do a second draft. It'll give the old cow a heart attack to see this tomorrow.

'Can you ask me these two pages?'

'OK.' I take her file. Her writing is dead neat and she

uses loads of highlighters. Yellow and pink and green. Very girly. I don't mind asking her the questions because it's the same stuff we do. Maybe History's one of the things I could get a C in. Vicky knows most of the answers and she pronounces the German words in a dead showy-off way.

'Oh lovely! You're helping each other.' Colette dashes in, all perfume and smiles, and grabs her keys from the top of the fridge. 'Vicky, love, I may be a bit late. Don't wait up.'

'Mum! It's Thursday!'

Colette laughs. She's wearing a skirt and her eyes are all sparkly. 'You sound like *my* mother,' she says, planting a kiss on the top of Vicky's hair. 'Bye – be good.'

'Declan! You haven't asked me about *Lebensraum*,' Vicky says.

'Sorry.' I look down the page but just then her mobile starts singing and vibrating.

She grabs it and takes a deep breath. 'Hi! How did it go?'

I lift the book with my essay in it and head up to the computer room. I'm a crap typist. I keep getting those wiggly green and red lines under everything even when I can't see what's wrong. But it looks great when I've printed it off.

I only know it's late because when I stand up to get the paper out of the printer I realise my hands are stiff with cold. I touch the radiator – it's cooling, which means it must be after ten. This is the longest I've ever spent on schoolwork. No wonder people at smart schools don't hang round the streets at night getting into trouble – they mustn't have time.

When I open the kitchen door Vicky still has her

History book open. There's a pile of plastic folders beside her stuff. My essay would look class in one of them. Shame to get it crumpled in my bag after working so hard. Only I don't want to ask her. Maybe I could just slip one into my bag tomorrow. She'll hardly notice. But no. I make myself ask.

'Yeah, no worries.' She didn't look up when I came in but she does now. 'That your *Macbeth* essay?'

'Yeah.' I can't keep the pride out of my voice.

'Let's see.'

I hand it over. She skims it and starts to laugh.

'Here, give it back!' I snatch for it.

She holds on. 'Declan – you can't hand this in as a final draft.'

'Shut up!' Hot rage floods my face.

'I'm sorry, I'm not being mean. You just mustn't have spellchecked it. Look, this is all one sentence. And you need to take a new paragraph every time –'

I bite my lip. 'It's only a stupid bit of coursework. I don't *care* about it.'

'I was going to say,' – she sounds quite kind – 'd'you want me to fix it up a bit for you? Just the spelling and that.'

'Oh. Would you?'

She shrugs. 'Yeah, I don't mind. It'll only take ten minutes, as long as you saved it. You did? Well, then, you make us some toast and I'll fix your essay. OK?'

'Yeah. Thanks.'

When it comes back it's still my essay but it's all in paragraphs with loads of full stops and all. I can't help smiling at it. Sykes will cream herself when I hand this in.

Chapter 24

VICKY

'I love Pizza Express,' I said as we sat down at a table in the window. The restaurant was all lit up for Christmas.

'Me too.' Rory grinned. He was wearing a long-sleeved black T-shirt and baggy jeans and looked *gorgeous*. I had finally decided on black trousers and a pink top. I saw Rory sort of checking me out when I took my coat off, while trying to look as if he wasn't – exactly the same as me. I hoped he wouldn't know that it wasn't only *our* first date – it was *my* first date *ever*.

I thought I'd be too nervous to eat in front of him, but when the pizzas came they looked and smelled so yummy that it was no problem. I would catch his eye and think, yes! Here I am on my first date with this lovely boy.

'So when will you hear about Cambridge?' I asked between mouthfuls.

'January.' He gave a little grimace. 'I hate waiting.'

'But you got on OK?'

He shrugged. 'I didn't make a fool of myself. But that doesn't mean I'm what they're looking for.'

I couldn't see how he could not be what they wanted but of course I couldn't say that without sounding totally sad so I just said, 'But, being head boy and everything – bet they loved that.'

He looked embarrassed. 'Well, I suppose it doesn't do any harm. Oh!' He sounded like he'd just remembered something. 'Tell Declan I did manage to get it in – about the horse show.'

I paused with a forkful of pizza halfway to my mouth. 'What do you mean?'

'He said I should try and put in about giving first aid to that boy. They were quite interested. Oh God, I don't even like thinking about it. You know – tempting fate.' He poured out some water and I wondered what it would be like saying goodbye to him if he did get into Cambridge. All the gorgeous, clever girls he would meet there … Then I wised up. It was December. If he went to Cambridge it would be next October, ten months away.

'Declan's going home on Sunday,' I told Rory. 'He and my mum have gone up to his house to give it a bit of a clean up for his mum getting out of hospital.'

'What was wrong with her? Sorry – that's very rude. I have a prurient interest in medical stuff.'

I wasn't sure what 'prurient' meant but I supposed it was something to do with wanting to be a doctor. I told him.

'That's pretty tough,' he said. 'My granda was an alcoholic.'

'*Your* granda?' I was shocked.

'Yeah, why not? Is this the first time she's been to rehab?'

I shrugged. 'I think so.' I didn't want it to sound like

I was *interested* in her, but neither did I want it to sound like I *wasn't* interested in what Rory was asking me.

'My granda used to be OK for years. Then – wham! He'd go on a huge bender. Is your aunt like that?'

'I don't know. I hardly know her.' I could hear the frost in my voice.

Rory poured us both more water. 'You really don't like Declan, do you?' he asked.

'Weeeell ...' I remembered my row with Fliss and Becca. We still weren't talking. I couldn't forget the things they'd accused me of. Poisonous. Jealous. I couldn't let Rory think stuff like that about me – I mean, it wasn't *true*, but I couldn't take the risk of him *misunderstanding* the same way they had. This week I'd made a massive effort to be nice to Declan. I'd even fixed up that weird essay for him. I couldn't decide if it was brilliant or crap: it was full of mistakes, but he'd thought of all this stuff I'd never even considered – like he'd really thought about the characters as people.

'I think he's dead on,' Rory said.

Join the fan club, I felt like saying, but I just smiled and changed the subject instead. 'We have exams next week.' Exams – not a brilliant topic for a first date.

'You're lucky to get them over with. Ours are in January, which kind of mucks up the Christmas holidays. Then we have our Upper Sixth formal the week after.'

He suddenly looked down at his half-eaten pizza and started forking up bits of spinach. Oh God, I thought. I wonder if he's already asked some girl to the formal, long before he met me. It was six weeks away. Maybe we wouldn't still be going out then. Were we even going out? I *thought* we were – I mean, he'd kissed me and taken me out for dinner but nothing had been said. No one I knew had ever been to the boys' school formal but it was every-one's ambition to be asked. I didn't want him to think I was fishing for an invite so I changed the subject.

'Are you looking forward to Christmas?' God, another clanger! What a primary-school thing to say. I might as well have asked him what Santa was bringing him. Christmas! Would we still be going out *then*? What would I get him? How much were you meant to spend? God, this was all so much more fraught than I had ever realised.

'Well, yes,' said Rory, not seeming to notice that I kept saying ridiculous things. 'Apart from revising and waiting to hear from Cambridge. It's always quite good fun, though, with there being so many of us. What about you – do you stay at your mum's?'

This was much safer territory. 'Yes, but I have a sort of second Christmas at my dad's on Boxing Day.'

'Double presents?'

'Isn't that the point of divorce?' I made my voice bright.

'So you don't really mind? Them being divorced, I mean?'

I frowned and took of gulp of water. 'Well, I was upset at first. I kept wishing Dad would come back. But then he married Fiona and she's actually lovely. So no, I don't really mind, not now. Anyway, that's enough about my family. What about yours? I saw your mum today with your wee baby sister.'

He laughed. 'She's cute, isn't she? It's quite an ego-boost having a baby sister. I mean, you have a crap day at school, your team loses, you get rejected by Cambridge – well, let's hope not – but she always thinks we're all amazing.'

'Hmm.' For the first time I wondered what Molly thought of me. She always squealed and kicked when she saw me on Fridays even though, I admitted, I never gave her much encouragement. I supposed she wouldn't always be a screaming baby and wondered if she might like having a big sister when she was big enough to know what that was. I imagined teaching her to ride, taking her shopping, reading her the stories I had loved. Maybe it would be OK.

* * *

Rory's hand tightened a little in mine and I smiled, though I didn't suppose he could see me in the dark. It was a cold, clear night, all the shops along the Lisburn Road lit up for Christmas. I usually hated walking but now I wished that the mile or so between Pizza Express and Sandringham Park was more like ten. I stroked his hand.

'Would you consider doing this again?' Rory stopped walking and swung me round to face him. Instead of speaking I tilted my face up and, without any conscious thoughts at all, kissed him. I couldn't believe I, Vicky Moore, who'd never had a boyfriend, was standing snogging in the middle of the Lisburn Road. Rory's mouth was warm and firm and tasted of mint and pizza. His fingers played in my hair. His body pressed against mine felt solid and warm. I shivered deliciously and buried my hands in his soft wool scarf.

Finally he pulled away and smiled down at me. 'So you don't mind going out with the boy next door? Not too much of cliché?'

I laughed. 'Not if you don't mind going out with the

girl next door.' My voice came out really normal but inside I was singing. Going out! He'd said it, so he must mean it.

'Ah, but you're only the girl next door *sometimes*.'

Far too quickly, we were at my house. Mum's car was in the drive and there was a light in the living-room window. I pulled Rory back behind the hedge.

'Showjumping tomorrow?' he asked.

I shook my head. 'Cam's giving me a lesson, which she won't usually do at the weekend. But *if* we win the final in two weeks we qualify for Dublin!' I realised I was babbling, but he looked as if everything I said was fascinating.

'And are you likely to win?'

I gave a little shiver. 'It's like you not wanting to think too much about Cambridge. Don't tempt fate. But Flight's on top form. I had a lesson on Wednesday night and he felt like he could jump a house.'

'I wouldn't want to see that,' Rory said, bending down to kiss me again. 'Far too scary.'

It was another ten minutes before I finally walked up the drive, all swollen with joy. Everything was so brilliant – Dublin looking likely, Declan going home and best of all, Rory, Rory, Rory! I thought of him walking up his identical drive three doors up. Did he feel like this too?

Childishly, I was looking forward to telling Mum about my evening – not *everything* of course. I flung my bag over the banister rail and put my hand on the living-room door handle. Mum's voice drifted out and I paused.

'…welcome here any time. I don't want us to lose touch.'

I held my breath, waiting for Declan to reply but there was just a murmur.

'I hope so, love. But if she isn't – well, you know where I am. I mean it – any time.'

Murmur murmur.

I yanked at the handle and crashed into the room. The two dark heads on the sofa looked so alike. Mum put her hand on Declan's and gave it a quick squeeze and the gesture seemed to squeeze out all my happiness.

Mum glanced up with a wide, bright smile and said, 'Hello, love, good evening?'

Such a big part of me wanted to flump down beside her and go over it all – how happy I was and how lovely Rory was and how he was coming round on Sunday evening to help me with my Chemistry revision. But I could see that she wasn't really interested. So I just said, 'Fine, thanks,' and backed out of the room to get ready for bed.

Chapter 25

DECLAN

I'm on my way to the muck heap with a wheelbarrow full of wet shavings and shit; it's heavy and stinky and the handles dig into my hands. I'd love to stop for a breather and watch Flight jumping but I don't want Cam to regret giving me the job.

'Well done, Vicky!' shouts Cam from the middle of the school. 'Do that again in the real thing and it should be next stop Dublin!'

The wheel hits a stone and a doughnut of dung drops off. I straighten my back for a moment and can't help glancing over at the school. Flight looks better than I've ever seen him – soaring over every jump with Vicky moving like she's part of him. It's split-second timing; I wonder if I'll ever be able to do that.

They finish off with three jumps in a row, just a bounce between each one. Vicky pulls him up and pats him after the last one. 'I think that'll do us!' she calls. 'Fiona's picking me up at two.'

She always does that – just rides and leaves. I don't

think I would if I had a horse. I'd want to *be* with it. Like Sally and Nudge.

'It's ten to now,' says Cam.

I've been around horses long enough to know that they can't put Flight out into the field like this. Even from where I'm standing I can see that he's dripping with sweat, his nostrils red pits. He looks like he just won the Grand National or something. I empty the wheelbarrow and try not to think about the way I like Flight. I don't *want* to like him more than the others but there's something about him. Maybe it's just because he's Vicky's.

'Declan will cool him off for you,' says Cam. 'I need to grab some lunch before the next lesson. Is that you finished with the beds, Declan?'

'Yeah.'

She runs me through the routine briskly: 'Saddle off, sweat rug on – run and get it, Vicky; it's hanging on his door – then walk him round the school till he's dry. Then turnout rug on and into the field – you know where he goes. Vicky, I said sweat rug! I thought you were the one in a hurry?'

By the time Vicky gets back I have the saddle off and resting on the fence with the stirrups run up properly. Flight rubs his sweaty face against my chest and I laugh because it feels nice.

'Don't let him do that,' she says. She flings the sweat rug over him and puts her hand on the reins even though I'm already holding him. 'Are you sure you can manage?' she asks. 'He's quite excited after jumping.'

'Yeah, it's fine.'

'And when you put him out – he goes in the far paddock – don't let him barge you at the gate. Can you manage the electric fence?'

I try to make my voice patient. 'Look, I put him out every morning when I was on work experience *and* brought him in every night.'

She chews her lip and fiddles with her stick. Fiona's red Audi swings into the yard. 'Hell!' she says. 'I'm late. Look, are you *sure*?'

'Yes.' Then – and I know this is going to annoy her but I say it out of badness – 'sure he knows me now, I've handled him so much.'

She narrows her eyes. Her face is pinched and she still hasn't let go of the reins. I gave them a gentle pull. A car horn blares, making Flight jump back and goggle at us with huge eyes. Vicky turns and stalks off. She doesn't look back.

* * *

I stand with Colette beside her car and think about all the places I've been in it in the last few weeks. Behind us, the light shines out of the open front door onto the path.

Colette nods in the direction of the house. 'She looks OK, doesn't she? Good form.'

'Yeah.'

'I'd be happier if she hadn't signed herself out, though.'

She's only saying what I've been thinking, so I nod. I take the bag she's holding out. 'Thanks for everything.' I mean something way bigger than thanks but that's all that comes out.

'Come here,' she says and hugs me so tight her hair tickles my cheek. Then she pulls back and looks at me. 'You'll remember what I said on Friday. About keeping in touch? I mean it, Declan. You'll see Vicky at the yard at weekends, of course, but –'

I don't say anything. Vicky's a total weirdo. She's nice as pie until she sees me within a mile of Flight, then she's a psycho. I don't think I'm going to be seeing too much of her at the yard. At least I hope not.

'I'll call in as often as I can,' Colette says.

'OK.'

'And Declan – what you just told me about trying to get those GCSEs and getting to college. You stick at it, OK?' She looks round the street. 'If I can do it so can you.'

'I'll try.'

'Your mum'll be really proud.'

I'm not so sure. Not when she knows it means going to the other side of the country. But I just nod.

'OK, love, better go.' She gets into the car. I lean against our gate and watch till the Golf disappears round the corner. Then I pick up my bag and go in.

The house looks the way it did when Gran was alive, tidy and shiny. There's a smell of polish, though Mum's already half-filled the ashtray with butts – not drinking must be making her smoke more – so that won't last. Colette and I worked for hours on Friday night, changing beds, hoovering, wiping everything. Colette filled the fridge with food too. I don't know if Mum'll be pleased or if she'll think Colette's trying to take over a bit but she's arranging the yellow roses Colette gave her and she smiles at me when I come in.

'Well, here we are, son,' she says.

'Yeah.'

She sets the vase on the mantelpiece. We both sit down and look at it. Mum says the flowers are lovely. I say they're lovely. We look at them a bit more. I say they really are lovely. She says they really are lovely. I wish she would just put the TV on and ignore me and act normal.

Then I think of something. 'Mum, I've got something to tell you. About school.'

Her head jerks up in alarm.

'No, it's good. Dermott reckons if I work really hard I could do OK. In my exams I mean.'

'What does he mean, OK?' She draws on her cigarette.

'Like, GCSEs. Enough to go to the tech.'

'Oh yeah? To do what?' She sounds interested.

'Well ... not sure.' For some reason I can't tell her about the horses yet. 'But if I get some exams I'll have a choice, won't I?'

'God, son.' She shakes her head. 'Sure you've never been much of a one for school work.'

Thanks Mum. 'Only cause I never bothered my head. But last week I worked dead hard. Look – d'you want to see my homework diary?' Mum hasn't seen my homework diary since first year. Gran used to look at it sometimes but, God love her, there was never much to look at. It's a bit of a joke – hardly anyone in our class does homework – but every Friday in extended form time Mr Dermott uncaps his green biro and does the rounds. Usually you just get a scribbled MD and the date, but this week on mine he wrote, 'Great reports from all your teachers this week. Keep up the good work.'

'See?' I hand it to her.

She takes the diary and the lines round her mouth disappear as her face relaxes into a smile. 'Och, son, that's great.' She sighs. 'I suppose that's Colette rubbing off on you. She was always staying in and doing her homework.'

'It wasn't Colette. I just wanted to.'

She reads what Dermott wrote again. 'Well, I suppose I'll have to keep you at it, won't I?'

'Yeah! You nag me to work and I'll nag you to –' I run into a brick wall.

She sighs. 'I know, son. Stay off the drink. Don't you worry, I'm not ending up back in there. Things are going to change round here.'

* * *

'I see your ma's out of the nuthouse? Don't worry, Kelly – a few days back with you'll soon send her back in.'

I hitch my schoolbag up on my shoulder and walk out the gates as if Emmet hasn't spoken.

Girly heels trip along behind me. 'Wait up, Declan, I'll walk you home.'

Great. But in a way it is nice to have company, even if it is only Seaneen.

She pulls a packet of cigarettes out of her bag. 'Want one?'

I shake my head. 'Nah. I've sort of gone off them.'

'God, Declan, you'll be serving on the altar next. Here, my granny says your mum's home. Is she OK?'

I shrug. 'I think so.' I don't want to tell Seaneen too much, but knowing her and her nosy old granny she knows it all anyway. 'She's not drinking, if that's what you mean. She's cleaning.'

'What?' She lights her cigarette.

'Cleaning the house. I'm scared to put a cup down. But I can live with it.'

We're at the top of my street and I can't help doing the light-in-the-window check. Something like a bird flutters in my chest until I see the glow of a lamp behind

the curtains, shining out into the dark December afternoon. Half the houses in Tirconnell Parade are lit up for
Christmas – the street's like Las Vegas – but that lamp's
enough for me. The bird stops flapping its wings and I
realise Seaneen's saying something about tonight.

'What?'

'I said, d'you want to come out later?'

'What for?'

'What for! Just to hang round. Me and Ciara and
Kevin. Maybe Sean. Come on, it'll be a laugh.'

For maybe half a moment I'm tempted. But Sean and
Kevin hang round with Emmet. Anyway, Colette's coming round later. 'Nah, you're OK. Got stuff to do. See
you, Seaneen.'

She seems to trip, then I realise she's lunging at me.
Her lips graze mine for a second, just long enough to
taste smoke and lip gloss – at least I suppose it's lip gloss.

'See you. If you change your mind we'll be around.'
She's away down her granny's path, pony-tail bouncing,
big earrings swinging. I don't fancy Seaneen – I don't
think I do anyway – but I can't help wondering what it'd
be like to snog her properly, feel those tits pressed against
you.

But I won't change my mind. I've got a bag full of
Maths and History. Psycho gave me back my *Macbeth*
coursework with, 'You have been hiding your light under
rather a large bushel,' in her angry red scribble. No idea
what that means but she gave me a B-.

And in two days' time I'll be at the yard with the
horses. So no, I won't change my mind.

Chapter 26

VICKY

All week I'd been avoiding Fliss and Becca – or they'd been avoiding me – but when I went to get a drink after my Science exam on Thursday there they were at the vending machine and there was no escape without looking like a total sap.

'Oh. My. God.' Fliss's usually perfect hair was greasy and stringy – evidence that she'd been running her hands through it in despair for the past two hours. 'That was the worst exam I have *ever* done. *And* after two hours of French! It's cruelty!' I didn't know if she'd seen me or not.

Becca fired a pound coin into the vending machine and bent down to retrieve a bottle of water. 'I hate Science. Can't wait to give it up.'

I leaned against the vending machine and decided to have a go. After all, it had been a stupid quarrel, not worth breaking friends over. 'The Physics was the worst. I didn't mind the Chemistry.'

'No way. The Chemistry was, like, *impossible*,' said Becca in her normal voice.

'Come on Becs,' said Fliss. 'Niamh is waiting for us.'

I sighed and pulled my blazer round me. Becca would make friends, if I could get her on her own – she was too sweet to like falling out with anyone – but Fliss could keep a fight going for ages. And it wasn't *fair*, I wasn't jealous. Or poisonous. Or any of those things. *They* were.

I glumped home on my own, trying to remember History dates all the way along the Lisburn Road. I remembered Declan asking me my History. It seemed much longer than a week ago. Life at home had snapped right back to what it was before he came. But it was *so* lovely never having to wait for the bathroom, never coming into a room to find Mum deep in conversation, never having to look at his sulky face across the dinner table. And Mum could say what she liked – *she'd* been in a really good mood since he moved out too. It was just … I wished he wasn't at the yard. I remembered his hands on Flight's reins last Saturday. The way Flight rubbed his head against him – he'd *never* done that to me. Ever.

'You're late, darling,' Mum said, as I walked up the drive. She was putting something in the car. 'You nearly missed me.'

'I know.' I put my schoolbag down. 'The Science exam went on forever. But it didn't seem as bad as usual.'

'Probably that revision Rory was doing with you last night?'

'Yeah, he's dead good at explaining stuff.' I thought I might have managed an A in Science for the first time ever. When Rory had offered to go over my Science with me I'd thought we could just do a wee bit of revision and kind of enjoy ourselves the rest of the time – we were in the dining room, and Mum was upstairs on the computer – but he'd taken it really seriously and hadn't let me lose concentration at all. I was starting to realise he was a pretty serious guy – it was probably having all those younger brothers and sisters. As long as he was serious about *me* I wasn't complaining!

'Fliss and Becca getting on OK with their exams?' Not for the first time I wished she didn't know me so well. I hadn't told her we'd fallen out but she must have guessed something.

'I think so. Where are you going, anyway?'

'To see Theresa and Declan – well, I'm going out for dinner later, but I wanted to call in to them on the way. I have a birthday present for Declan.'

'I didn't know it was his birthday.'

'It's next week, really. And to be honest, it gives me an excuse to call without Theresa thinking I'm checking up on her.'

'Oh. You never used to get him a birthday present.'

'Well, no, but it's different now, isn't it?'

I didn't answer.

'Look, love, I'd better go – want to get there before the traffic's totally impossible. There's some of last night's chilli in the fridge.'

'OK.' I didn't say 'Give my love to Declan.' I picked up my bag and went in. The kitchen felt cold and empty. I looked at the chilli in the fridge and decided I wasn't in the mood for it. I didn't want to revise for History on my own. I might have texted Becca if only Fliss hadn't snubbed me at the vending machine. I dragged out my History books and sat staring at them. At least there was only one more day of exams – English and History – and then on Saturday night Rory was taking me to one of his friends' eighteenth birthday party, which somehow seemed a really grown-up thing to be going to. And it was only just over a week until the final and Flight was going better than ever. So there was a lot to look forward to. I couldn't understand why I felt so – I tried to work out what it was – *unsettled*. Must be pre-menstrual, I decided, getting up to put the kettle on.

It was only later, after she'd come in, that I realised I hadn't asked Mum who she'd gone out to dinner with.

* * *

'Morning, Vicky.' Fiona turned round from spooning some revolting sort of mush into a wriggling, head-twisting Molly who bashed her hands on the tray of her high chair and shrieked with delight when she saw me.

'Hi Fi. Hi Molly.' I yawned and felt the teapot on the Aga.

'It's just made,' said Fiona. 'Good girl, Molly-moo.'

'Molly-*who*?' I wrinkled my nose and took a mug out of the dishwasher.

'I know.' Fiona laughed. 'I said no baby talk but …' She changed the subject. 'You're late this morning.'

'Tired after my mocks. Can't wait to see Flight.' I put some bread in the toaster.

She lifted Molly's bib to wipe her face and Molly screamed. 'This is the last weekend before the final, isn't it?'

'Yeah. I wrote about it yesterday in my English exam. "Describe the proudest achievement of your life." I did it all about us going to Dublin and winning the championship. It was really descriptive. I think I should get an A star.'

'But it hasn't happened yet!' Fiona sounded horrified.

'I couldn't resist it. Anyway,' I pressed the button and caught my toast, 'Flight's jumping like a champion. I can't wait to ride him today. Why don't you come with me? We could go on the farm trail again.'

'And what about this monster? I can't exactly strap her to my back.'

'Oh. What about Dad?'

'He's playing golf.' Then she said the stupidest thing I'd ever heard in my life. 'Why don't you get Declan to go with you? He can take Joy. I've told Cam he can exercise her whenever he likes.'

'What? But he's a beginner. And what about Sally?'

'Sally doesn't have time at weekends. And he's a very *good* beginner, Vicky. Cam says it's a long time since she taught anyone with so much potential. She really thinks a lot of him.'

'Who thinks a lot of me?' Dad came in, dressed for golf in a very dodgy jumper.

'Ha ha. No, I was saying to Vicky, Cam thinks a lot of Declan. And it's quite unlike her – she doesn't really get close to people.'

'What d'you mean?' I asked.

Fiona handed Molly to me and I let her pull at my collar a bit. 'You know how she is – keeps to herself. Runs the business brilliantly but keeps the customers – even people like me who've been there for years – at a distance. Have you ever been in her house?'

I shook my head.

'Nor me. But Declan has. She brings him in for a cup of tea before he starts work. Says he could do with it after the walk from the bus stop.'

'Huh.'

'Well, I think it's nice. She must have been so lonely losing her family like that.'

'It was a car crash, wasn't it?' It was kind of common

knowledge at the yard, but at the same time no one ever gossiped about it, at least never to me.

'Joyriders,' said Dad with a sort of satisfied look at Fiona. 'The sort of scum Fi's all for giving second chances to. Three of them in a stolen car. Came onto the M1 without looking.'

'But *don't* talk about it at the yard,' Fiona warned.

'Of course I won't.' But my mind was whirling. Cam's family killed by *joyriders* – I wondered if Declan knew that. I wondered if she'd be so keen on him if she knew about his own little escapade. I wouldn't *tell* her, of course. I just wondered.

* * *

The yard was quiet. Cam was teaching, but when I went to the big shed to get Flight I stopped at the sound of a soft voice talking affectionate nonsense.

'Good boy, let's see that hoof, you're enjoying that, aren't you?'

Sounded like old Jim. I stopped in the doorway. Flight was tied up outside his stable and Declan was grooming him. The electric light was on and his coat gleamed like burnished copper. He was resting a hoof, head down, totally relaxed, ears flickering back and forwards at Declan's voice. Jealousy punched me in the guts. He *never* stood like that for me.

'What are you doing?'

'Oh.' He looked a bit embarrassed to be caught out talking to a horse. 'Cam asked me to groom him.'

'Well, I'm here now. I'll take over,' I said. I knew I should say thanks. He handed me the body brush and went away. I ran my hand over Flight's shoulder and it was like silk.

'Can I get in to muck out?' It was Declan with a wheelbarrow. I straightened up and he pushed past me into the stable and started forking up the dung. I leaned over the half-door to watch. I wanted to be able to find fault with him – after all, Dad was *paying* for this – but he was annoyingly quick and competent. I took out my irritation by yanking the plastic curry comb through Flight's tail, which was full of mud – obviously Declan hadn't got that far. In seconds my eyes were full of tiny mud-specks.

'He looks great. ' Declan paused and looked out.

'Hmm,' I said. Like I needed *him* to tell me how my horse looked!

'Are you going to jump him? Only Cam's got a lesson so the school's not –'

'I know.'

'I was only saying.'

I fetched Flight's tack, making a mental note to take it home for cleaning. This time next week would be the final – and the end of term – and nearly Christmas. And Rory was taking me to a party tonight. I knew I was being stupid to let myself get annoyed about Declan being all over Flight. Because at the end of the day, what-ever fuss Cam made of him, *he* was always going to be the one shovelling the shit, while *I* was the one saddling up my four-thousand-pound horse.

Declan pushed out past me again and for the first time I noticed that he was wearing proper riding boots instead of the steeky trainers he usually wore. He caught me looking.

'Your mum got me them,' he said, even though I hadn't asked. 'Early birthday present.'

'Oh.' I couldn't think of anything to say to that.

'She's in great form, isn't she?'

I shrugged. 'Yeah, I suppose she has been in extra good form this week.' And if you think I'm hinting that it's because *you're* not around any more, then good! I thought.

But that's not what he thought.

'As long as he's worth it,' he said, brushing up the front of the bed. 'None of my mum's ever have been. But then – a teacher at the university. That sounds OK, doesn't it?'

Something cold opened out inside me. I swallowed. 'What are you talking about?'

'This Brian. Is he nice? Have you met him yet?'

I'm going out to dinner later. And last week it was the cinema. And I had been too stupid to work it out. But she'd told *him*.

The bottom fell out of my stomach. I hauled on Flight's stirrup leathers, grabbed my hat and pushed past Declan and out of the barn. Without waiting to warm up I kicked the surprised Flight into a trot and belted out of the yard.

Chapter 27

DECLAN

From the battering of Flight's hooves on the concrete I can tell Vicky's stormed off.

I go back to mucking out. Flight's bed looks perfect – even Jim grunts less at my beds now – so I push the wheelbarrow next door to Nudge's, which is bogging as usual.

What's her problem? Does she hate Colette's boyfriend? I thought she'd be *less* nasty now I wasn't living in her house, not *more*. Maybe she's just raging at her mum having a boyfriend. I wonder when Colette told her. She didn't exactly tell me – I just overheard her talking to Mum about it.

But I'm trying not to think about Mum. She wasn't up when I left the house this morning but last night she was all sort of, 'Och, son, would you really be bothered heading away up there on a Saturday? It's awful far,' and I kind of know she'd rather I stuck around home. I sigh and scoop up a big pockle of shit with the fork.

Vicky can be as mean as she likes; she's *not* going to

spoil being here for me. She's only ever here to ride Flight anyway – rides him and goes home or back to her da's or wherever. Like he's just some toy she can pick up and put down. There'll be hours and hours every weekend when she'll be nowhere in sight and I can just get on with it. Get on with *my job*. All week the thought of coming here has kept me going. Kept me working when the words on the page were dancing and blurring. Kept me in the house every night with that clingy look in Mum's eyes.

I've read all that stuff about the tech so often that I know it off by heart. And sometimes I can't believe it's anything to do with me. Other times, like now, finishing off Nudge's bed, noticing that it's taken me a quarter of the time it used to, hearing the noise of hooves and Cam shouting orders in the school and just breathing in that warm, damp horsey smell, I know this is the right place for me to be. And Mum can sigh and Vicky can sulk as much as they like.

Girls are weird anyway. Like Seaneen. Haven't been able to shake her off for weeks – Thursday night she *kissed* me, for God's sake, and then yesterday she just stuck her nose in the air and bounced out the door with Kevin.

'Declan?' It's Cam. 'How are you getting on?'

'Just Joy's and then that's me.'

She looks into Nudge's stable and smiles. 'We'll send you off to college knowing how to muck out anyway.' I like the way she says this, like it's a definite thing. 'OK,' she goes on. 'I'm heading out to pick up some rugs from the cleaners soon. You'll be OK on your own? When you finish here, can you groom and tack up Sparky and Hero?'

'Yeah.' She trusts me. Vicky can just piss off, jealous bitch.

I make an extra effort with Joy's bed, because Cam said Fiona's offered to let me ride her any time I want, and Cam says that's fine as long as I have all my work done first. 'When the lighter nights come in the spring, you could head off into the farm trail after work.' I can't wait. Being out there in the fields with a horse and no one else, looking over at the mountains – it must be wicked. Like being a cowboy. Princess Vicky doesn't know how lucky she is.

When she clatters back into the yard she doesn't look like she thinks she's lucky. Flight's foamy with sweat and he shifts and fidgets when she flings herself off, like he feels her bad mood.

I pull down the clean shavings from round the edges and spread them over the bed. Vicky's face, red-cheeked, appears over the half-door.

'Sucking up to Fiona now? You don't really think you'll be able to ride Joy, do you? Face it, Declan. You're only here to do the dirty work.'

I bite down hard on my lip, the way I do when Emmet McCann tries to wind me up. Don't let her get to me. She'll be out of here in half an hour, until tomorrow. This isn't about me. It's about Brian.

But I can't help my hands tightening on the fork.

She smiles when I don't answer – not a real smile – then starts talking in this dead ordinary, conversational voice, 'Do you know how Cam's parents died?'

I set the fork on top of the wheelbarrow and start brushing back the bed. 'Yeah,' I mutter. What's that got to do with anything?

She scratches Flight's sweaty face. 'They were killed in a car crash.'

'*So?*'

'*So* guess who caused it – *joyriders*.' She says it carefully like it's a foreign word she's just come across.

My breath shudders in my throat.

'Yeah,' she goes on. '*Joyriders*. Surprised you didn't know that. But then Cam doesn't know much about you, either, does she?'

I grab the broom handle tighter in my suddenly sweaty hands.

'Well, not *yet*,' says Vicky. She gives that smile that isn't a smile again.

Just concentrate on sweeping and breathing. Breathing and sweeping. She wouldn't do it; she's only trying to scare me.

'Vicky!' Cam's voice flits through the open door of the barn. 'I'm leaving now. Come if you're coming.'

'Don't go without me!' shouts Vicky, all sweetness. 'I've got something important to tell you.'

She throws Flight's reins at me. 'Since you're still working here – well, for now – you can put him out for me.' And she leaves without another word.

For a few moments all I can do is lean against Flight and swallow down rage. I breathe in the salty, hot tang of him. Leather and sweat and something sweet and alive that's just horse. I never smelled that smell until three weeks ago and now it's as familiar as cigarette smoke.

But it's over.

I know it is.

Who have I been kidding? 'Course you can do it,' Mr Dermott kept on saying. 'You're not stupid.' But I am stupid. Stupid to have believed in this.

Every second I stand here Vicky's telling Cam.

Flight whiffles in my ear and cocks his tail. Automatically

I go for a shovel. I hear her voice in my ear: 'That's all you're good for – shovelling shit.'

Flight rubs his nose against my arm, leaving a trail of snot. I look at him standing there, tack on, stirrups not even run up. Ready.

I don't have a conscious thought. It's like the night Emmet came to the door and said, 'Look what I got!' And the engine still running in the Peugeot 306 in the street. And Gran in the living-room, and me knowing she wasn't well, and thinking, it's not up to me, Mum should have stayed in herself if she was that bothered. And Emmet laughing, 'Come on, man. You up for it or not?' And me pulling the door closed behind me and saying, 'Aye, might as well.'

Next thing my foot's in the stirrup and I'm swinging my leg over his back. He grunts in surprise when I yank him round, out of the yard and across the road to the farm trail.

'Come on!' I push him on and on, up the hill. He swings along in a powerful trot that eats up the path. We get to a downhill and I feel myself slipping and bouncing in the saddle. Sit back, I remember Cam telling me. Sit deep, feel the reins, and the horse will slow down. But this horse doesn't want to slow down. Ragged and juddering we career down the hill like a skateboard with a wonky wheel. It shakes the crap out of me.

The ground flattens and Flight lunges himself into a mad canter. I grab his mane and my arse finds its way back to the middle of the saddle. This is better than the trot. Better than running. His hooves pound the ground, striking out *last time last time last time*. For a few seconds it feels sweet, a million times faster than Kizzy. There's nothing ahead of us but the path stretching between fields. Mud flies up from his hooves. Speed and air take over. I don't give a shit what happens. The wind whips tears from my eyes and I'm blinded for a second before they run down my cheeks. I lean forward. Flight snatches the bit and then there's speed like there's never been and the ground flows past me and I'm terrified and elated and I never want it to stop.

Something flies out of the hedge. Flight twists; there's nothing in front of me, then the ground leaps to meet me.

It whacks me so hard it forces the breath out of me. I pull myself up and look for Flight.

But the path stretches ahead, empty.

'Fuck!' I jump up and run. My heart hammers. The ground pulls at my legs and my face burns in the cold air. Shit shit shit. Let him be OK. I don't care what she tells Cam. Just let Flight be round the next corner.

I'm running and fighting to breathe and praying and I think I can't go any further and then there's one more bend in the path and there he is, just beside the gap in the fence, head down, nosing at the undergrowth. He's fine.

My heart gives a huge leap. 'Flight!' I cry. 'Thank Christ!' I dash forward, my feet breaking twigs. Startled, he shies, catches his leg in his reins, and pulls back in horror.

'Whoa, there, it's OK, boy.' I stretch out a hand but he's out of reach.

He flinches away, the reins break with a snap and next second he's ducked out through the gap. There's a car coming.

I'm right behind him but the car gets him first.

The squeal of brakes, the flash of metal and a high-pitched scream – I never knew horses could scream. A tangle of horse and car.

And Flight's body falling through the air. His legs flail and buckle.

He gives a grunt, and then he's still.

Chapter 28

VICKY

Clean rugs were piled in the back seat of Cam's Land Rover. I leaned back in the passenger seat and inhaled their sweet, chemical smell. Looked at Cam's hand changing gear. No rings, like Mum. Mum used to have a sort of white mark on her finger where she'd worn her engagement and wedding rings for so long. It was only in the last year or two that you couldn't tell there'd ever been rings there. She'd put them in her jewellery box. 'I'll keep them for you,' she'd promised. 'For your eighteenth, maybe.' The engagement ring was really pretty with three sapphires. When I was younger I used to sneak into her bedroom and try it on.

Brian. Why hadn't she told *me*? All that getting her hair done. And going out. And being so cheerful. And I'd thought it was just getting rid of Declan. And he – *he knew*! Again I saw them on the sofa last Friday night; the two dark heads bent together, her hand covering his.

'So?' Cam's voice broke into my thoughts. 'Hello?'

'What? Oh – sorry! I was thinking.'

'About next week?' She smiled. 'He's going well. You've put a lot of work in.'

'So have you,' I admitted.

She shrugged. 'Well, as long as you tell everyone where you learned when you win. Drum me up a bit of business. Now – what was it you wanted to talk to me about?'

'Um …' I bit my lip. Was I really going to say it? Nasty Me wanted to all right, but Nice Me wouldn't let her. Cam would think I was a bitch. And she'd be right. 'I just wondered if you'd have time to clip Flight again this week. And pull his mane? Just so we can be a *really* good advertisement for your yard.'

She laughed. 'I'll see. Probably. Declan works so hard he's been getting all the tack cleaned, which leaves Jim with more time during the week. He's an absolute god-send, you know. I'm going to ask him to come up every day in the Christmas holidays. Do you think he'll want to?'

Go on! said Nasty Me. *Perfect opportunity*.

But I couldn't. Maybe my threat would be enough – he'd always be wondering if I was going to say something, and then maybe he'd leave of his own accord and I'd be totally happy – apart from *Brian*.

We turned into Cam's road. She peered ahead and frowned. 'Something up ahead,' she said, changing gear and slowing down; 'looks like some sort of hold up.'

'Probably Stanley's cows again.'

I was only half paying attention. Should I phone Mum and confront her about this Brian? How long would I have to wait before she told me of her own accord? Maybe I could talk to Rory tonight. He was picking me up at Dad's and we were going to his friend's eighteenth in Hillsborough. I was going to meet his friends for the first time!

Suddenly the windscreen filled with trouble – an accident – and Cam stopped. Whatever was going on was happening right at the open gate to the farm trail. I peered out, sudden dread clutching my stomach. A car at a weird angle, like it had swerved, and something on the road, struggling; something brown …and the blood on the road … it had to be Stanley's cows.

But as I jumped out and ran up the road, the sun hit metal – a stirrup – and I knew.

Prone in the road in front of the car that had hit him, blood pumping from his back leg, eyes glassy, was Flight.

* * *

'I heard you crying,' Fiona said. I felt the bed give as she sat down beside me.

I gulped and turned over on to my back. Tears, hot then quickly cold, ran down into my ears. I'd lost track of how long I'd been lying there. The afternoon had passed in a nightmare of vets and phone calls and cups of tea. And Fiona and Cam saying over and over again that they couldn't believe it. Trying to piece it all together. I'd wanted to go home to Mum but she wasn't answering her phone – probably out with Brian.

'Come on, Vicky.' Fiona pulled me to her. 'This isn't going to help anyone.'

'I c-can't help it.' I hid my face in her shoulder. She smelled of perfume and baby.

'I know.' She stroked my hair like I was a child.

'If that car had been a second later or if it had been going a tiny bit slower –' I sobbed.

'You have to stop torturing yourself. It wasn't *your* fault.'

'I know whose *fault* it was!'

Fiona sighed. 'I still can't believe he … And then just to run away like that!' She held me away from her and gave me one of those straight looks. 'Vicky, are you *sure* you don't know why he did it?'

'I told you, I don't know! Why will no one believe me?' But I felt my eyes slide away from hers.

'Well, he must be feeling a lot worse than you.'

I pushed her hands away. 'How can you even *care* how he feels?'

'I just wish I could understand what got into him. You're *sure* he didn't think you'd asked him to take him out?'

'Of course not! He's a joyrider and a thief. He just takes what he likes. I *told* you!'

'Look, Vicky.' She gave me a little shake. 'You need to get a hold of yourself. You're going to make yourself sick.'

'I don't care.' Fresh sobs shook me at the memory of Flight lying in the road, blood gushing from his back leg and the vet shaking his head.

'Yes, you do.' She set me away from her and pushed the straggles of wet hair from my scorching cheeks. 'Now, listen. It was a terrible accident. A terrible shock. But you have to keep positive. You heard what the vet said.'

'He's going to d-die!'

'He is *not* going to die.'

'You didn't see the blood! You didn't see the bone sticking out!' I retched at the memory and she took my hands.

'I know.' Her voice was very gentle. 'But the vet said he'd seen worse. He said there was a fair chance of a full recovery.'

'In a year! And not *definitely*.'

'Oh honey, nothing's definite. For the moment just be glad he's alive, eh? Look, it's nearly seven. Rory's due at eight.'

'I told him I wasn't going to the party!' It was nearly a scream.

'He still wants to come and see you. He must really like you. Now why don't I run you a nice hot bath?'

I sat up and sighed. Rory would *really* need to like me to be able to fancy me like this. But somehow it seemed totally unimportant.

* * *

'You shouldn't miss your party,' I said. 'I'm not exactly much company.' We were in the little den at Dad's – a small room full of Molly's toys and bits and pieces of mismatched old furniture living out their days. Fiona had lit the fire for us and it cracked and sparked in a friendly way but it couldn't stop me shivering. Dad had even given me a glass of brandy to calm me down and warm me up but all it had done was make my head ache.

'Don't be daft.' Rory took my hand and began playing with my fingers. It was strangely soothing. 'As if I would. There'll be other parties.'

Tears pricked the backs of my eyes at the thought of how much this would have meant to me last week and how little I cared now.

'I just feel so ...' but I didn't have a word for it.

Rory traced a tear down my cheek and I thought how ugly I must look. 'Tell me exactly what you think happened.' I could imagine him as a doctor, caring for his patients, listening to them, never hurrying them.

'It was Declan. I told – asked him to put Flight out and he, he must have, I don't know, just taken him. We reckon he took him onto the farm trail, fell off and then Flight r-ran across the road.' I bit my lip to stop the sobs that threatened to burst out every time I thought about Flight lying in front of the car.

He stopped playing with my fingers and his face got serious. 'Vicky, it doesn't make sense. I saw Declan the other week with that runaway horse. He was so *responsible*. Like he would have done anything to make sure the horse was OK.'

'So? What's that got to do with it?'

He sighed. 'It doesn't add up. Why would he just take him?'

'You don't *know* him!' I was shaking with rage. The little voice inside that had always kept Nasty Me well hidden when I was with Rory was silent now and she was having her chance. 'That – that *bastard* nearly kills my horse and *I'm* the one getting the third degree! If he was so *responsible* why did he steal my horse?' I could hear hysteria surging into my voice and Rory was looking at me like he didn't recognise me. 'Why did he just run home to his drunk mother and his joyrider friends? He didn't even care enough to stay around! I *told* everybody what he was like and no one would listen! Well, I was right!'

'Vicky! You're acting like you hate him!' Rory pulled away.

'I *do* hate him! I've *always* hated him!' Rory looked more and more horrified as words spewed out of me. 'How could you expect me to feel anything else?'

'But he can't have meant it! It was an accident!'

'It still shouldn't have happened.'

Suddenly his eyes narrowed and he said, 'What did you say to him?'

'Say?'

He shook his head. 'Listening to you like this ... You're so full of hate. I just don't think you're telling me everything.'

'God, Rory! You're like everyone else! They all take his side! C-Cam and Fiona – and, and *Mum* –'

He stood up. 'Have you ever thought everyone might be right?'

'Wh-what do you mean?' I swallowed.

He rubbed his hand over his hair and spoke as if the words were hard to say. 'Look, Vicky, I don't *know* what happened. But I do know there's more to this than you're letting on. And I'm sorry. I liked you and everything but I ... I can't ...' His voice trailed off.

Suddenly my mind snapped into focus. 'You're *finishing* with me? Because of him?'

'*No.*' My heart rose, but fell at his next words. 'It's not because of *him*, it's because of *you*. I knew you were a bit jealous; I worked out you were a bit of a princess – I'm sorry, but you are – but I didn't know you were so vindictive. I can't ... I can't just sit here and hold your hand and tell you how sorry I am when you're like this. You need to grow up, Vicky.'

I watched him leave. Another scene in the nightmare.

* * *

I thumped my pillow and tried to find a cool, dry spot on it. I knew if I cried out loud Fiona or Dad would come in but I couldn't forget Rory's words. *Grow up, Vicky.* So I'd lost him as well. It's Declan's fault; it's all his fault –

my friends, my boyfriend, my mum, my horse: all gone because of *him*. That's what I *wanted* to think. God, to offload it all on him – it would be so easy!

It's not because of him, it's because of you.

For hours Nasty Me and Nice Me fought it out. And I knew Rory was right. No matter how wrong Declan had been, taking Flight like that, I knew he would never have done it if I hadn't made that threat. But I wasn't really going to tell her! Yes, but he didn't know that. He believed I would. And *why* did he believe that? Fresh tears ran down my face. Because I'd been such a bitch; he had every reason to believe I was capable of taking it one step further.

And now – oh, I was pretty sure I'd got my wish. I couldn't see him turning up at the yard again. Flight wouldn't be rubbing his face against him and nickering at him and closing his eyes with pleasure while Declan groomed him. I didn't need to worry about that any more.

But Flight might not be doing all those things with me either. Not if he was dead.

Chapter 29

DECLAN

You can't put a dead horse on top of the wardrobe. It's too big.

Every time I close my eyes the scene plays across my eyelids like a film. I want to press stop but I can't. The car with its wing all smashed in. Flight down on the road. The blood – oh Christ, the blood. People standing around, shouting – but there's no soundtrack. Just their mouths opening and closing. Cam. Vicky. The man in the car. In the next scene Vicky's lunging at me but Cam pulls her back. Flight. The blood. The car.

The next few scenes are in fast forward. The ones where I'm going home. Running. Then walking. I don't even know if I'm going the right way, but then there's a scene where it's dark and I'm limping down Tirconnell Parade. I see my hand turning the key in the lock. See my hands yanking off my new boots in the hall and throwing them into the corner.

From somewhere Mum's voice comes at me, 'What time do you call this? … worried sick … dinner's ruined …' See

Mum taking a plate out of the microwave. Her face – worried and pleased with herself at the same time. Me sitting at the table looking at a plate of bones and blood. My throat closes. Why can't she see? I can't tell her but I want her to know without being told.

Then it flashes back to the road. Flight. The car. The blood. Over and over.

* * *

'Thought you were working Sundays as well?' Mum leans against the kitchen doorframe, yawning. She pulls her dressing gown tighter round her.

It's after one o'clock. She was up until three. I heard the TV. I've been up for hours. I put the heating on but my insides are full of ice. I ache everywhere from the fall and the long walk. But it's not enough.

I shrug. 'Nah. Don't think I'll bother. You were right. It's too far away.'

She feels the kettle, switches it on and yawns again. 'Aye, you're right, son. Better sticking round home. I mean, horses!' She says it like it's something ridiculous. 'Not really you, is it?'

I shiver at the word 'horses' and she gives me a funny look. 'Are you sickening for something?'

I shake my head.

The phone rings in the hall and she shuffles out to it. Our phone hardly ever rings. Except – oh God, it'll be Colette. I make Mum a cup of tea, trying not to listen.

She comes back in. 'Mrs Mulholland. Do I want anything from Tesco's? Her Mairéad's taking her. She's one nosy cow.'

I grab this harmless subject. 'Och, Mum, she's just being nice.'

'Nice!' She humphs around a bit, looking for a lighter. She takes her tea into the living-room, switches on *EastEnders*, and lights a cigarette.

I hover in the doorway. 'Mum? Are you not getting dressed?'

'Jesus, Declan! It's Sunday. Would you give my head peace? What does it matter?'

'D'you want me to go to the shops for you?'

'I don't need anything at the shops! Why is everybody obsessed with the bloody shops!' But she laughs. I haven't heard her laugh for ages. I want to ask her if she's happy being home. I want to ask her if she still feels like drinking.

I don't want to be here if Colette phones.

In the end the weather decides it, flinging rain at the windows in bucketfuls. I go upstairs and lie on my bed listening to it until the room grows dark around me.

* * *

The park shuts at teatime in winter but it's easy to shin over the broken-down side of the fence. I sit on the swing, pull my coat round me and unwrap the vodka bottle from its brown paper bag. They don't ask for ID in the offie on the main road. It's the cheap stuff, a half bottle; didn't want to use all my birthday money. 'Happy birthday, Declan,' I say and unscrew the lid. Not much of a taste, not like beer or whiskey. But if it does the job for Mum – or did – there must be something in it. I'm not drinking it for the taste.

Cold at first then, as I start downing it faster, a tongue

of fire reaches down into my stomach and licks. But the bottle stays cold in my hands. I scuff my feet against the ground to push the swing and I wait to feel something. Or *not* to feel. That's what I'm after. Stop feeling. Stop thinking. Stop the film playing. It's been four days now and I can't make it stop.

At first all I feel is the drink swishing up and down with the movement of the swing. The more I drink the horribler it tastes so I down it faster, even though my throat gags, just to get it down.

And wait to start not feeling. Swinging and waiting. How long does it take? My hands freeze on the bottle so I gulp down the dregs and fling it away. Hear it smash on the ground behind me. Loud in the empty park.

I stuff my hands into my pockets and lean back on the swing and look at the stars. Then I lean too far and have to grab for the chains to stop myself falling backwards, and they're even colder than the glass so I start to laugh cause I'm being so stupid. I catch myself on – sitting on a swing on my sixteenth birthday. 'Wise up, Declan,' I say out loud. My voice sounds stupid. The hot tongue has stopped licking me and I'm shivering inside and outside.

I stand up and the ground tilts and it reminds me of the first time I got off a horse and my legs buckled. So much for not thinking. If you could just wipe your head clean. Better still, wipe out what you did. How far back would you go? Last week before you took Flight? Or before that? Last month, fighting Emmet? Last year, leaving Gran and getting into that car?

If you could make it all not have happened.

'Fuck this!' I shout. I wait for an echo or something but there's just the empty park. I have to get out but I can't find the broken-down bit of fence and when I do, it seems to have got harder to climb and I nearly wreck myself trying to get over it. Then I have to lean against it for a bit before I can start walking. Down the main road past Barry's flat. I must have got out over the wrong bit of fence. Shouldn't be round here.

My ma's going to kill me, I think. But how can she kill me for being like her? Colette said you didn't have to do the same as your parents but Colette's wrong.

A wee old man gives me a nervous look and steps aside to pass me even though he has to go on the road for a few steps. 'Never worry yourself, granda!' I shout after him. 'I'm just like my ma,' and start laughing again except this time it turns into heaving, tearing sobs and I can't stop.

Until I see who's coming up the road towards me. Emmet with a couple of his mates. He's got his head down, texting, and he doesn't see me, but he might look up so I juke down the alley beside the bookies but then I know he's going to come down here too. I don't know how I know but I do so I start to run and the alley's full of dogs' piss – at least I hope it's only dogs' piss – and more broken glass and I've got a stitch and I have to stop and lean against the wall and then the sobbing in my throat turns into retching and I'm puking my guts up.

And the stupid thing is, he never followed me. He probably didn't even see me.

The other stupid thing is that the film never stops. I'm on my knees in a pissy alley puking and crying and wanting to die and the film just plays on and on and fucking on.

* * *

'Kelly? Kelly!'

Behind me, Seaneen gives me a poke with her ruler. I open my eyes and glance round. Everyone sniggers.

'What? Oh – sorry, sir.'

Payne looks up at the ceiling and sighs. '*If* it's not too much trouble, Kelly.'

I squint at the board. A meaningless jumble of numbers. My headache beats out my pulse and my mouth's so dry that my 'Don't know, sir' only comes out at the second go.

'"Don't know, sir." If I'd a pound for every time …' Payne gives an exaggerated sigh. 'Thought your new-found work ethic was too good to last. OK, Walsh. What can you do with it?'

Maths lasts for years. I go to the toilets on the way to History, splash cold water round my face. At least there's nothing left to throw up.

When I come out Emmet McCann's blocking the corridor. 'How's the gee-gees, Kelly?' he asks with a smirk.

'Piss off, McCann.'

'Yeah,' he goes on, all conversational. 'Must run in the family. *Riding*. I suppose your ma can give you tips, can't she? Being the expert. Or should that be *sexp –*'

I have him up against the wall so fast he doesn't have time to get the last word out.

Dermott's door flies open and he pulls us apart.

Emmet yanks at the V-neck of his jumper. 'Sir! He just grabbed me for no reason!'

I don't say anything. My breath comes fast through my nose.

'Right. McCann – off with you. Kelly – in here now.'

Dermott's never called me Kelly before. In the class-room he leans against his desk, folds his arms, and looks me up and down. 'Well?' He's got green ink smudged on his shirt sleeve.

'What?'

'You were meant to be staying away from him.'

I shrug.

'So what's the story?'

I shrug.

'Declan.' He sighs. 'Look, whatever's got into you this week – don't think I haven't noticed – you need to sort it out.' His voice isn't cross any more. It's sort of kind. I clench my jaw so hard it cracks and the pain is welcome. *Sort it out.* I start to make for the door, but he holds me back. 'Not so fast. I've something here that might cheer you up.' He rummages in a pile of papers on his desk. 'Where is it? Ah yes.' He hands me out a leaflet. It's about getting a grant if you go to college away from home.

'Oh.' I look at it in disbelief. It belongs to another life. I start to tell him it's OK, I've changed my mind, I won't need it, and then I think of all the hassle of explaining to him. How can I tell him I've wrecked everything? How can I tell him I've killed a horse?

Him with his leaflets and his downloads and his bloody enthusiasm. So I just go, 'Thanks, sir.'

On the way to History I shove it in the bin in the corridor. I stick it right down into it so he won't see it.

* * *

'Kevin told Sean that Emmet McCann told him he's going to get you,' Seaneen pants, catching up with me at the end of Tirconnell Parade.

'Do I look worried?'

'Just telling you. Here, hang on.' She drops her bag and grabs my arm while she stands on one leg, takes off her shoe, fiddles with it a bit and then puts it back on. 'That's better.' She doesn't take her hand away.

'Can I get my arm back?'

She flounces away. 'God, Declan, you're hard work. I don't know why I bother with you.'

'Neither do I.'

'So what did you do to Emmet McCann?'

'Got him against the wall. Then Dermott came out.'

'He's a nasty get. Like that da of his. D'you know what that Barry said to me last week in the chippie? "God, those are quare tits, love." Perve.'

'Yeah.' I don't want to get into a conversation about Emmet. Or Barry. Or anything. I just want to go home and sleep.

'Hey, there's your Colette's car.'

'What? Oh, shit.' I scudder to a halt. My insides turn to stone. Then ice.

Seaneen gives me a funny look. 'What's wrong? Last week you couldn't wait to get home and see what she'd bought you. Hey – when is your birthday?'

'Dunno. Yesterday.'

'*Declan.*' She stands in front of me, blocking my path. 'Come on. Tell me what's happened. Last week you were all bizz about everything and now – it's like somebody's dead.' She puts her hand on my arm again.

I let out a long, shuddering breath. It's like when Dermott was nice to me earlier. I can't stand it. 'Piss off, Seaneen. I never asked you to hang round me.' I shake her hand off.

She turns without another word and marches away.

I try to sneak into the house and up the stairs but Mum catches me in the hall. 'Colette's here. Come and say hello.'

I grit my teeth and push open the living-room door.

'I was just leaving,' Colette says. She looks the same as always. 'Why don't you come out to the car with me? I've got Christmas presents for you and your mum.'

I've no choice but to follow her into the street. She waits until she's handed me the plastic bag. Then she looks me right in the face and says, 'You haven't told your mum, have you?' And I see that she doesn't look the same as usual, that her face is as cold and disappointed as her voice.

I can't answer. I swallow. Try to meet her eyes. I shake my head.

She fiddles with her car keys. 'Well, she's worked out that something's wrong. And she's imagining far worse.'

'*Worse?*'

'She said you came in drunk last night. She thinks you're on drugs.'

'I wish.'

'Oh for God's sake, Declan, don't be so pathetic. You have her worried sick.' Her voice is like a knife. 'Look – I'm not stupid. What really happened? You didn't just take Flight out for no reason, did you? Vicky won't tell me anything. She just cries.'

I can't answer. Can't believe she's saying his name out loud. I wish she would hit me or something.

She shakes her head. 'You've done something stupid. Worse than stupid. But there's no need to go round act-ing like this.' She's never sounded this angry, not even when I thumped Vicky. 'You haven't even asked how Vicky is, let alone Flight.'

'Flight? But he's ...' I can't say the word.

'He isn't dead, Declan. Is that what you thought?'

I nod. Bite my lip as hard I can.

'Oh, he may never recover. He could still be put down. We won't know for months. But he's alive.' When she speaks again her voice is dead sad. 'I can't believe you just ran away, Declan. That's the bit that really... You never even phoned.'

I stare at the ground, willing the tears behind my eyes to stay there. 'I'm sorry.'

'Yes, well.' She doesn't sound impressed. 'It's not me you need to apologise to. Look, I have to go.'

Two Rs in 'sorry', Kelly.

And I hear the car door slam.

Chapter 30

VICKY

Becca made friends first. She hunkered down beside me at the lockers and said, 'Katie Maguire told Niamh what happened to Flight.'

I nodded. Concentrated on not crying. All week I'd only felt like I was half-here. The days had dragged and it was still only Thursday. 'Should you not be in PE?' I asked. Becca hated getting into trouble.

'I was at the school nurse. Period pains. You?'

'Just couldn't face it.' It was the first time I'd ever mitched class.

'Is he going to be OK?'

'We don't know. He won't die or anything, it's not like that, but he … he might never be sound again.'

'I don't really know what that means,' Becca admitted.

'It means I might never be able to ride him again. He might be lame for life.'

'Oh. But he won't die?'

I sighed. 'His injury won't kill him. But if he … if he doesn't get better … Well, no one wants to keep a lame horse.'

Her round face was shocked. 'You mean – you couldn't just keep him as a pet?'

'I'd *want* to,' I reassured her. 'Course I would. But it costs a lot to keep a big horse like Flight. If I wanted another one I *could* ride – well, Dad wouldn't pay for two.'

She grimaced. 'But it hasn't happened yet? I mean, he might be OK?'

'Might be. We won't know for ages – six months, maybe a year.'

'Poor old Vicky.' She moved closer to me and gave me a hug with one arm. 'Look, babes, I'm sorry we fell out.'

'Me too. I wanted to text you when it happened but I just … I don't know … I didn't want you to think I was, like, emotionally blackmailing you into making friends.'

'I wouldn't have thought that!'

'Fliss would have.'

'Not when she hears what's happened. Was Rory good?'

I gave a dry little laugh. 'He dumped me.'

'He *what*?' Her eyes widened.

Tears pricked the back of my own eyes. 'Dumped me. He said … said…'

Becca tightened her arm round me. 'How could he dump you just when you needed him?'

'It wasn't like that. I don't blame him. Neither will you when I tell you what I did.'

'What *you* did?'

So I told her. She was the first person I'd told. I knew Mum and Fiona both guessed I'd said something to Declan but I was too ashamed to tell them, especially after the way Rory reacted. Cam, though she'd been brilliant with Flight and texted me all the time to tell me how he was, was kind of distant, as if she guessed there was more to it than I was telling. But Becca and Fliss had already told me what they thought of my attitude to Declan. Becca could say told you so if she wanted. I was too miserable to care.

But she didn't. She kept her arm round me and made comforting noises, and when I'd blurted out the whole story she gave me two tissues and said, 'Poor old Vic. I bet you'd give anything not to have said it.'

'Course I would! I … I can't forgive him, Becs,' I admitted. 'Not after what he did. I'm mean, I'm *sorry* and I know it was partly my fault and I feel so *guilty* but every time I think about Flight lying in the road like that …' I couldn't go on.

'I know.' She squeezed my arm. 'I don't think anyone could expect you to forgive him just yet. But you will some day.'

'I won't.'

'You will. And Vic? You *really* need to talk to your mum about this Brian.'

The bell made us both jump. 'Chemistry,' said Becca with a groan. 'Can't mitch that. You okay to come or shall I bring you to the nurse? I'm sure she'd let you lie down for an hour. You look awful.'

I was tempted for a moment. 'No, it's okay. But Becs, will you talk to Fliss for me? Tell her – you know, everything.'

'Course I will. And look, let's meet in Starbucks after school?'

'The three of us? OK.'

* * *

Fliss slid into the bench beside me and Becca and set down two steaming mugs of hot chocolate and a Diet Coke. She wasn't as easy to make friends with as Becca. Becca was all hugs and warmth and forgiveness but Fliss was tougher. Oh, she'd make friends properly and mean it, but she wouldn't let you just forget about what she'd fallen out with you about in the first place.

'I wonder how *he* feels about it,' she said. 'He must feel worse than you.' It was more or less what Fiona had said.

'It's not his horse, though,' I said. 'I bet he *is* sorry – how could you not be? – but he just ran away, couldn't even stay and face me.'

'D'you blame him, though? *I* wouldn't be able to face you if I'd wrecked your horse,' said Fliss. 'Remember when I broke your phone in Year Nine?'

'Fliss! You can hardly compare them!' said Becca before I could reply.

'But the principle's the same,' insisted Fliss. 'You were really nasty about that, Vic – no, I'm not casting up, honestly. I just mean you're very …' She thought for a moment, like she really wanted to get the right word. 'Possessive, I suppose. That's what I meant when I said about you being so jealous and that. You know the way you are with your dad having the new baby and that. And being so mean about Declan. And now your mum and this Brian.'

I stirred my hot chocolate with the wooden stick thing. I knew Fliss wasn't saying all this just to be nasty but it was hard to listen to.

'I don't *like* my mum having boyfriends, you know,' she went on. 'I know I always make a joke of it but I used to wish my mum was like yours, that she stayed in and focused on me all the time. But I suppose they deserve a life too.'

'Yeah.' Becca joined in. 'I used to be really jealous of you and your mum too, Vic. Like, whatever you do, your mum thinks you're great. OK, so she's a bit annoyed with you at the minute, but you know what I mean. I'm never going to be good enough for my mum – if I get As she wants A stars; if I come second in a test, why wasn't it first? I feel like I'll never be clever enough, thin enough, pretty enough –'

'Becs!'

She waved away my sympathy. 'No, this isn't about me; I just wanted to remind you, you're pretty lucky.'

It was what Mum was always trying to tell me. And Rory, saying I was a bit of a princess.

Fliss rubbed my arm and made me smile at her. 'Vic, babes, don't get all sulky. You're *our* friend. If your friends can't tell you the truth, who can?'

'I know.' My voice was very small. 'I just feel like I've *lost* everything. Flight and Rory and –'

'You haven't lost *us*.'

'I could have, though.'

'But Vicky, you need to ask your mum about Brian,' said Fliss. 'You can't just keep putting it off. I bet you're being all huffy with her and she doesn't even know why.'

'OK.' I ran my finger round the inside of my mug to cream off the froth. 'I'll ask her tonight.'

* * *

I stared at the receipt. Carphone Warehouse. £39.99. Mum hadn't got herself a new phone, had she? No, she'd said she'd wait for my old one which I was going to give her after Christmas when I got my iPhone from Dad. So what was this all about? She hadn't forgotten about Dad's present and got me a phone herself, had she? I hoped not – not a forty quid one!

Mum came into the kitchen. 'Vicky? What are you doing? I asked you to get me my purse, not analyse the contents of my bag!'

I held out the receipt. 'It was just – I hoped you hadn't got me a phone. Because dad's getting me an iPhone. Remember?'

She took the receipt off me and sighed. 'Don't worry. I know you wouldn't thank me for it. It was a Christmas present.'

'Oh. Who for?' Then I knew. 'Mum! How could you?'

She sat down opposite me at the table. 'I got it a while ago. I wasn't sure what to do with it; it seemed a bit mean not to give it to him.'

Despite all my good intentions and the pep talk from Fliss and Becca I couldn't help my eyes flooding with tears at the injustice. 'It was a bit *mean* for him to nearly kill my horse!'

'I know.' She rolled the receipt up in her hands and started playing with it. 'Look, I don't know if I did the right thing. It just seemed … petty or something not to.'

'You mean…?' Gradually I took in what she was trying to tell me. 'You *gave* it to him? You've *seen* him?'

Mum pinched the bridge of her nose as if she had a headache. 'This afternoon.'

'Did he say anything?' I didn't know why I was asking. Like anything he said could make a difference now.

'He said sorry. I didn't make it easy for him, you know, Vic. I think he realises how serious it is. He seemed to think Flight was dead.'

I shuddered. 'Well, if he was so worried why didn't he get in touch?'

'I asked that.'

'And Mum, he *doesn't* know how serious it is! Flight may never be sound. We don't have a full team for Saturday. That driver's suing Dad because his car's a write-off.' Tears burned my cheeks. Again.

'I told him he'd have to apologise to you.'

'Well, he needn't waste his breath.'

'Do you really mean that?'

'I don't know!' I sobbed. 'I'm just ... it's all so mixed up.'

She stroked my hair. 'Vicky – I think he's pretty cut up about it. I mean, if that makes you feel any better. He hasn't told his mum – I suppose he's scared of worrying her, you know she's a bit fragile – and I got the impression he was bottling it all up. At least you aren't doing that.'

I tried to laugh and gave a big snottery gulp. 'That's true.' Then I thought of the things I *was* bottling up. I wasn't ready to tell her what I'd said to him. But the other thing... 'Mum,' I said, looking her in the eye. 'Why did you tell him about Brian? And not me?'

For a second the disbelief on her face made me think she was going to say, 'Brian? What on earth are you talking about? There is no Brian.' But she didn't. She just looked puzzled. Maybe a bit guilty.

'*I* didn't tell him about Brian,' she said slowly. 'I told Theresa. I suppose she must have told him. It wasn't a secret.'

'It was from *me!*'

'Oh Vicky, I'm sorry. I was waiting for the right moment. And then with the accident – it just seemed too much for you to cope with.'

'But you told *her*!'

'Do you not tell Fliss and Becca things you don't tell me?'

'Yeah, but –'

'It's the same thing. Well, partly it was to have something to talk about. Theresa can be pretty hard work. But it was more…' She sighed. 'No, you're right, I should have told you. But it was only a date at first. I didn't know if it was going to lead to anything. I didn't want to make a big deal out of it for no reason.'

'Mum! Even having a date is a big deal for you.'

She gave a dry sort of laugh. 'You know, Vic, you've had it easy. Dad left me for Fiona. He's still with her *and* you like her. I've never had a boyfriend since your dad. Not even a date, until now. You've never had to deal with any of that. How many boyfriends has Fliss's mum had?'

'But at least Fliss's mum *tells* her!'

Mum just tore on as if I hadn't spoken. 'And I've lost count of the men Theresa's had. Some of them, from what your gran used to tell me, pretty unpleasant. But I have *always* put you first.' She was starting to sound quite fierce. 'And you know what, Vic? I'm lonely. I'm fed up being on my own every weekend. I'm only thirty-six, for God's sake. And I'd like to meet somebody while I still can.'

'So, what about this Brian, then?'

'He's a lecturer. I met him at the Open Libraries Festival. He was doing a talk on Seamus Heaney. We got chatting. He's forty-two. Divorced.'

My voice scrambled in my throat. 'Has he got kids?'

'No.'

'I suppose that's something.'

'Oh Vic!' She laughed. 'We've only been out a few times. I'm not about to move in with him.'

'I should hope not!'

'I'm sorry I didn't tell you before. And I'm *really* sorry you found out from Declan. That must have been hard.'

'It's OK.' I didn't want to go too far down this road.

'So, can we just relax and have a lovely Christmas, like we always do?'

'Yes.' I gave her a quick hug. 'Do I ever get to meet him?'

She smiled. 'Let's take it a day at a time. But if we're still seeing each other in the New Year, then yes, of course.'

'Mum, it's Christmas next week; course you'll still be seeing him in the New Year! You need to be more positive!'

'And *you* start being a bit more positive about Flight, OK? Remember what your gran used to say – if you visualise something, you could make it happen. You just visualise jumping Flight over those big fences that scare me.'

I thought of Flight standing at the back of his stable, resting his bandaged leg, eyes dull with pain and boredom. 'I'll try,' I promised.

Chapter 31

DECLAN

I lean over the sofa to hug Mum and drop the wee box into her lap. 'Merry Christmas, Mum.'

She looks at the necklace and smiles up at me. 'Och, son, that's lovely. Here – put it on for me.' She holds her hair away from her neck while I fasten the chain. It's an angel – silver with a tiny gold halo. Well, maybe not real gold – it was £15.99 in Argos.

'It's a guardian angel,' I tell her. Then I think this sounds dead gay. 'I mean, you know, like a good luck thing.'

She pulls it away from her neck to look at it. 'It's gorgeous.'

She's trying so hard. She's cooked a proper Christmas dinner and everything. She went to the Spar herself to get the stuff. Yesterday she even went over to give Mrs Mulholland a Christmas card and stayed for ages talking to Mairéad.

I'm trying hard too. Colette made me feel so crap the other day. *Don't be so pathetic. She's imagining far worse.*

So no more wandering the streets. No more drinking. I stay in and watch her and try to act normal. Oh, it's all still there – the road, the car, the blood – but sometimes for a few minutes at a time, I can forget about it. In the mornings, for the first few seconds, it's like it never happened. But it always comes back.

Mum's present is an iPod. 'I know that's what all you young fellows want,' she says. I don't think she knows you need a computer to use it. 'Don't forget Colette's,' she says, handing me a rectangular package.

It's a mobile. Nothing flashy, but it's slim and black with a camera. She must have remembered that I didn't have one. She must have bought it Before.

'I'll do the dishes, Mum. You stay here and watch TV.' Doing the dishes is a good excuse to get away. Even if it's only as far as the kitchen.

Mum's been cleaning like a demon on and off since she got home but now the kitchen looks like someone's made a feast for twenty, not a dinner for two. Colette did proper cooking like this every night, but her kitchen never looked like this. Neither did Gran's when she used to do Christmas dinner for the three of us. This is a dead mean thought so to make up for it I give everything a really good scrub and put all the dishes away. Usually I just let them drip. The tin she did the chicken in – where does that go? I remember seeing it in the top cupboard. This is the cupboard I never used to be able to reach, but when Colette and I were cleaning in here and she got me wiping out the cupboards I noticed I could. God! Why does *everything* make me think about Colette?

I lift the tin and slide it in. Right to the back. It hits something hard and clinks. I stand on tiptoes and try to move the other dish out of the way.

Only it isn't a dish. It's a bottle of vodka.

I stand back down normally and breathe out slowly. It can't be. It must have been there before. But Colette and I cleaned out that cupboard.

Well then, it's just … Maybe she just likes to know it's there. Doesn't mean she's been at it.

But it's half empty.

I stack the other dishes away. Wipe the surfaces. Put the leftovers in the fridge.

Not thinking about the bottle of vodka totally wins out over not thinking about Flight.

'Declan? Have you fallen asleep in there? What about a wee cup of tea?' She sounds so normal. She's *been* so normal. Well, not normal for her. But normal like a normal person.

Still not thinking, I put the kettle on and find the teapot. Milk. Mugs. I bring the tea in and she smiles.

'Thanks, son. We've had a lovely Christmas, haven't we?'

'Um. Yeah.' How can I say anything? She hasn't been drunk. I always know. And it's Christmas. I sit on the arm of the sofa and look at *EastEnders*. 'You're bang out of order!' yells Phil Mitchell. I hate Phil Mitchell. He looks like Barry.

Then I hear my own voice, louder than Phil's. 'Mum? Why's there a bottle of vodka in the cupboard?'

She takes a sip of tea but under the silver angel a red stain creeps up her neck. 'A bottle of vodka?'

'Don't tell me it was from before. I know it wasn't. And don't say you haven't been drinking it. I'm not stupid, Mum.'

'Declan, have you seen me drunk since I got home?'

I shake my head. Try to drink my tea but it's too hot.

'Look, I have a wee glass now and again. That's all. It's just a wee treat. It's no big deal.' She tries to reach her hand out to me, but I move away, spilling the tea on the sofa arm. 'Watch what you're doing!'

'Thought you were off it?' My voice sounds sulky. Childish.

'I *am*. For God's sake, Declan. Look, I know I was overdoing things a bit before. But it's all sorted now. I can take it or leave it.'

'But you were meant to have stopped.'

'Does Colette never take a wee drink?'

'Mum, that's different!'

'Why?'

Because Colette's not an alcoholic. But I don't say it.

'Am I the one who came in legless last week?'

'That's not fair!'

'Oh, but it's fair for you to lecture me?'

I sigh. I'm not going to win. She twists everything. But maybe she's right. If she's only having a glass every now and then. That's just – what do you call it? – moderate drinking.

But my mum's not a moderate drinker.

* * *

Mum sets the phone back in its holder. 'Well,' she says, '*she's* happy, all right. Spending New Year's Eve with this Brian. Must be serious.'

'Oh, right.'

Mum sighs. 'OK for her, isn't it?'

'Well,' I shrug, 'she's been on her own for ages.' I still can't think about Colette without my face smarting at the memory of that day before Christmas. 'It's not me you need to apologise to.' I've even thought about it. But I can't *imagine* phoning Vicky. Well, I can imagine it. It always ends with her slamming the phone down. I've even thought about writing it. But she'd think – and Colette'd think – that I was chickening out of a proper apology. And they'd be right.

And Cam. I wish I could apologise to Cam.

'Maybe it's time I went out and met someone nice,' says Mum. 'What d'you think?' She smiles at herself in the hall mirror and rubs her tongue over her teeth. Then she frowns at me. 'Any word of you getting off your arse and getting yourself a life?'

'Mum!' I've stayed in every day since I found the bottle. Stayed in until my head throbbed with being indoors. Stayed in to make sure *she* was OK. It's been so boring I even started doing a bit of revision for my mocks. Not that there's any point now. 'You used to nag me to stay in and stop running the streets.'

'Well, there's a happy medium, son. You're sixteen. You shouldn't be sitting in with your mother.'

God, she makes me sound like a sad bastard.

'And, you know,' she goes on, sort of proudly, 'it's not like you need to keep an eye on me. I haven't been near that bottle since Christmas.'

That's true. I keep trying not to go and look in the cupboard but I can't stop myself. And the level hasn't changed. I thought she might have filled it up with water but I tried it – well, I got as far as sniffing it but the smell brought back my birthday and made me gag so I reckon it was vodka, all right. So maybe she's right – she can take it or leave it now. Sometimes I think I've caught the brightness in her eyes, the slight redness of her cheeks that means she's been at it – but I could be wrong.

'Ah, go on son. Away out and see your friends.'

'I'm not leaving you on your own on New Year's Eve.' No need to tell her I don't seem to have any friends.

'Well, I might head over to Mairéad's for an hour. Sure, she doesn't get out much with those wee twins.'

'Oh. OK then.' For the first time I notice she's wearing her good leather trousers and she's got make-up on.

I've hardly been out the door for ages and the raw air catches at my throat. It's like breathing for the first time in days. The footpaths are starting to freeze and they're flashing light/dark in all the flickering lights. Tirconnell Parade is still lit up like Las Vegas. I stuff my hands deeper in my pockets and trudge on. There's nowhere I want to go. I nod alright to Chris Reilly, Kevin Walsh and a couple of girls from the year below. The girls are sliding on the icy footpaths, half-falling and grabbing at the boys and laughing. I wonder where Seaneen is.

I head on past the chippie, the offie, the sweet shop, and cut down through the waste ground beside them to the main road. There's a row of cars outside the chapel even though it's not Sunday. Gran used to drag me to Mass all the time. Haven't been in the chapel since her funeral. Gran was a great one for Confession. Every Saturday when I was wee I had to wait for her in the pew and not move or fidget. If I was good she took me to the Cosy Café on the way home for jam doughnuts. One time she wouldn't take me because I got my toy car out and ran it down the aisle. The Cosy Café's boarded up now.

I wonder what it'd be like to go to some priest and say you'd nearly killed a horse. I wonder what he'd give you – a few Hail Marys, maybe. How could that make you feel any different? Gran always used to say she felt great after Confession. She used to stay in the wee box thing for ages, but she can't have had many sins.

Past the chapel there's the new flats. Well, people call them new but they've been there a few years now. I can't help glancing up at Barry the Bastard's window and my stomach clenches when I see the light.

I think about going to the park, but I had enough of the park on my birthday.

My new phone tells me it's only ten o'clock. Sod the bloody New Year. It'll be the same as every other year. I get to Fat Frankie's just before he shuts and get a chip. Haven't had proper chips for ages – not since that time with Rory after the show. Rory telling me I should work with horses. I bet he and Vicky aren't walking through some shithole estate eating chips on New Year's Eve.

Walking past Seaneen's house I have to step on to the road because of the big silver Jeep mounting the footpath in front of me. A drug dealer's car. Then the registration jumps out at me – BAZ 67. Quick glimpse of fat bristly neck. I bend over my chips so he can't see me, and the sharp vinegary smell nearly knocks me out. A blast of music and laughing comes through the open door of the house. If I hadn't told Seaneen to piss off, would I have been invited? Then I catch on. Seaneen's house is Mairéad's house. *That's* where Mum's seeing in the New Year. Not sitting with a cup of tea and Jools Holland on the TV. At a party. A party with drink. A party with Barry McCann.

I wrap the chips into a parcel and go straight through our house to the back yard to put them in the wheelie bin.

It's not even a surprise to see the three vodka bottles wedged down between plastic bags and the chicken carcass from Christmas day. They're not even wrapped up. It's the cheap import stuff. The stuff she gets off Barry.

And when a Flight-haunted sleep finally takes me, it's no surprise to be dragged up out of it by the giggling and shouting and key-scraping of Mum getting in. This time, she is legless.

And she's not alone.

Chapter 32

VICKY

I scuffled along Sandringham Park in the cold drizzle. Even though it was the first of January there were still soggy clumps of leaves in sad heaps. Mum was still in bed. Dad and Fiona and Molly had gone to Fiona's parents' holiday cottage on the north coast. They'd invited me but I didn't want to leave Flight. Mum had gone out with Brian the night before so I'd ended up sitting home on my own. Becca had invited me round to hers and I'd got ready and everything but in the end I hadn't felt like going. I just stayed in and went to bed early. Which is why I was wide awake and restless while the rest of Belfast slept off its hangover.

I was so intent on looking down that I didn't see Rory until I nearly crashed into him.

'Oh my God! Sorry!' I said and my heart stopped. This was the first time I'd seen him since he dumped me. But it was bound to happen some time.

Rory blushed. 'Oh, hi, Vicky. Um – happy New Year.'

'Yeah. Happy New Year.'

I thought he would just walk on but he hovered. He was all hopped up in a big overcoat with a wee woolly hat and he looked gorgeous. I had greasy hair which I'd pulled back into a plait and was wearing the quilted jacket I usually only wore to the yard.

'So – how have you been? How's Flight?' He sounded nervous, like he wasn't sure if it was OK to ask this or not.

'Cam thinks he's putting more weight on his leg. But he gets bored being in the stable all the time.' I bit my lip. 'Did you have a nice New Year?' I was coming out with total crap but I didn't want him to just say goodbye and head up the street away from me.

He smiled. 'The usual. We always do this big family thing. Loads of cousins and grannies and stuff. It's a bit corny, to be honest, but my mum would be so upset if I said I didn't want to be there. Even though I grew out of it when I was about twelve. You know what family parties are like.'

'I don't, really. My family's kind of small and kind of ... well, split.' I didn't just mean Mum and Dad. I was thinking about Declan and his mum. I didn't *want* to think about him; I just couldn't seem to help it. I bet he hadn't been sitting in on his own on New Year's Eve, either. I bet he'd been out partying with his horrible joyriding friends.

I scuffled at some leaves. We seemed to have reached the point where there wasn't anything left to say. Then at same moment we both said, 'I'm sor –' and gave short, embarrassed laughs.

'You first,' he offered.

My stomach shivered but I had to say it. 'It's just I'm sorry about ... well, you were right about me being nasty to Declan. I did say … something … to him and I suppose it made him so angry he just took Flight without thinking. I kind of know it wasn't on purpose. What you said –'

'Look, I feel bad about that,' he interrupted. 'I was way too harsh.'

'It's OK,' I said. 'You did make me sort of wise up to myself. Other people – my friends – had told me the same thing but I wouldn't listen.'

'Still, my timing could have been more sensitive.'

'Your timing was *crap*,' I said and suddenly we were both laughing, a proper laugh this time.

'Look,' he said, 'are you busy? I mean, were you going anywhere special?'

I shrugged and tried to sound casual. 'Just waiting for Mum to surface so she can take me up to see Flight.' I hoped my voice didn't sound as full of anticipation as I felt.

'I could take you up. If you wanted to, I mean.'

'OK. If you're sure.'

And that's how, half an hour later, I was looking over Flight's half-door with Rory standing beside me, so close that I could feel the rough wool of his coat. The yard was deserted. All the other horses were in the field and poor Flight looked so lonely stuck in his stable. He nickered and limped over when he saw us at the door.

'He's happy to see you anyway,' said Rory.

I couldn't help feeling pleased. 'He never used to do that. But then … well, to be honest I suppose I just used to come up and ride him and go away again. I never spent much time just *being* with him. When – well, *if* I'm ever able to ride him again I think I'll kind of know him better.'

'Well, that'd be good, wouldn't it?'

'*Don't* start telling me this was a blessing in disguise,' I warned him.

'Course not. Can you show me his leg?'

'OK, Doctor Marshall.'

He got all interested in the wound, especially when I showed him the drain that was still in it, though it was coming out later in the week. I could look at it now without flinching but I couldn't answer all Rory's questions about it.

'Look, any time you want a lift up here to hold his paw or whatever,' he said when we were walking back to the car, 'just give me a shout. I mean, I have to revise but it's nice to get a break.' He half-looked away and started rummaging in his coat pocket for the car keys.

'Hoof, not paw!' I said.

'I know. I'm not that stupid. It made you laugh, though, didn't it?'

* * *

'So, are you guys, like, back together?' Becca's voice on the line was high-pitched with excitement.

'No. *Ssshh*,' I warned her, as if Rory could hear from three houses away. 'Just friends.'

'Yeah, right. He *totally* still likes you.'

I sighed. 'Oh, Becs, I totally still like *him*! Meeting him today was the only nice thing that's happened since – well, since the accident.'

'It's certainly cheered you up, babes.'

Mum said exactly the same thing when I ate all my dinner for the first time in ages. The problem was, I thought, stacking the dishwasher for her afterwards, I couldn't *really* text him and ask him to take me to the yard; it would be too much like running after him.

But before I went to bed my phone bleeped and it was a text from him! GOOD 2 C U. GLAD WE R FRIENDS AGAIN. I MEANT IT ABOUT TAKING U 2 C FLIGHT. 2MORO?

And I replied: OK, WOT TIME?

* * *

'God, it's freezing,' Rory said, hugging himself and pulling his scarf tighter. I wished he would hug *me*. He opened the car door and jumped in.

'Don't suppose there's anywhere round here to get a nice hot cup of coffee?' he asked when he'd started the engine.

I looked round the frozen fields. 'Afraid not. Nowhere closer than my house. But I could make you a cup. I think we have some of Mum's homemade mince pies left.' I held my breath. We'd been going up to the yard together for the last three days but this was the first time either of us had suggested taking it any further. And Mum was back at work today – the house would be empty. I fiddled with my seat-belt, keeping my face hidden in case it gave away how much I wanted him to say yes.

'Yeah,' he said, 'that sounds good.'

Before Rory had dumped me I had made him quite a few cups of coffee, when he'd been helping me revise and stuff, but now it seemed much more of a big deal. It mattered that it was strong enough, that I gave him the cup he'd once said he liked, that there was the right amount of milk. And I knew I was being stupid – it was only a cup of coffee, for goodness' sake, and he *definitely* didn't fancy me any more – he never even *looked* at me that way – but for some reason I felt really nervous.

The funny thing was, Rory did too. He kept putting his cup down and he took a second mince pie without seeming to notice that he'd only eaten half of the first one.

And then he said it. 'Vicky. I don't know if you know but ... next week ... it's our school formal.'

'Is it?' I managed to sound really casual.

'And I know it's really short notice but I wondered if ... I mean I know we're not ... but I thought you might like to come with me.'

'Oh!' My mind raced. OK, he wasn't asking me out again, but he was asking me to his *formal*! If ever there was a good omen this must be it!

'So, will you come?'

'Umm, what date?'

'Friday the eleventh.'

'Oh. That's my mum's birthday.'

His face fell.

'Of course I can come!' I put down my coffee cup and hugged him – just a hug. Friends could hug; I hugged Fliss and Becca all the time. But it felt lovely – he smelled just the same. And he didn't pull away immediately.

'And do you have enough time? To get a dress and all?'

'Oh yes! My friends and I are going to hit the sales. Big time!'

* * *

Fliss was still in Donegal so Becca and I went into town. There were loads of formal dresses but most of them you wouldn't be seen dead in – too tarty, too glittery, too frumpy, too clingy. But then in Karen Millen I found my dream dress. Turquoise with spaghetti straps that crossed over down the back and a skirt that was slinky but not tight.

'Wow!' said Becca. 'There is no way he'll be able to resist you in that!'

I did a twirl and tried to see what my back looked like. 'Are you *sure* it suits me?'

In some ways Fliss would have been better to shop with. If something looked minging she'd just raise her eyebrows and say, 'I think not, Miss Moore.' Becca always wanted to please you. But I didn't need Becca to tell me the dress was amazing.

I held my hair away from my neck. 'Up or down?'

Becca squealed. 'Let me come and do it for you! You know I'm ace at hair. We could have the back up, in a sort of twist, and maybe curls coming down at the front.'

'Could you do that?'

'Easy. And Fliss can do your make-up and nails. She's got that lovely silver stuff. Look, we'll come and be your personal beauticians! Straight after school.'

'School!' I remembered in horror. 'I can't be at school till four and then have time to get ready by seven. No way!' I was taking the turquoise dress off very carefully – it was the only size twelve in the shop.

'Course not,' agreed Becca. 'That's why you're getting out at lunchtime. Your mum'll write you a note, won't she?'

'I think so.'

Becca held the dress in front of her while I pulled my jeans back on. 'So, have you met this Brian yet?'

I pulled my jumper over my head. 'No. She keeps

saying *soon*. She said in the new year. *Now* she's saying her birthday. I think she wants to see what he gets her.'

'What's that got to do with *you* meeting him?'

'Well, if he buys her a CD and takes her to Pizza Express, then maybe it's not that serious and there's no point.'

'I like Pizza Express!'

'Me too. But they're *old*. They can afford posher places.'

'So if he buys her a diamond necklace and takes her to the Merchant Hotel then it is serious and you can meet him?'

'Well, yeah. I suppose. Something like that. Not that she's exactly the diamond necklace type.'

'So d'you reckon they're having sex yet?'

'Becca!' I threw my shoe at her. 'Stop it! Yuck!'

'You're being quite cool about it, though, aren't you?'

I remembered the first time I'd heard about Brian. Then pushed the thought away. 'I suppose.' I picked up my bag and pulled back the curtains of the cubicle. 'OK. Shall we go and buy this dress, then?'

Chapter 33

DECLAN

'Right, Declan?'

'Oh, hiya, Cathal.'

Great. Reduced to walking into school on the first day of term with Cathal Gurney. Between sniffs he tells me about the Xbox 360 he got for Christmas. 'And I've got all these new games, so I have.'

It's easy to zone out, keeping half an ear and both eyes open for Emmet McCann. I've kept out of his way all over Christmas but I haven't forgotten what Seaneen told me.

Mr Dermott rubs his hands together. 'Well, 12D.' He's even more all bizz than usual. 'New term; new challenge. All ready for your mocks?'

A lot of groaning and 'Aye right, sir', and 'No way, sir'. It's only our year doing exams. Everyone else has normal classes while we go to the assembly hall. There's desks laid out in rows. One for everyone in Year Twelve. It looks sort of important and scary and real.

It's not though. It's just the usual crap. *Write a letter to your French pen pal inviting him/her to come and stay at your house. Tell him about all the local attractions!* I can just imagine some poor frog arriving at 13 Tirconnell Parade.

Monday, Tuesday drag by. This is the first time in my life I ever did any revision but it doesn't seem to make much difference. By Wednesday afternoon the assembly hall stinks of deodorant and stale farts. School ends early because of exams and I've been making myself head straight home – see if I can catch her before she starts – but I know I'm being stupid. Last night I found a bottle in the cupboard under the stairs. She never used to hide them before.

She hasn't been falling down, passing out, throwing up drunk – not since New Year's Eve anyway.

She hasn't been crying, pyjamas all day, bad-tempered drunk.

She hasn't been on a bender, round at the Bastard's flat, lost weekend drunk.

But she has been drinking.

Last week I thought Mum going back on the drink was the *worst* she could do. But it's not.

'Oi Kelly!' It's Emmet. I swing round but there's no one else in sight. I don't think he'd jump me without a couple of mates.

'What?'

'See your ma?'

I look round. 'No. Where?'

Emmet yanks my bag off my shoulder. 'Don't try to be clever, Kelly. You tell your slag of a ma to keep away from my da. Get it?'

I grab my bag back. 'Look, McCann, if you think I *want* my ma anywhere near your da –'

'Yeah, well tell her! She better keep away. My da was all right when she was locked up. Then the minute she's out, she's sniffing round.' His voice rises to a high-pitched whine. You'd nearly think he was going to cry. He's pushed his fat face so close to me that I smell cheese and onion crisps. His nose is so squashed that his forehead seems to jut out further than it.

'Piss off, McCann.' It's just words. I can't really be bothered. And all the time I'm trying to block out that 'she's sniffing round'. I wish Emmet would just deck me one and get it over with and preferably knock me out for about a month.

He doesn't. He just says, 'You watch your back, Kelly,' and slouches off in the other direction, trying to look tough.

* * *

'Here's your tea, son.'

'It's half four!' She's got that jitteriness that means she'll fight with you as soon as look at you. Three or four glasses, I'd guess. She's got lipstick on and her big gold hoop earrings. That means she's seeing him.

'Och, sure I knew you'd be hungry after your exams.'

Not chicken kiev and chips in the middle of the afternoon hungry.

She hovers round the table. 'What are you up to tonight, son?'

'Nothing.' I push chips round my plate. I spear the chicken and a gush of snot-coloured garlicky mush spurts out. I saw this thing about chicken farms on TV. It would put you off. I set my knife and fork down.

'Are you wasting that good food?'

'It's not good food. It's crap.'

'You wee frigger. I stood and made that for you. Many's the one wouldn't have bothered.'

'Aye and many's the time you didn't bother.'

'Your trouble is you got spoiled at Colette's.' She lights a cigarette with a shaky hand. 'I should never have let you go there, getting stupid ideas on the Malone Road.'

'Yeah, well, you weren't exactly in a state to do much about it, were you?'

She goes on as if I never said anything. 'You've been a miserable get since you got back from there. Sitting up in your room, sulking. God knows it was bad enough when you were running wild and up to all sorts. Now I suppose you think you're too good for round here? Just like her.'

'That's not fair. Colette was dead good to me.'

'Oh, I bet she was. Easy for her, isn't it?'

I get up and scrape the food into the bin under the sink. 'Don't worry, I'll stay out of your way when Barry comes round.'

'Oh, so that's what all this is about? Look, what's he ever done to you?'

I rub the scar on the back of my hand. That's the only mark that ever showed. He did it cause I told the peelers it was Emmet driving the car. I thought it would get me out of being sent away but it didn't work, though I only got two months. Emmet got three and his ma kicked him out. I reckon that's what Barry has against me – having Emmet living with him cramps his style. And he dumped Mum cause I squealed. I can't believe she went crawling back to him but she's totally stupid about him. Of course he's never laid a finger on *her*. I've heard him often enough: 'I wouldn't hit a *woman*,' like he thinks this makes him Mother fucking Theresa.

And now she's standing here with her make-up on and she won't listen to a word against him.

'I just don't like him coming round here.'

'Well, maybe I'll go to his, then.'

I shrug. 'Go ahead.'

At least when she's fighting like this she's not crying and clinging. 'Fine,' she says. She grabs her bag. 'And maybe I'll not rush back.'

'Good.'

* * *

I hate this, waking at four or five. That's the hardest time to not think. It's freezing. I roll over to look at the clock radio and realise what's happened. The electric's off. I noticed last night it was nearly out of credit. I throw off the duvet and head to the window. It's grey and damp but it's not getting-up-time dark. I should have set the alarm on my phone. But I don't bother with my phone much.

Last time I went out and left her sleeping it off… My stomach lurches. I make myself push her bedroom door open. The room's empty. She hasn't stayed at Barry's for ages. But I knew last night – that's the way she goes when she's gearing up for a serious bender.

Breakfast is a dead loss. The milk's OK but there's only a few cornflakes left. The bread's a bit stale – it would be OK to toast but that's no good without the toaster working.

There's no hot water, of course. I give myself a bit of a sniff to see if I should have a cold wash or go to school the way I am. It would founder you in the bathroom so I just fire on some extra deodorant under yesterday's shirt.

Dermott's on late duty. 'Come on, Declan!' He gives me a funny look. He's been doing that a lot. 'Everything OK, lad?'

For a millisecond I wonder what it would be like to be the sort of person who could say, 'No, actually. Nothing is all right. My mum's on a bender with a psychopath. I've wrecked my whole future. I've nearly killed a horse and I can't stop obsessing about it. And I can't stand it any more.'

But I'm not that sort of person. 'Slept in.'

'OK. Straight to the hall. English first, isn't it?' He's not really listening. He's looking behind me. 'Shelley McIlroy! This is the third time this week!'

Everyone in the hall turns and stares when I walk in. Payne and Sykes are invigilating; just my luck. Payne gives me the third degree then walks me down to an empty desk like I can't be trusted. It's right beside Emmet McCann.

Sykes heaves her fat arse off the chair at the front and grumps along the aisle with a paper. 'You've lost fifteen minutes,' she hisses.

Like I care.

I dashed out so fast I forgot my pencil case. All I can find is a buggered biro and when I try to write my name on the page it comes out scratchy. So I have to put my hand up and ask for a pen.

'I am not a stationery supplier,' says Sykes. 'It is your responsibility to come prepared.'

I push my chair back from the desk. What's the point? I'm about to stand up and walk out when a pen slides onto my desk from the person on my other side. 'Here.' It's Seaneen Brogan. The pen's pink with a fluffy pom-pom on the top but it writes OK.

There's the usual stupid comprehension thing. An advert saying Portrush is class and we should all go there. Then a letter to the *Belfast Telegraph* – but you can tell it's only made up – saying Portrush is a dump. And you have to compare them. I don't know, never been there. It looks OK in the advert. But I suppose that's the point.

Section B. Writing to inform, explain and describe. Usual shite. Describe your proudest achievement. Now which of the many could I possibly choose? I could make something up about scoring a winning goal in football or something. But I don't think I can be bothered.

I can't do this.

I sigh and look round. Beside me Seaneen's scribbling away, her curls bouncing on her neck. The tip of her tongue is resting on her spiky little teeth. Not in a Cathal Gurney sort of way – it looks cute. I wish I hadn't told her to piss off.

Emmet McCann snuffles like a pig. He can't breathe properly ever since I broke his nose. Every few seconds he gives a big rattly snort. It's minging.

'Eyes on your own work!' barks Sykes. Yeah, like anyone's going to copy off Emmet McCann.

I start doodling on the back of the paper. A blob. Then it turns into a dog, or maybe a horse. 'This is the best work experience report I've ever seen,' said Mr Dermott. 'You should be very proud.'

And I was. I'm not now. But for that time – what was it, two weeks? – before I wrecked it … I close my eyes and see the stable yard. Not the road outside and the car and the blood and the people shouting. I'm looking over the half-door at my first halfway decent attempt at a bed. 'Aye, you're not the worst,' says Jim. Flight's breath frosting the spotlit evening. The fat weight of a well-stuffed hay net. The happy munching of a yard full of contented horses. The soft shine of clean leather.

My eyes are open now and the pen is covering the page faster than I've ever written before. I don't do what Sykes always tells us and check my full stops and paragraphs and that. I just write. Smells. The tickly, sweet smell of haylage. The salty, damp tang of a tired, sweaty horse. Even the steamy, rich smell of a fresh heap of dung.

And the hot stink of the blood pulsing out of Flight's leg, pooling on the road –

Stop it! You weren't that close. You couldn't smell it. But I can now. Like that mad old bitch Lady Macbeth. *Here's the smell of the blood still.*

My hand shudders to a stop, suddenly so sweaty that the pen skids out and lands with a thud beside Emmet's foot. I grab it. Payne's head jerks up from the crossword.

For the first time I look at what I've written. My breath shivers. Cam. Kizzy. Flight. No way can I let Sykes see this. Scrunching up the paper is so quick I don't even know I'm going to do it till it's done.

'What the … Declan Kelly! What are you doing? Give that to me.' Payne's beside me, grabbing for it.

I close my hand tighter round the ball of paper. Sharp edges dig into my fingers.

'Fuck you!' I push the desk away. It overturns, crashing into Kevin Walsh's in front. He swings round. 'Oi! Watch out, Kelly!'

Still gripping the exam paper I kick the chair over and run out of the room.

Chapter 34

VICKY

Fliss lent me a lovely silvery pashmina for the formal and Becca tried out different hairstyles on me every breaktime until Mad Max chased us out of the toilets.

'God, you are *so* lucky,' Fliss sighed for the hundredth time on Thursday morning at the lockers. There was no sign of Becca. 'Does Rory have any nice single friends?'

'I haven't met his friends. You have to remember it was the shortest relationship in history. And,' as Fliss opened her mouth to argue, 'we are just friends.'

'But he's asked you to the formal. He *must* want to get back with you.'

'He probably just doesn't know many girls.'

'So, have you seen him since he asked you?'

'No, they have their A2 mocks. That's weird, isn't it – exams all week and then a formal on Friday?'

'I suppose it stops them obsessing all week about their fake tans and their hair appointments,' said Fliss wisely.

'I don't think boys are like that,' I said. 'They just wear tuxedos, don't they?'

'Yeah.'

'Boring. I'd hate to be a boy.' I thought of the fun I was going to have getting ready for the formal with Fliss and Becca to help.

'They do look gorgeous, though, don't they? You're *so* lucky.'

And we were back where we'd started.

Becca dashed in and dumped her bag just as the bell clanged through the corridors.

'Hi babes,' said Fliss. 'Thought you weren't coming.'

'Got my report. The postman came dead early. Mum wouldn't let me leave till she'd interrogated me about that B in Maths.'

'Oh God, *reports*.' That gave us something else to obsess about, for a few minutes anyway.

The envelope with the school crest was still on the doormat when I let myself in after school. It was addressed to Mum, but I didn't think she'd mind me opening it.

She didn't, especially when she saw it. I thrust it at her as soon as she got in from work. All As and a couple of A stars. It was my first ever A in Science, thanks to Rory's private coaching. Though of course it could well be the last.

I watched Mum's face as she read down the grades and comments. 'Victoria is an able pupil who has applied herself diligently to her studies. This excellent report augurs very well for June.' I bet Mad Max hated having to write something nice.

'Good girl,' said Mum, giving me a hug.

I decided to cash in on her approval. 'Mum, d'you think you could take me up to see Flight tonight? Just for ten minutes? *Please*?' I did puppy-dog eyes.

'I'll take you after tea.'

It was pretty decent of her, I thought, as I sat beside her in the car watching the wet hedges blow and scratch against the windows. I was glad Flight would be tucked up warm in his nice stable. He was munching his haylage but turned round to look at me when I slipped into the barn.

'Poor old fellow; he must be bored,' I said, scratching behind his ears the way he loved.

'He's more settled,' said Cam, who was doing her evening rounds. 'And look, see how well his wound's closing over.'

He nuzzled at me. 'He's way more affectionate,' I said.

'It's because you're spending more time just being with him,' said Cam. 'And he's definitely making good progress. Though of course it's early days.' She looked at my face. 'Don't look so scared, Vicky. I've got a good feeling about him.' This was the most she had said to me since the accident. I leaned my head against Flight's warm neck and wished I was brave enough to confess about threatening Declan.

Mum offered Flight a treat, warily. 'I still don't understand how it happened,' she said. This was the first time she'd seen Cam since the accident.

Cam sighed. 'No. It must have been just a moment of madness. It was so unlike him, though.' Then her voice hardened. 'First and last time I'll take anyone on for work experience.'

'I've been expecting him to get in touch with Vicky to apologise,' Mum said as if I wasn't there. 'But so far …' She shrugged. 'And he owes *you* an apology, too,' she went on. 'I mean, this isn't the sort of thing that does your business much good, is it?'

'Well, it happens. All too often, unfortunately, with the roads getting so busy. Flight's not the first horse to dump his rider and run over that road. We've just been lucky up until now. I'm going to get a gate put on. I meant to before, but you know what it's like – it takes something like this…'

On and on they went until I could have screamed. All this obsession and speculation about what he'd done and why he'd done it. And all the time I was the only person who *knew* why. I looked at my poor, damaged show-jumper resting his mangled leg and tried to filter out their voices.

Driving home I kept the conversation firmly on the formal. Starting with the need to get out of school early. 'Rory's picking me up at quarter to seven,' I reminded her. 'And there's no way I could get ready in three hours.'

She laughed. 'OK. Just this once. But I'm not writing a note saying you have to have time off to beautify yourself. I don't want Mrs Maxwell to think I'm that sort of mother. I'll say you have an appointment.' Then her voice changed. 'Picking you up? Rory's not *driving*, is he?'

'Course not! We're all meeting up at his friend Phil's house for cocktails, and he's leaving the car there. Then we're getting taxis to the hotel.'

'Cocktails?' Mum looked disapproving.

'Cock*tail*,' I promised. 'Look, Mum, you know I'll be sensible. I'm not going to let anything stop me from having a perfect night.'

Chapter 35

DECLAN

Payne looks me up and down.

'I will talk to you *when* you've tucked your shirt in *and* done your tie up properly.'

I heave as big a sigh as I dare. Fixing my tie I get a whiff of sweat fighting against the deodorant I put on this morning. The sweat's winning. I tuck my shirt in and look Payne in the face.

'Right,' he goes. 'So what was all that about?'

'All what?' I know fine rightly.

'That...' He searches for the word. 'Ridiculous out-burst yesterday.'

Ridiculous outburst. Makes me sound like a two-year-old in a tantrum. He looks not far from a ridiculous outburst of his own. I don't really listen. 'Blah blah ... disturbed entire room ... upset other pupils ... abused school property ... shouted obscenities ...' Load of crap. 'Then,' he finishes, folding his arms like this makes him dead impressive, 'you absented yourself from the premises without permission, and missed your afternoon examination.'

'I'd have failed anyway,' I mutter.

'That is neither here nor there!' he roars. 'I want an explanation.'

I sigh. A month seems to have passed since I ran out of school yesterday. A month of expecting Mum to come home, of looking for money for the electric, of freezing my bollocks off in the dark and going to bed with two duvets. And if I'd found money for the meter I wouldn't be standing here with bloody Payne. I'd be at home eating chips and watching TV with the heating turned up high. At least in school it's warm and if I stick it till lunchtime I'll get my free dinner.

'Kelly? I do not tolerate dumb insolence.' Payne is the original Mr Zero Tolerance. But if I talk he'll say I'm being cheeky and he won't *tolerate* that either.

Out in the real world – well, the assembly hall – I should be doing my History exam. A few weeks ago I thought I could have got a C in History. If yesterday's 'ridiculous outburst' feels like a month ago, that ridiculous optimism belongs to another lifetime. So I don't give a shit about missing History. I can stick it out here.

I fold my arms. And wait.

'You need to learn to control your anger, Kelly.'

'That's not fair!' How can he say that when I'm not even speaking?

He gives a half-smile. Triumphant because he's got me to talk. 'Well, you were suspended last term for fighting – for breaking a boy's nose, let me remind you. And here you are, in trouble again.'

'That was ages ago.' He's right about controlling my anger. I'm trembling. I dig my hands into my pockets. Try to breathe slowly. Payne's eyeing me nastily. I can see the broken veins on his cheeks. He wants me to react. It would be so easy to take a swing at him.

'And look at you!' he goes on. 'You're a mess. Have you no pride in yourself? No self-respect? That uniform looks like you've been sleeping in it for a week.' He wrinkles his nose as if to tell me he can smell me. Maybe he can. I can smell myself, even through the sickly, bitter coffee that Payne's office always smells of.

I set my mouth hard. Don't react don't react don't react.

'You can stay here until you're prepared to give me an explanation. I could just suspend you instantly, but –'

I don't want to get sent home. If I could think of something to say that would get Payne off my back I would. But my brain's too fuzzy.

'I'll talk to Mr Dermott.' My voice surprises me.

Payne gives a dry laugh. 'Oh, you will, will you? And who are you to say who you'll talk to and who you won't? This is a disciplinary matter and as such *I* am dealing with it and you will talk to *me*.'

No I won't.

'Sir, can I sit down?'

He's about to say no, then points at a grey plastic chair. 'If you must.' Payne sits too, at his desk, and lifts the phone. 'I'll have to phone your mother,' he says, 'if you won't cooperate.'

Suddenly the room's boiling and airless. I wipe my hands on my trousers. This bastard knows how to break me.

'Sir, she hasn't been well. Please don't disturb her.'

He curls his lip. 'Should have thought of that before, shouldn't you?'

He starts looking something up on the computer.

Probably my phone number. Then I realise he can phone our house as much as he likes. She's not there. Unless she's come home in the meantime. How long's it been? Two nights and a day and a half. She used to go on benders like this. Then she'd be dying for days and that'd be her off the drink for ever. Until the next time.

So let Payne phone.

But he doesn't. The bell makes me jump and when it dies away he glances at the big timetable on the wall by his desk and says, 'You say you'll talk to Mr Dermott?'

'Yeah.'

'He's free now. Oh no –' He checks another sheet. 'Invigilating. But *I* will go and take his invigilation and *he* can come and try to drag some sense out of you.' He makes it sound like he's doing me a big favour. He takes up the phone again.

In no time Dermott's big face peers round the door. They have a quick *mutter mutter* in the corridor then Payne buggers off.

'Alright, Declan?' Dermott sounds brisk and casual, like he just walked into tutor group. Then he looks at me closely and his voice changes. 'You're not, are you?'

Please don't be nice to me! Shit! Why did I say I'd talk to him? This is far worse than Payne. I let out a long breath and stare at the floor.

'You want to get offside for a bit?'

I glance up. 'What d'you mean?'

'Well, I don't like it much in here.' He looks round the grey office. It's all timetables and discipline policies and filing cabinets. 'Do you?'

I shake my head.

'I'm not teaching until after break. And you seem to

have abandoned your History exam. So why don't we repair to a local hostelry and I'll buy you a cup of tea?'

'What about Pa – Mr Payne?'

Dermott raises his shoulders in a gesture that *might* mean 'sod Mr Payne'. 'Come on,' he says. 'I'll risk it if you will.'

There's a café at the school gates where we sometimes beak off class to get chips. It feels weird walking in with a teacher. Dermott notices me eyeing up the Ulster Fry the waitress is carrying to the table beside us.

'Hungry?'

I can't let Dermott buy me a fry! Then I think, what the hell, he's a teacher, he's rich. I didn't ask to come here. 'A bit.'

'I'm meant to be on a diet.' He frowns at his big, soft belly.

'I won't tell anybody.'

He laughs. 'Well, it would be very rude to sit and watch you eat, wouldn't it? Go on then!' He orders two Ulster fries. It's the best food I've had for ages. Even eating with a teacher doesn't spoil it.

But the fry doesn't last for ever and finally Dermott pours us both out a second cup of tea and gives me this 'come on, come clean' sort of look. 'I understand there was a bit of an, er, incident in the English exam?'

'Yeah.' I start rolling my serviette into a tube.

'I thought things had been going better?'

'They had.' Past tense.

'Until…?' he prompts me.

I know I have to talk – I can't let Dermott take me here and buy me a fry and not give him what he wants. And he'd feel crap telling Payne he couldn't get anything out of me.

But if I say anything about Mum I know what'll happen: he'll be on to Social Services. And when Mum comes back – because she always does – things'll be worse than ever. So I'll have to give him a *bit* of what he wants.

I'll tell him about Flight.

The very thought makes the Ulster fry turn to lead inside me. I take a swallow of tea and try to find the words. 'I lost my job.'

Dermott raises his sandy eyebrows. 'But that – what was she called? – Ms Brooke seemed to think you were the bee's knees.'

'Yeah. Well, not any more.'

Slowly, looking at the pattern on the table, I tell him the whole story. What Vicky said. Watching her drive away with Cam, all ready to tell her about me. Knowing it meant the end. Taking Flight.

Flight's been up on that wardrobe for so long I thought I could just keep him there. I haven't let him jump down for ages. And now that Dermott's forced me to let him down, it's like he's kicked over the whole wardrobe. Loads of stuff crashes down with him.

But I'm not stupid. I keep a grip of myself enough not to say anything about Mum and Barry. It feels like I talk more than I've ever talked in my life. Dermott doesn't interrupt. He nods and says 'uh huh' and flinches a bit when I tell him what happened. I don't hold back the details. The car across the road, Flight struggling, the blood. Once I start the words come spurting out like puke.

'And is that when she sacked you?'

I shake my head, rolling the serviette up the other way. 'She never sacked me. I mean, she would have, but I just, you know, took off.'

'Like you did yesterday?'

I shrug. 'I suppose. I started writing about it for the story thing, and then … well, I couldn't hand it in, so I just, you know…' Ridiculous outburst.

'And this happened when?'

'Fifteenth of December.'

'But that's nearly a month ago!'

'Yeah.'

'And who've you told?'

'No one.'

'Declan!' He shakes his head. 'Not even your mum?'

This is where I have to be careful. 'She knows I don't work there no more.'

'And your cousin? How did she take it? I assume you've apologised?'

I shift a bit and start pleating the serviette into concertina folds.

'Declan?'

I bite my lip. Shake my head. 'It's not that I'm not sorry!' I burst out. I clench my fists hard and bite the insides of my cheeks. There's burning behind my eyes and if I cry here, in public, in front of Dermott –

I suck in a long breath.

Dermott glances at his watch, then asks for the bill. 'Of course you're sorry,' he says. 'Anyone can see that. And your cousin's clearly to blame too. But you're only going to start feeling better if you *say* sorry. Write it down if that's easier.'

I frown. 'They'll think that's just a cop out. Like I'm too chicken to say it properly.'

'Well, it'd be better than nothing, wouldn't it? Why don't we head back to school, and you sit down and write a couple of letters?'

'I dunno.'

'Look, it'll make you feel better, if nothing else.'

I shrug. I don't see how writing a letter is going to make any difference. But I suppose I could write them just to keep Dermott quiet. I don't have to post them.

Dermott pays and shrugs himself into his teacher anorak. I pull my blazer on. Heading out of the steamy warmth of the café into the cold street, it feels like we've been away from school for ages, not just a period.

Pulling a scarf out of his pocket, Dermott looks down at me and says, 'I wish you'd told me all this before, Declan. Or told *someone*.'

I shrug.

'You don't like asking for help, do you?'

'I dunno.' Never thought about it.

He goes on like he's thinking out loud. 'You don't like asking for things and you're ...'

What's he going to come up with? I don't mind what Payne and Sykes say about me but –

'Passive.'

'*Passive*? How come I'm always getting into trouble if I'm passive?'

'I mean, you let things happen to you. Bad things.'

I scuff my feet on the footpath.

'If you don't mind a bit of teacher advice: try to take action a bit more. I don't mean kicking over tables. Or thumping McCann – though you wouldn't be the first to be tempted. I mean, when things go wrong, talk to someone. Don't just bottle it up and hope it goes away.'

He means, don't put stuff on top of the wardrobe. Not that he knows about the wardrobe.

'OK, sir.'

'Come on then. Back to the asylum.'

Teacher advice. Who listens? But Dermott – he's a good bloke; he's been around since Year Eight, so I let him sit me down in his classroom while he teaches some cheeky wee brats and I write two letters. At first it's impossible and I scrunch up more paper than I did during the ridiculous outburst but in the end I get it done. They're very short. And in a way he was right. Even if Vicky and Cam still hate me, even though it won't make Flight better or get me my job back, even if they tear them up without reading them, I feel better. I remember Gran every Saturday after confession – that clean look.

And that other thing he said about not letting bad stuff just *happen*. I can't *stop* Mum drinking. Maybe it's not even my fault. But I *can* stop her pissing off and leaving me with no electric in frigging January.

So after school, if she's not back, I know what I'm going to do. I'm going up there to get some money off her. To Barry's. He won't like it. But tough. I'm going to do it.

Chapter 36

VICKY

'OK. You can look now.' Becca handed me the mirror.

I gasped. It wasn't that I didn't look like me, but I looked like a shinier, airbrushed version. My hair was pulled back with loads of tiny, sparkly turquoise clips and the bits hanging round my face were curled into loose ringlets.

'Wow! You are so clever! Thank you!' I hugged Becca though she cried out, 'Mind your curls.'

'Let's see.' Fliss came in from the loo. 'Oh, very sophisticated. Clever old Becs.'

'I used to cut my Barbies' hair all the time,' said Becca. 'I used to want to be a hairdresser when I grew up.'

'Bet your mum loved that.' I half-turned to admire the way she'd caught the back of my hair up in the little clips. The mirror gave me a tilted view of part of my room, looking like a beauty parlour. There was make-up all over the dressing table and the wonderful turquoise dress hung on the wardrobe door, waiting for me.

'Yeah, well, I was like, six, or something.'

'OK, let me check that make-up,' demanded Fliss. 'More lippy, I think. And don't forget to take it with you. You'll need to put more on after the meal.'

My stomach somersaulted at the idea of food. 'There's no way I'll be able to eat!'

'Course you will.' Becca gave my arm a squeeze through my fleecy dressing gown sleeve.

'You have to eat to soak up all the alcohol,' said Fliss, just as Mum came in with a tray of glasses full of something fizzy.

'What's that about alcohol?' she said, her parent radar obviously working overtime.

'Wow! Champagne!' said Becca. 'Thanks, Mrs Moore.'

'It's only pretend,' said Mum. 'I don't think your parents would take too kindly to me plying you with drink.'

'Oh, well, it's still lovely,' said Becca, taking a sip.

'Hey, Mrs Moore, you're looking pretty good yourself,' said Fliss, who could always talk to people's parents.

For the first time I looked at Mum properly. She was wearing a new dress – OK, it was a bit homespun and hippyish for me, but it was a pretty, rusty colour that looked good with her dark hair and eyes. I hoped Brian was going to take her somewhere nice.

'It's my birthday,' said Mum. 'And do you think you girls could stop calling me Mrs Moore? It makes me feel about ninety.'

Anyway, I thought, Fiona's Mrs Moore now. When Mum and Dad got divorced Mum said she was going to go back to being Ms Kelly but I'd begged her not to. 'I'll die of embarrassment if you have a different name from me,' I said when I was starting senior school. She'd said

OK but I could tell she didn't really like keeping Dad's name. I wondered what Brian's name was.

'You're, like, half the age of my mum,' said Becca.

Mum laughed. 'I was a child bride,' she said. 'And no, I wouldn't recommend it.'

If she went out with Brian for, say, a couple of years, and then I went away to uni – Glasgow or Edinburgh, I thought, though lately I'd been thinking Cambridge might be nice if I was clever enough – well, I supposed she could marry him then. She'd probably be a bit lonely when I left. Then I caught myself on and laughed.

Fliss gave me a concerned look. 'Don't let the excitement go to your head, Victoria,' she said in Mad Max's voice.

'It must be nearly time for the dress,' suggested Mum. 'I want to see you in it before I go.'

The silk shimmied over my body, cool and creamy. Mum did up the criss-cross lacing at the back. I turned round to face my beauty therapists. 'Well?' I breathed nervously.

'It's gorgeous!' They all stood back and looked at me.

'God, you are so lucky!' cried Fliss for the billionth time. 'There is no way he won't jump on you in that dress.' Then she caught Mum's eye and shut up, thank God.

'You don't think I should have got a fake tan?' I said to change the subject.

'No, Vicky; it's January. You don't want to look like that crowd in Year Eleven – they're orange!' said Fliss, sounding so firm that I relaxed.

In my silver sandals my toenails, painted by Fliss, twinkled. 'I feel like a princess,' I couldn't help admitting. 'Thank you so much – you guys are the best friends in the world.'

'We know,' said Fliss. A car horn beeped in the street. 'Hey, that's my mum. Better go.'

'Text us all the goss!' they ordered, shrugging themselves into coats which looked suddenly clumsy and heavy beside the cold silk of my dress. 'Bye, babes!'

When the doorbell went I shrieked, 'I'll get it!' and was gliding – my dress seemed to make me glide – across the hall before Mum could stop me.

A man. An actual *man*. Old, I thought at first, but it was only because he was grey. I supposed any hair was a bonus at their age.

'Hello,' he said. 'You must be Vicky.'

OK, not the most original, but then he was probably a bit taken aback to see a girl in a ball gown instead of Mum in her hippy dress. I willed myself not to blush under Fliss's careful make-up. 'Um, yes,' I said. 'I'm going to a formal.'

Apart from being grey, Brian was short and beardy with round glasses. He was definitely the absent-minded professor type in his tweedy jacket and not-terribly-new-looking chinos. But he didn't look like he would break Mum's heart. Mind you, neither did Dad.

'Where are you taking Mum?' I asked, just to be polite.

'I've booked a table at the Rowan Tree.' He sounded a bit anxious. 'Do you think that's all right?'

I relaxed. 'She's never been there, but I have. I really like it. The crème brûlée is amazing.' I had only been to the Rowan Tree once, for Fiona's birthday, but it would do no harm for Brian to think I went there all the time.

'Oh. Well, that sounds a good endorsement,' he said. He blinked. I wondered if he had met many girlfriends' daughters. I sort of suspected that this was as new to him as it was to me and I couldn't help liking him a bit more for it.

Then Mum was there. 'Vicky, you shouldn't have left Brian standing on the doorstep,' she said. Her voice sounded a bit high or breathless or something. She had her coat on already and her cheeks were pink. They didn't kiss or anything, thank God. Mum kissed me instead – very carefully because of my make-up.

'Have a lovely time,' we all said at the same time and Mum laughed. 'Careful with drink,' she whispered.

'Mu-um! I've told you a million times I am not going to do anything to spoil this night!'

I waved goodbye and checked my reflection in the hall mirror. Just a tiny rub of lip gloss, I decided. Twenty to seven. In five minutes Rory would be here. Then this magical night would *really* begin.

Chapter 37

DECLAN

I look at myself in the hall mirror. Even in the half-light I look like shit. *Do you have no self-respect, boy?* There's no way I'm going to face Barry in a dirty school uniform with BO so I force myself to have a cold wash – not a shower, I'm not that brave – and get changed. The house is like a fridge but hopefully not for much longer.

If I get the money I'll buy stamps on the way home and post the letters before I chicken out. Dermott gave me envelopes and all. I find a pen – for a minute I think, 'Where did this gay-looking pink thing come from?' before I remember it's Seaneen's – and write Vicky's address on hers. Then I look at Cam's. I force myself to think about Cam. She liked me. I mean, she must hate me *now*, but she liked me *then*. I know her address – Old Farm Stables, Mill Road – so I write it out and put both envelopes in the pocket of my fleece with the pen.

The chill from the house follows me out, clinging round me. I pull my woolly beany hat out of my pocket and over my head. It's raining and the street's empty.

Walking past some of the houses I smell dinner – frying meat, chips. If I get the money I'm going straight round to Fat Frankie's. *When* I get it. Think positive.

I have my head down against the rain so I don't see Seaneen till we nearly bump into each other.

'Alright, Declan?' She sounds quite friendly.

'Oh, hiya.' I kind of want her to stay so I try to think of something else to say and end up going, 'Here's your pen.'

'Oh, that's OK.' She grins and takes it. The rain's frizzed her hair and she's holding a brown paper bag to her chest. You can see the patches of grease and smell the salt and vinegar.

'You been for chips?'

'Yeah. My ma's got the plates warming. See you.' She crosses over the street to her house. I imagine them all sitting round the TV, the wee twins getting their fish cut up for them, Mairéad pouring out big glasses of Coke.

Pity she was so keen to pour out big glasses of vodka on New Year's Eve. Pity she invited Barry the Bastard and my mum to her stupid party. But I know Mum and Barry would have sniffed each other out anyway.

Barry's flat's up on the main road near the chapel. I've hardly ever been in it. It's pretty well known for knock-off booze and cigs and stuff; they say Barry can get you anything you want. It's been busted a few times but the pigs have never got anything. He's not stupid.

Walking up the main road, taking my time even though I'm getting wet, I wonder if my dad would have turned out to be a lowlife like Barry. I like to think not but how would I know? 'You're very like him,' Colette told me a few times, and I don't know if that's good or bad. My dad was dead at twenty-two. Too reckless, Gran used to say when she talked about him, which was hardly ever. The day Colette brought me home, when Mum was inside sober and arranging the roses and everything was still OK, she'd said, 'If I can do it so can you.' I thought she meant I was like her, a bit, and I liked that idea. But then what Dermott said – *passive* – makes me sound like *Mum*. The way I've felt for weeks – dragging myself round, not leaving the house, not getting washed some days and feeling this heaviness weighing me down – is that what it's like being her? Is that why she drinks?

Even what I did on my birthday – I knew I was an eejit, but it didn't stop me.

I love my mum – I think – but I don't want to be like her.

The main road's busy. People late from work or early for a night out. I stop at the crossing. Press the button. WAIT. Red man. I sort of don't want the green man to show up but soon he's beeping away and I've got to cross.

What's the worst he can do? He's not going to like me coming round but Mum's not going to send me away without the money. She can't be so drunk she won't understand that I can't live without electric and food all weekend. Maybe she's even ready to come home. She might not even still be drunk. Maybe she's slept it off and she's just waiting for that kick up the arse that'll get her home and she'll be dead glad to see me and she'll say, 'You know, son, I was just having a final fling there, but it wasn't like it used to be. That's me finished with Barry. That's me finished with the drink. I never knew how fed up I was with it until you showed up. You've rescued me, son.'

Yeah right.

Past the waste ground. Past the shops. Way too soon the block of flats rears up. It's on the first floor. Up the concrete steps. Follow the iron handrail. His is the first door you come to, just at the top of the stairs. Maybe he'll be out. But through the wee window at the top of the door I can see light.

I swallow. It's not too late to turn back.

To what?

I square my shoulders. My first ring is annoyingly feeble so I push the bell hard. The low drone of a TV gets louder – someone's opened the living-room door. Oh God, let it be Mum.

Then the door's pulled open just enough for Barry's big gob to look out.

'Yeah?'

I take a deep breath. 'I need to talk to my mum.'

'She's not here.'

For a second I believe him. Christ, she could be lying dead somewhere. Two days and nights and I haven't done anything to find her. Then I wise up. She *said* she was going to Barry's; where else would she be?

'She is here.' I can't get over how confident I sound. 'I need to see her.'

'She's out of it.' He sounds disgusted.

'What d'you mean?'

'You know fine rightly what I mean.'

'I need to get something off her.' I am not going to say please, not to him.

'Oh yeah?' He laughs. His belly, straining under a Manchester United top, blocks the doorway, solid, like a sweaty, nylon drum. I wish I was brave enough to put my fist in it.

'I'm not leaving till I see her. She's my mother.'

'And this is my house. So piss off and don't come whingeing round here again. Do you need your ma to come home and tuck you in? Read you a wee bedtime story?'

'Piss off.'

'Don't you get cheeky with me, you wee shit. D'you think I've forgotten what you did to our Emmet? I'm going to have to take him private to get his nose sorted out properly. Never mind grassing him up to the pigs.'

I want to say, 'Wise up, his fingerprints were all over that car; the pigs aren't stupid,' but I don't. Don't react. Stay focused.

'Look, if you could even just bring me out her purse. I need … I just need to get something.' I keep my voice dead steady.

But Barry laughs. 'Aye, right. Think I'm going to let you rob her blind? Take advantage of her when she can't defend herself? No way, sonny. Just take yourself off.'

He goes to slam the door. Instantly I thrust myself half inside the flat, but just as quick he grabs me and throws me out again. Something – the door or the doorframe – whacks into my left shoulder. Pain knocks the breath out of me and I grab my arm.

'Got the message?' he snarls.

I've no free hands and he's hulking there, huge and horrible. I've never defended myself against him. Not once. But I feel my knee draw back – it's like slow motion but at the same time it happens dead fast – and wham it between his legs. Feel the contact with his balls through his loose trackie bottoms. Disgusting.

With a grunt he grabs at his groin, and I step back, excited and terrified.

But Barry recovers fast. 'You … wee … bastard,' he breathes. His fist gets my jaw so fast and hard my head feels like it's going to jerk off.

Before I can get a breath he's got me with both hands. When he grabs my left shoulder my whole body vibrates with pain.

'You were told to fuck off my property.' His voice seems far away. 'Now don't come round here again.'

It's not a hard punch really. But there's nothing behind me except the empty space of the stairs. As my body hurtles down I have no thoughts, only the bang bang bang of each step until some instinct makes me grab for the handrail, then it's more of a bump bump slither to the ground.

Above me I hear the door slam.

Then nothing.

* * *

Cold. Concrete. I open my eyes and my head splits in two. Every breath sends a shudder of pain through me. I close my eyes again. Just stay like this, inside the pain, don't try to move. Eyes still shut, I test myself. Legs seem to work. Arms: a dagger of pain stabs me when I try to move the left one. I let out a moan.

Stop it. Get a grip.

Using my right arm, I raise myself onto my hands and knees. Risk opening my eyes. Grey concrete. Red flecks. Blink. Something drips. Rain. No, blood. I dash my hand up to my face and it comes away warm, wet, red. I swallow. I'm on the road with Flight. He's bleeding.

No, no, no. Come on. OK, sit up. The ground tilts and settles. Not the road. Hallway of Barry's flats.

Go on, stand up. Yes, you can. Hold the wall. OK. Breathe. You're standing up, you're fine. One step. Go on. And another. Yes, you can; you have to.

Outside door. Too heavy with one hand. No, I've got it.

Outside hits me with cold, damp air that knocks a bit more sense into my head. Keep moving. Don't meet anyone's eye. Don't let anyone stop you or you'll be down that road to the hospital and questions and social workers and all that shit. You just need to get home.

But the further I walk the worse I feel. It takes so much effort to keep going that if I want to think at the same time I have to stop.

So. It's Friday. Barry pushed me. I know that so I don't think I'm concussed or anything, only dazed and a bit sore. Frigging sore. I'll just go home and sleep it off.

But I failed. I didn't get the money. What if I go home and go to sleep in the dark and cold and don't wake up?

You don't like asking for help, do you, Declan?

My phone jabs against my hip. It probably got buggered in the fall. I pull it out. If it's wrecked I'll go home. If not –

It's OK. Not even cracked. 18.43, says the screen.

A man stops beside me. 'You alright, son?'

'Yeah, bit of a fall. I'm nearly home.' I wave my good arm vaguely at the next block and he goes on his way looking relieved he doesn't have to get involved.

Shops, closed now. I lean against the wall of the bookies. Come on; she said to keep in touch. She said, 'if you needed anything'. And it's Friday. Vicky won't be there.

OK. Breathing hard, I push in the number. It rings. And rings. No one there.

Suddenly I know I can't make myself do one more step. Despair floods me. I can't do this any more.

Come on! I breathe in slowly. Try again. I hit the green button and Colette's phone bring-brings in my ear again.

On and on and on.

Chapter 38

VICKY

The doorbell and the phone rang at exactly the same time. I freeze-framed in the hall, the silky dress swishing round my bare legs, and chose the door. I took a deep breath and opened it, feeling ridiculously shy.

Rory didn't look like a stranger exactly – he looked the way the mirror told me I did – a glammed-up version of his normal self. But I certainly got what Fliss meant about boys in tuxedos.

I wanted to say, 'Wow!' but I reminded myself we were only friends.

Rory took a step back. 'Vicky! You look gorgeous. Give us a twirl.'

Half-mortified, half-delighted, I did, knowing the dress's back was its best bit – the plunging line and the criss-cross straps.

'You look pretty amazing too,' I said.

Rory bowed. It was as if we were both playing a part in a costume drama or something. I just hoped the final scene would be the hero and heroine in a big romantic clinch. 'Your carriage awaits, madam. Sorry it's not a stretch limo.'

'Oh no, they're terribly vulgar. I'd much rather have a – what is it again?'

He laughed. 'A Clio.'

'I'll just get my coat.' The silvery pashmina wasn't warm enough on its own for a January night, so Fiona had lent me a lovely, long, black wool coat. As I lifted it from over the banister the phone rang again.

I hesitated – how important could it be? It was only the landline. Mum and I both had our mobiles.

Oh, what the hell. I grabbed it. 'Hello?'

For a second I thought, 'Oh my God! Heavy breathing! It's a pervert. Thank God Rory's here!'

Then I recognised the voice saying, 'Colette?' It was Declan.

'No, it's Vicky,' I said. 'Declan,' I mouthed to Rory.

'Oh.' There was a funny noise, like a gasp or a sob. And I caught on. He wasn't phoning for a chat. Something was wrong. My imagination fast-forwarded. Theresa – the stupid cow had done it again. Well, he'd have to try Mum's mobile. Except that wouldn't be fair – she was out for her special birthday night.

'Look, what's wrong?'

But I couldn't make any sense out of the reply. 'Here, you try,' I whispered to Rory. With a mixture of relief and foreboding I handed him the phone.

'Declan? What's up, mate?' He sounded calm, grown-up and in control. 'OK … OK …' he was saying. 'Where exactly are you?' He flapped his hand at me. 'Pen and paper!' he cried. I rifled in the drawer of the hall stand and came up with a pencil and a slightly furry Post-it. What was he writing? I glanced at the clock. Five to seven!

'Right,' Rory said. 'I've got it. See you in ten minutes, max.' He hit the button, then swiftly punched in 1471 and scribbled down a number. 'Just in case,' he explained. 'I think I know where I'm going but –'

'Look, will you *please* tell me what's going on?'

Rory sighed. 'I don't know for sure. I couldn't get much out of him, only that he seems to be hurt in some way. I couldn't just tell him we were going out, could I? Look, we'll have to give Phil's a miss, but we'll go straight to the hotel after we sort this out. Come on.'

We dashed out. A thin rain was falling which made me fret about my curls turning to frizz. Rory thrust the Post-it at me and started the car. I read his scribble – the name of a shop and a phone number. I hoped it meant more to him than it did to me.

'D'you know where we're going?'

'Roughly.' He indicated left out of Sandringham Park. 'I think he said something about a fall and being on the main road near his estate.'

'Hmm. So, what – we give him a lift home?'

'I don't know. He sounded pretty bad.'

'OK.' I tried scenario two. 'So we take him to A&E?' And *then* go to the formal, I added silently.

'And dump him there?' He sounded hassled. He was driving faster than usual.

'It's *your* formal. It's not like you can just miss it. You're head boy!'

'God, I hope not. Maybe we can pick up his mum or a friend to stay with him.' He didn't sound that hopeful. 'Look, can you text Phil? Tell him we won't make it to his.' He handed me his phone.

Scrolling down his contacts – not many girls, I was glad to see – I tried not to let myself imagine scenario three. The one where whatever this was was so bad it made us miss the whole formal.

Because that sort of thing just couldn't happen.

The rain was full on now. Rory had to put the wipers on fast, and it was hard to see properly as they slashed across the windscreen. But there was no mistaking the hunched figure on the low wall beside the waste ground.

'Quick! Over there!'

He indicated and pulled over. I hoped Declan would just dash into the car – I really didn't want to get out into the rain – but he showed no sign of moving.

Rory looked at me. 'Come on, Vicky.'

I took a deep breath, wrapped the pashmina round my head and followed him out into the street, hovering behind him as he squatted down beside Declan.

'Bloody hell.' It was the first time I'd heard Rory swear.

Declan lifted his head and I gasped. Even in the dark you could see the blood running down his cheek from his hairline.

'Shit,' I breathed. 'What happened to you?' He tried to answer but his teeth were chattering too much. 'Here.' I pulled off Fiona's coat and wrapped it round his shoulders. I kept my arm round him and his whole body shook against me.

Rory touched Declan's arm. 'OK, Declan, mate, we're going to take you to hospital. Can you move?'

'Thought you weren't meant to move people?' I said. This was the one bit of first aid I knew.

'Depends,' said Rory. 'Where does it hurt?' God, he sounded like a doctor already.

'Dunno.' Declan dashed some blood away from his eye and I tried not to notice how it got on Fiona's coat when he pulled it round him again with an awkward, one-handed movement.

'He's bleeding loads,' I whispered.

'Scalp wounds do bleed a lot,' said Rory. 'But it's probably not too bad. Can you remember what happened, Declan?'

'Fell down some steps.'

'Were you knocked out?'

'I think so, yeah, but I'm OK. I walked round here. Don't need to go to hospital.' He tried to stand up, but his legs buckled and I had to grab him.

'You need to be checked over,' said Rory. He sounded so calm and grown-up, like he did this sort of thing all the time. 'Vicky, give him a hand to the car.'

Somehow we manhandled him into the front of the car and I climbed in behind him.

And knew, without a doubt, that this was scenario three.

* * *

The average waiting time tonight is two and a half hours. I'd been reading the sign on the counter of the Accident and Emergency reception obsessively, but it never changed. Maybe they just kept it like that all the time.

'You look like Lady Macbeth.' Rory sat down and handed me a plastic cup of something that was meant to be coffee. I glanced down at my dress. Dark smears of blood stood out against the turquoise silk.

'Oh, Rory, your formal. I'm *so* sorry. I feel awful.'

Rory shrugged. 'It's not your fault.' He blew on his own drink and smiled.

'He's *my* cousin.' I looked round the dismal room,

trying, as I had been ever since I got in, not to look at the woman opposite who was clutching a kidney bowl and retching. Trying to filter out the wailing of a hundred children.

'I suppose *someone* would have stopped and helped him,' Rory said. 'But I'd rather it was us.'

'Yeah, me too,' I said. 'Oh well. At least we didn't have to wait two and a half hours.'

'Ha! Don't be fooled. This is only where the triage nurse sees him. Then they work out how long he should wait.'

'No way! You mean we could be here for ages?'

'Yep.'

'But he's really hurt! Surely they'll take him quickly?'

Rory shook his head. 'Compared to a lot of people he's fine, Vic. He's conscious, he's walking and talking.'

'Just about!' A wee boy with a black eye ran past my legs and nearly made me spill my coffee. I slanted my eyes at him in the nastiest face I could. 'Well, he'd better get seen to before that wee brat! There's nothing much wrong with *him*.' I felt an overwhelming urge to black his other eye.

'Honestly. I've come in with my mates with far worse from rugby, and they've had to wait hours.'

The woman with the kidney dish was called, thank God. I checked the clock on the wall. Amazingly, since it felt like we'd been here for ever, it was only five past eight. At the hotel, Rory's friends would probably just have finished their starters. I looked at him. His trousers were a bit damp and he'd undone his bow-tie, but basically he looked OK. Unlike me, he wasn't covered in blood.

I took a deep breath. Part of this whole nightmare had been OK because of being with Rory. But …

'Look, *you* could still go. You won't have missed that much if you leave now. No, listen,' I said as he started to protest, 'I'll be fine here. I'll give Mum a ring after they sort Declan out. You said it would be hours yet, so she can enjoy her meal and everything. Then we can take him to our house. Maybe he'll tell her the whole story.'

'No,' he said. 'I'm not leaving you.'

'But I'd be fine. And you're head boy. It's your –'

'Vicky.' He covered my hand with his and squeezed it. 'We're in this together. You're not getting rid of me.'

I bit my lip, tasting lip gloss, to stop the smile I felt wasn't appropriate. 'OK,' I said simply. I left my hand in his.

Just then Declan appeared from the nurse's room. He was holding a piece of white stuff to his forehead. He'd been cleaned up a bit but he still looked terrible.

I shifted my skirt to let him sit down. 'Well?'

'Have to get stitches in my head – no, staples, she said. And an X-ray.'

'Ouch!' I imagined a stapler stabbing through my skull.

'I've had staples,' Rory said, 'when I fell off my bike. It's not as bad as it sounds.'

Declan held out a piece of paper, where the nurse had ticked a box saying his injuries qualified him as 'medium priority'.

'D'you want to phone your mum?' Rory asked.

'Nah, she hasn't got a mobile, and –' He seemed to run out of words and I tried to imagine not wanting to tell my mum immediately if anything happened to me.

Declan seemed to notice our clothes for the first time. Shiny tracksuits and football tops were clearly the dress code in A&E on a Friday night so I suppose our formal wear – even if mine was a bit bloody – made us stand out. 'Were you going somewhere?'

'Oh, no,' I said. 'This is how we always dress on Friday nights.'

'But you … oh God, I'm so sorry. I wouldn't have … I didn't know…'

'It doesn't matter. Some things are more important.'

'I thought it'd be Colette.' He sounded panicky, desperate.

'She's out for her birthday,' I said. 'Look, it's *fine*. Honestly. Don't worry.' I put my hand over his. It felt cold and dry, and there were grazes all over his knuckles. Oh my God, I was practically holding his hand. 'We'll phone my mum in a bit,' I said.

Half eight. Twenty to nine. Nine o'clock. Half nine.

* * *

'Vicky! You should have phoned me immediately!'

I returned Mum's hug and exchanged a sheepish smile with Brian who was standing just behind her, fiddling with his car keys. 'I didn't want to spoil your birthday.' Now that she was here I felt tearful.

'Oh, your lovely dress!'

I looked down at it. 'I know.'

'Where's Declan?' She gestured at his fleece on the chair beside me.

'Getting X-rayed. Rory's with him. He got two staples in his head.'

'Ouch,' said Mum and Brian together. I wondered how much Brian knew.

'Where's his mum?'

'AWOL. He won't say much.'

'Vicky.' Mum sounded serious. 'I know how you feel about him. But if his mum's – well, *drinking somewhere* –'

'Even if she's not,' I put in quickly, 'he'll have to come home with us. He needs looking after.'

Before she could reply, Rory and Declan came slowly along the corridor. Declan hesitated when he saw Mum but she pulled away from us and hugged him. 'Oh God,' she said. 'I'm not hurting you, am I?'

He didn't answer but he hugged her back, and both of them had tears in their eyes. The familiar jealousy started to rear up but I pressed it down. Remembered where Declan's *own* mum was – probably; he didn't even *know*. Suddenly I knew what Mum had been getting at all those weeks she tried to make me realise how lucky I was. It was nothing much to do with living in a nice house and having a horse and computer and an iPhone and all that.

All the same, I had to look away. At Rory.

'Nothing broken,' he said. 'He's cracked two ribs. His shoulder's the worst – he says he grabbed at the banister to break his fall and he must have given it a real wrench. The rest's only bruising.'

He nodded at Brian and they shook hands, very man to man.

I grabbed Declan's fleece and Fiona's coat. 'Can we go home now?'

Rory and I went out alone to his car. Walking out of the hospital, breathing the cold, damp midnight air, I shrugged off the horrible stuffy air of the hospital.

Rory put his arms around me and I leaned into him, feeling that we'd been through something big together. Bigger than a formal – which was only a dinner and a disco in a posh dress, really. Even though we weren't kissing, only hugging, I felt closer to him than ever before.

'Ouch!' he said and pulled away suddenly.

'What?'

'Something sharp just stabbed me!'

I was still clutching Declan's fleece. The something sharp was an envelope poking out of the pocket. I pulled it out. It was grubby and smeared with blood and pebble-dashed with gravel.

It was addressed to me.

Chapter 39

DECLAN

2.35. 2.37. 2.37 still.

I try not to look but the clock's right in front of me and I can't move my head cause it's full of concrete. When I close my eyes the concrete turns to cotton wool and then the film starts up again. The Flight film's all mixed up with Barry and the steps and waiting by the waste ground and Mum. Sometimes I forget I'm here in Colette's house and I'm still at the bottom of the steps, only Flight is there too, bleeding everywhere and I hear footsteps and I think it's Mum but oh, God, it's Barry –

'Hey.' Something touches my arm and I flinch. 'It's OK; you're dreaming.' Colette.

I can't be dreaming, I'm not asleep, but it's too hard to try to tell her. I open my eyes. 3.19. Colette's sitting beside me, still holding my arm. My breath pushes out in painful gasps. The sheets are twisted sweatily round my legs and my T-shirt's stuck to me.

'Sorry,' I whisper.

'You didn't wake me. I'm meant to be waking *you*, every hour, just to check you haven't gone unconscious.'

'I haven't.'

'Good.' She pushes the damp hair back from my forehead, very gently, avoiding the place where the staples are. 'You feel hot.'

I try to shift but darts of pain from my shoulder stab through me.

'You can take more painkillers soon,' says Colette. 'Can I get you anything else?' While she speaks she straightens out the sheets. I can feel her getting ready to go, thinking about her own, nice, quiet room. The only thing I want, apart from the pain to go away, is not to be on my own.

'No,' I say. *You don't like asking for help, do you?* 'Uhh – would you stay with me?'

She sits down beside me. 'Of course I will. It'll seem better in the morning.'

I close my eyes but I'm wide awake.

'Declan, love,' she whispers. 'Where's your mum?'

'Barry's.'

'Drinking?'

I can't nod, it hurts my head too much, but for some reason I don't want to say yes.

But she knows. 'Oh, Declan.' She sounds sad. 'Why didn't you tell me? Why didn't you phone?'

'You know why.' I bite my lip.

'Because of Flight?'

'Uh-huh.' I'm not hot now. I'm shivering.

'That wouldn't have made any difference.'

'You couldn't have done anything.'

'I could have … oh, I don't know. How long has she been at Barry's? I thought they split up ages ago?'

I wish. 'Dunno.' When I try to think my head throbs. 'Wednesday.'

'Wednesday!'

'It's OK. I don't mind. It was just –' I remember the cold seeping through the house like despair. 'The electric ran out and there was no food. That's why I went round there.'

Colette sighs. 'I've always known she drank. But not like *that*.'

What does she mean *always*? Mum only started drinking – really drinking – when I got into trouble. If my head wasn't so sore I'd ask her but the effort of thinking up the words is too much.

When Colette speaks again it's her remembering voice. 'I suppose she always drank too much, even when we were kids. She and your dad used to get carry-outs and drink in the park. Everyone did. Well, except me. I was the goody-goody.'

'She drank *then*?'

'Oh yes. They always said there was nothing else to do. I used to worry because your mum's mum died young – when we were eighteen. And *she* was an alcoholic. But Theresa always told me to lighten up, that I was just *boring*. She calmed down when she got married. Then when Gerard died I suppose it was one of the ways she coped.'

My head tries to adjust to this new idea of Mum drinking before I was born. Drinking when I was a kid. When *she* was a kid. A bit of a laugh down the park. I remember my birthday. The smash of the empty bottle. Puking in an alley. That hadn't been a laugh.

'But it got worse when Gran died.'

'Maybe. And you probably started to notice more then, because your gran wasn't around any more.'

I shiver.

'Declan, you do know Gran had a bad heart, don't you? She didn't … it wasn't anything to do with you, her dying. I mean, just in case you ever worried about that.'

The pain in my arm's clutching me tight. I don't want to cry but the pressure's building up behind my eyes.

'OK,' Colette says. 'More painkillers, I think.' She pats my good arm. 'I won't be a minute.'

She comes back with two cups of tea, the tablets and a hot water bottle, and helps me to sit up. My whole body feels like someone jumped on it wearing hobnailed boots. I wonder where I'd be now if I'd fallen down the whole flight of steps. Or if I hadn't phoned Colette's number. Or if Vicky had told me to piss off.

* * *

I stretch out my foot and wiggle the tap for more hot water. It gushes out in a lovely swirl. My bruises look darker under the water and the cuts stung when I first got in but now they've stopped. Colette put some sort of smelly stuff in the water – lavender or something. 'It'll help your aches and pains.'

I close my eyes and think about washing myself but if I just lie here the dirt'll melt away in the hot water.

'Declan!' I must have been half-asleep because I jolt and splash at Colette's voice. 'I've left you some clothes on your bed.'

I remember what my own clothes were like last night – bloody and torn. I can't put them on again. Does that mean I'll have to wear girls' clothes? Vicky's *knickers*? But the trackie bottoms and sweatshirt neatly folded on the bed look like boys' all right and the boxers definitely are.

'Rory left them in for you,' Colette explained.

My head's OK but the rest of me is one huge ache. I lie on the sofa with a duvet, sometimes watching TV, mostly half-dozy. Colette footers about, in and out of the room, but dead quietly. It feels unreal. I just lie there in Rory's too-big old clothes and concentrate on not thinking.

I jerk out of sleep to find Vicky sitting beside me reading a horsey magazine. When she sees I'm awake she chews her lips and says, 'Um, hello.'

'I thought you'd be at your Dad's,' I say. 'Is it not Saturday?'

'I'm going in a while,' she says. 'I wanted to see you first. I got your letter.'

For a few seconds I don't know what she means. Then I remember. 'Oh.'

There's an embarrassed silence; I feel crap and I suppose she does too.

'I wanted to say sorry,' I say at last. 'Like, right from the start. I just didn't know how to.' She doesn't reply; she's not going to make it easy. I swallow. 'I know sorry's not enough, and I know a letter's a bit ... but anyway, I ... you know...'

She looks at her magazine. 'I know it was partly my fault. But I honestly *didn't* tell Cam. I wouldn't have done that. I was just ... I was jealous of you. The way you were with Flight. It seems so stupid now. And last night ...' She looks like she's going to cry.

I don't know what to say. I never thought for a second that she didn't tell Cam. My head's throbbing again. I lean back against the arm of the sofa and close my eyes.

'Are you OK?'

'Yeah.' I try to keep my eyes open.

'Will I get you a cup of tea?'

'OK, thanks.'

I kind of know she doesn't want to say any more for now and that suits me. I drink the tea and she goes to her dad's and I ride out the afternoon on a fuzz of painkillers. I'm never really asleep but I'm not awake either.

But when the doorbell goes it makes me jump. Rory? But the voice that's following Colette's down the hall, getting louder, isn't Rory's. It's Mum's.

She pushes in, in front of Colette. 'Oh, my baby!' Her face is blotchy and puffy. She looks wrong in this room. 'Oh, Christ, look at the state of you.'

I struggle to sit up. 'I'm OK.'

Colette's eyes suddenly blaze. 'No, he is *not* OK,' she says. She turns to me. 'Don't you dare pretend everything's OK!'

Mum's eyes, huge in her thin face, dart from me to Colette.

'You weren't so worried about him when you let that … that *animal* throw him down the stairs and leave him. God, Theresa, you're lucky he wasn't killed!'

'I know, I know, you don't have to tell me!' she sobs.

'*Someone* has to tell you! You do know you left him on his own with no electric, no heating, no *food* – God, Theresa, I know you have a problem but that's just –'

'Don't you dare tell me how –'

I leap up. 'STOP IT, BOTH OF YOU!'

There's a stunned silence. The only thing I can hear is my own harsh breathing and somewhere outside a car starting. The shouting and jumping make my head swim and I slump back down on to the sofa. Mum plonks herself down beside me. She reeks of smoke and drink and too much perfume and under that, stale sweat. She's my mother and the smell of her makes me heave. She tries to put her arm round me, wrecking my shoulder, and I flinch away with a yell.

'Oh, baby, I'm so sorry.' She explodes into hideous, snotty crying. 'I never knew. God's my judge, I never knew.'

I hunch over and try to block her out.

Colette folds her arms and looks at Mum like she's disgusted. 'Theresa, have you *any* idea what would have happened if he hadn't had the sense to phone us?'

'I know, I know.' Her mood does that sudden flip that makes her so hard to keep up with. 'I was asleep, I never even heard the door. And then when I was heading out this morning I found this at the bottom of the steps.' She pulls my beanie hat out of her pocket. 'And ... and bloodstains.' She shudders.

I wish she would shut up. I don't want all this drama. I want everyone to leave me alone. But no chance.

'I done no good till I found you, son! None! And when you weren't at home I was heart-scared.' She fumbles for her cigarettes and then catches Colette's eye. 'Oh, for Christ's sake, Colette. I suppose you don't even let people smoke in your precious mansion.'

'It's her house,' I find myself bursting out and she and Mum both give me funny looks.

'Come on.' Colette suddenly takes charge. 'I think you and I need to have a chat, Theresa. I'll put the kettle on and find you an ashtray. Declan,' she turns to me, 'just give me a bit of time with your mum, OK?'

You're welcome to her, I feel like saying, but I don't. I'm just glad Vicky isn't here to see my mum like this. I switch the football on and leave them to it. I don't care what they're saying.

Mum's eyes are red when she comes back in but she's calmer. 'I'm sorry, son.'

'You always say that.' I press my lips together so tight that I'm biting them. I've always made it too easy for her. I always let on to believe her because I've always *wanted* to believe her, but not this time. I worked it out while I was half-watching Newcastle hammer Liverpool – this time she went too far. Nothing has ever been as bad as waking up at the bottom of those steps, watching my blood seep into the concrete and knowing that my mum was upstairs, hammered, letting it happen. Nothing. Not Gran – and God knows I felt bad enough about that, I know what everyone was saying. Not being sent away; not even finding her unconscious the day all this started.

'I know.' She tries to take my hand but I fold my arms even though it wrecks my shoulder. 'Look, I … I've got a drink problem.' She looks down at her hands.

'I kind of noticed.'

'Come on,' she wheedles. 'Don't make this harder for me. I've been telling myself it wasn't too bad, I could handle it. I wasn't drinking in the mornings; I was keeping the house clean, but …' Her chin wobbles and I dig my nails into my arms. If I press hard enough will I draw blood? Probably not; my nails are pretty bitten. 'It was getting worse, wasn't it?'

I shrug, then decide to answer for once. 'It's not just the drinking.' I spin round to look her straight in the face. 'Look at me, Mum. This is what that psycho did to me. Just for asking to speak to you! He's always hated me; he blames me for Emmet getting in trouble. But this is …'

I give up.

Now she's the silent one. She picks at the skin on her

hand. It reminds me of when she was in the hospital and I know what I have to say.

'I'm not coming home. Not if he's still going to be around and not if you're drinking. I can't take any more.'

I'm ready for her to argue but to my amazement she looks me in the eye and says, 'I know, son; I don't blame you. I'm … I'm going back to the unit. Today, if they'll take me. I have to get off the drink. And this time I'm going to do it properly, I swear. I *swear*, son, whatever it takes. And you're going to stay here – Colette wants you to.'

'And Barry?'

'I'm finished with him. No, I mean it, Declan. I mean it. Seeing what he did to you…' She reaches out a shaking hand to touch the cut on my head. I try not to flinch from her touch and instead, my eyes fill with tears. At first I try to stop them, like I always do, cause Mum hasn't seen me cry for years, and then I think, well, maybe it's time she did, and I let them roll down my face.

Chapter 40

VICKY

'Here. Take her while I do some lunch, will you?' Fiona dumped a wriggling Molly in my lap and my sister's little hand grabbed for one of my plaits. Dad had gone straight to golf after dropping me off.

'Ouch! Molly-moo, you little devil,' I said, tickling her tummy.

She shrieked with laughter and so did Fiona. '*What* did you just call her?'

'Moll – oh, right. That's your fault. It's infectious.'

Fiona hovered in the doorway. 'She loves you. Look at how excited she is to see you. I think she missed you last night.'

I looked at Molly's fat red cheeks. 'God, last night. I hope I never have to do anything like that again.'

'Your mum said you and Rory were fantastic – by the time she got there you'd dealt with it all.'

'Well, not really. I mean, we took him to get patched up but there's still loads to sort out. Mum was trying to get in touch with his mum when Dad picked me up this morning. Theresa's been drinking for days.' I smoothed Molly's thin blonde fuzz over her pink scalp and thought of the gash on Declan's forehead, the staples stabbing in to close the wound. 'Fi?'

'What?'

'Just … well, I'm glad Dad married you.'

'Where did that come from?'

'Instead of some psycho stepmother from hell.' I shivered at the thought of Barry, even though I'd never met him and hopefully never would. But I'd seen what he could do, all right.

'Well, thank you.' She mock-bowed but I could tell she was pleased. 'I suppose I'd better make you a nice lunch for that.'

'Ga!' said Molly.

I pulled the end of my plait out of her mouth and followed Fiona into the kitchen, Molly on my hip, her fat little legs clinging round my waist. 'Fi, I have this letter I found in Declan's pocket.' I took it out of my jeans pocket, a thin, crumpled, grubby envelope. 'It's addressed to Cam. I think it's an apology. D'you reckon I should give it to her?'

'Let's see.' She dried her hands on a tea towel and picked it up. 'Been in the wars a bit, hasn't it?'

'You should have seen Declan.' I wondered if this was the time to tell her there was blood on her coat but decided not to. Mum would leave it into the cleaners. 'He wrote me one, too. I read it. He said … well, about the accident and stuff, that he was sorry.'

'And you think this is the same sort of thing?'

'Must be. I'm just worried if I give it back to him he might change his mind and not give it to her.'

'And why would that matter to you?' She narrowed her eyes and gave me one of her very straight looks.

'Well –' I ran my finger over the name and address. 'Look, I … I haven't told you everything. About the accident. It was my fault, too.'

'I guessed.'

I heaved Molly higher up and searched for the right words. It was a pretty incoherent explanation but it was honest.

Fiona poured soup into a pan and set it on the Aga before she replied. 'I knew you must have done *something* – or more likely said something – to make him kick off like that. And I knew how jealous you were. You do have a very hurtful tongue when you want to, Vicky.'

'I know. Rory guessed too – that's why … Well, anyway, I know it was my fault too and if Flight doesn't get better I'll never forgive myself.' I struggled not to cry.

'But you've forgiven Declan?'

'Yes, I've forgiven *him*.' The words felt strange in my mouth. *I've forgiven him.* But I had.

'Does he know?'

'Yes. I wish I'd told him ages ago. I felt *so* much better after I talked to him.' And I realised, as I said it, that telling Fiona was a huge relief as well, even though I hated admitting to having been such a bitch. I'd already had a bit of a confession session with Mum the night before. We'd stayed up for ages, talking. 'I want to tell Cam now, and then … yes, I will give her this. D'you think *she'll* forgive him?'

Fiona pursed her lips. 'He abused her trust. I think she's pretty sore about that.'

'But if I tell her what I said? I was *really* nasty, Fi. He told me about Mum having this new boyfriend and I just … God, I don't even want to think about it.'

Fiona stirred the soup. 'Tell her what you told me. Give her the letter. It's all you can do.'

'I just feel I want to make up to him for being so horrible. And I kind of realised last night – I mean Mum's always tried to tell me but I wouldn't listen – he has a pretty crap time at home. He loved it at the yard – I think he was even hoping to work with horses properly – and I did my best to wreck it. Deliberately.' It sounded so horrible.

'Have some lunch and then we'll head up there together, OK? I'll take Molly in the pram and show her the horses while you speak to Cam.'

'Thanks, Fi. Then I want to stay for a bit and spend some time with Flight. Cam said I could start leading him out in hand to graze a bit.'

'Good idea. Put that monster in her high chair and we'll have some soup.'

* * *

'Look: he's definitely putting weight on that leg.' Flight pulled at his head-collar rope and moved his teeth over to a juicier-looking patch of grass.

Cam, walking past on her way to the tack room, arms full of tack, smiled. 'He's enjoying getting out for a graze, anyway. And the swelling's down a good bit.' Fiona pushed Molly's pram out of earshot and started showing her the horses in the field.

I slid my hand inside Flight's rug and gave him a scratch on his warm, hairy shoulder. 'He's brilliant. Aren't you, my love?' Then, as if I'd just remembered, though in fact I'd been waiting for the right moment since we got here, 'Oh! I meant to give you this.' I held out the blue envelope.

She put the saddle down on a wall and took it, frowning. 'What's this? Fiona paid your livery bill yesterday.'

'It's an apology. From Declan. I got one too.'

She turned the envelope over as if she didn't really want to open it. 'Bit late, don't you think?'

I swallowed. 'Cam, there's something you don't know about that day – about why he went off on Flight, I mean – and I think you should know about it before you read the letter. I mean, I think you've probably guessed that I … said stuff to him. Because everyone said it was so unlike him. And I *wanted* to tell you; I just couldn't.'

She folded her arms and waited.

And I told her what I'd threatened. I played with Flight's mane the whole time, plaiting and unplaiting the same lock of red hair over and over until he twitched his neck in protest. 'I *wouldn't* have told you,' I finished. 'At least, well, I was going to but in the end it seemed too mean. But Declan believed me when I said I would. I suppose he just …' my voice trailed off and for the first time I met Cam's eyes. They were very green and very cold.

'I already knew,' she said.

'About the joyriding?'

'Right from the start. It was in the report his school sent.'

'And you still let him work here? *Why?*'

Cam shrugged. 'He was a good worker. One of the best I've ever had. And he loved the horses. I don't just mean he liked the riding and the fun stuff, but all of it. There was something special about him. Well, I *thought* so.' She started pressing round Flight's cut – that was all it was now – frowning. 'And I suppose I thought it'd be a good chance for him to try a different sort of life. Maybe if someone had done that for … Well, anyway.' She straightened up. 'I was wrong.' Her voice was brisk.

'Please, Cam, just read it,' I begged.

'You've changed your tune,' she pointed out. 'One minute you didn't want him near the place, then suddenly you're pleading his case. Why?'

'Because I know how much it was my fault. Because he *is* special with the horses. Everyone could see it. I could see it too, but I wouldn't admit it because I was so … so jealous.'

'I know you were.' Cam turned the envelope over. 'The way he was with Flight – you hated that, didn't you?'

I bit my lip and nodded.

'He has a real affinity with horses,' she said. 'Oh, I know he doesn't know much yet. In a way, that was a help. He didn't have preconceived ideas. You know, lots of people just see horses as showjumpers or machines or, you know, fit them into our routines, expect them to be what we want. He didn't know any of that. He just accepted them as – well, as horses. As themselves.'

'I know. That was what I hated.' I scratched Flight's neck. 'So – will you let him come back?'

She shook her head. 'That kind of recklessness – there's no place for that on a yard full of valuable horses. No matter how good he is. I'm sorry, Vicky; I'm not taking him back just to make you feel better.'

Flight rubbed his head against my chest. I rubbed his ears and nodded at the letter. 'But you'll read it?'

'I'll read it,' she said. 'But I'm not saying it'll make any difference. Put that saddle away when you've a minute, will you?'

And she set off towards her house, stuffing the envelope into her body-warmer pocket like a used tissue.

Chapter 41

DECLAN

'Declan, for you!' Colette's voice yells upstairs. I click the mouse and sigh. I never heard the phone but whoever it is, I don't want to talk to them.

'Declan!' This time she sounds impatient. I shut down the computer and drag my feet down the stairs. It still hurts to move much.

Colette's hovering in the hall, looking sort of shifty. 'There you are! You've got a visitor.'

Oh, God. This is worse than I thought. At least on the phone you can cut someone off.

'Come on.' She sort of propels me into the living-room and leaves me at the door.

And sitting on the sofa, looking round, taking everything in, but sort of nervous, too, judging by the way she's chewing on her fingernail, is Seaneen.

'Hiya,' she goes, like she just bumped into me outside the chippie. She shakes an envelope at me. 'Dermie asked me to bring this round.'

It's a Get Well card, a funny one. Looks like everyone's

signed it – Cathal Gurney's writing takes up half the card – and tucked inside it is a piece of folded paper. I unfold it and read: 'Hope you're feeling better. You might like to know that you got four Cs in your mocks. So all you have to do is repeat that in June and you're on your way. Congratulations. Looking forward to seeing you back at school soon. Martin Dermott.'

'So what's he say?' Seaneen demands.

'Just teacher stuff.' I look at her properly for the first time. She's wearing a short denim skirt and for once her curls aren't pulled back from her face, but bouncing loose like a lion's mane. She's wearing make-up.

'How did you know where to come?'

She grins. 'Well, I knew it was this street. And I've seen your Colette's car often enough. So I got the bus to the Lisburn Road and then just walked up the street looking up all the driveways until I found it. I got some funny looks, right enough.'

The idea of Seaneen Brogan going to all that trouble ... I shake my head. 'What if Colette'd been out?'

'Oh.' She says it like it's no big deal. 'I was going to knock on a few doors. I'd have tracked you down in the end.' She looks round. 'Your Colette's house is massive! But,' she lowers her voice, 'it's not very swanky, is it? I thought it'd be more posh. When Chantelle's da got his claim their new house had all like marble fireplaces and white carpets. But this is all bookshelves and those hippy rugs.' She sounds dead disappointed. Then she grins. 'You don't look as bad as I expected, anyway. I thought you'd be battered black and blue. Everybody's saying Barry McCann threw you down the stairs of the flats and split your head open.'

'Well, yeah, sort of. I got staples.'

'Yuck!' She screws up her mouth. Then, 'Can I see?'

'If you want.'

She comes over to me and I push back the hair on the side of my head to show her. 'Wicked!' She traces round the wound with cool, soft fingertips. She slides them down my cheeks and suddenly the feel of her fingers on my face makes me catch my breath. 'Your face isn't marked,' she says. Her lips are inches away. There's a tiny scratch on the bottom one; a darker line showing through her pink lip gloss. She smells like strawberries.

The door opens. Colette nearly wets herself when she sees us. 'Oh – sorry! I was just going to … no, I know, Declan, why don't you take Seaneen out for a coffee? You haven't been out the door since you got here.'

'OK, back in a sec.' I dash upstairs. It would look a bit sad to get changed but luckily I've got my new jeans on and my favourite blue hoody. Colette went round to our house a couple of days ago and brought loads of my stuff over. I quickly brush my teeth, rub a bit of something in my hair – some stuff of Vicky's but it seems to do the job – and make a face at myself in the bathroom mirror.

Colette waylays me on the stairs. 'Here.' She slips me a tenner. 'Go out and enjoy yourself.'

'We're only going to Starbucks or somewhere.' I don't want her to think it's a big deal.

'She's very pretty,' Colette says.

'Shh!'

She laughs. 'Go on. And tell Seaneen not to worry about buses; I'll take her home later.'

It's weird being outside. I breathe in the dry, cold air, and shake off the feeling of indoors that's been clinging round me. It's even weirder walking down Colette's street beside Seaneen. Sometimes her hand bumps mine. I sort of want to take her hand; I don't think she'd mind, but I don't know. I put mine in my pocket to make things simpler.

'God, it's lovely round here, isn't it? Bit quiet, though. I think I'd get bored. Jesus, would you look at the size of that!' She stares up every driveway we pass.

'How come you're not at school?' It's only three o'clock.

'Community service – visiting the sick. Got out of netball to come here. Dermie gave me a note.'

Hope that's not how she really thinks of me – 'the sick'. I try not to let her see that I'm knackered before we get to the end of the street. I can't think of anything to say but Seaneen looks in the windows of some posh shops and seems happy enough.

And then when we're sitting in Starbucks looking at each other across two mugs of hot chocolate, it's easy.

'So, how did your mocks go?' I ask, trying not to end up with a moustache of cream.

'Brilliant! Two Bs, three Cs. But I got an F in Maths. I'm crap at Maths.'

'Me too.'

She looks surprised. 'No, you're not. You got a C. I know because I had to count up your marks with you not being there and I found this one he'd left out – I mean, some Maths teacher, he can't even count – and it brought your mark up to a C. And you could see the old bastard was raging, like he didn't want you to pass.'

Can't believe that morning in Payne's office was less than a week ago. 'Yeah, well, I'm going to get dead good at Maths just to sicken him. It's one of the ones you have to get for Tech.'

'Tech?' She looks like she's going to ask me a question but all she says is, 'Maybe you could help me?'

'I didn't exactly get an A star, Seaneen.'

'You got fifty three per cent. I got twenty nine. That's twenty four per cent better.'

'See? You *can* do Maths.'

She laughs. Her hands are cupped round her mug. The nails are long and painted pink but one nail, on her wee finger, is short and raggy. I wonder if that's the one she was biting when she was waiting for me at Colette's. I look down at my own hand and it doesn't seem to be attached to my brain when it slides across the table and touches hers.

Her eyes widen and she looks straight at me, then uncurls one hand from her cup and places it over mine.

'Thanks for coming,' I say.

'Thanks for the drink.' Her cheeks are sort of pink.

'D'you want another one?' I want to keep her here as long as I can.

'OK, but I'll go and get it. You?'

'Nah, it's OK.' I try to give her the money – there's enough for one more drink, but not two – but she won't take it. While she's up at the counter I try to look at her without her noticing. Even though she's small, her legs look dead long in her short skirt and black boots. The way she leans in to give the guy her order you can see the shape of her arse. In a nice way.

'God, you could buy a quare feed in Fat Frankie's for the price of a drink in here,' she says, putting her cup down. Then instead of sitting back down on the chair opposite, she slides into the space beside me on the bench thing. I can smell her perfume and the chocolate on her breath. She acts dead casual. Neither of us mentions that she's changed her seat. She just starts yakking away – school gossip, estate gossip – but all the time she's half-turned towards me and she's stroking my hand. Her other hand is on my leg and it's getting pretty obvious that when I said I didn't fancy Seaneen I was wrong.

Finally she says, 'So, when are you coming home?'

I bite my lip. 'It'll be a while. You know my mum's –'

She squeezes my hand. 'I know; she phoned my mum yesterday. Look, it'll be different this time.'

'Maybe.'

'And you know Barry's away back to Siobhan? More fool her for taking him in. He's probably shitting himself in case you try and do him for assault.'

I heave a huge sigh and the girls at the next table turn round. I look down into my empty cup. So Barry's back with Emmet's ma. That'll probably keep Emmet off my back too.

'And Declan?' Her voice isn't as sure as usual. '*I'll* be there. I mean, if you … if you want –'

Her hand tightens on my leg and she leans closer. I push her hair back. It's heavy and light at the same time, springy and soft, and my fingers get tangled. Then my mouth finds hers. She tastes of chocolate and chewing-gum and lip gloss and spit. It's not a quick kiss like the last one. It's slow and soft and pretty soon her tongue flickers into my mouth and licks along my top gum, which is the sexiest thing I've ever felt, so sexy it makes me ache and it's just as well we're in public because I could nearly explode with wanting more but at the same time this is enough for now.

I pull away first, but I keep my hand on the back of her neck so she knows I'm not really pulling away. 'I do want.'

'Took you long enough.' She sounds cross but she's smiling. 'Come on.' She stands up. 'That guy's giving us dirty looks.' She holds out her hand and I take it.

* * *

Seaneen and Vicky eye each other up across the kitchen like two dogs not sure whether or not to be friends. Seaneen doesn't hesitate when Colette invites her to stay for her tea. 'I'll give you a lift home afterwards,' she says. 'I'm going to Brian's and I can drop you on the way.'

The women do all the talking. Seaneen gets Colette to tell her some of the stuff Mairéad used to get up to.

'No way! My mum had pink hair? But she says I'm not allowed to dye mine.'

'But yours is a lovely colour,' says Vicky.

'I'd like blonde highlights. Is yours totally natural?'

'Yeah.'

'God, you're so lucky.'

They're all doing that girly thing, talking about nothing. I can imagine Seaneen round at our house saying, 'Go on, Theresa. Tell us about the time you and my ma mitched off school and Sykes caught you.' Seaneen looks dead pretty when she laughs. She's telling Colette something about her dad and my dad trying to start up a band years ago. I'm listening but then Vicky catches my arm.

'Look, Declan, tonight Rory and I are going up to the yard. I want you to come too.'

I swallow. 'I don't know, I never...'

'Declan,' she says, 'you have to, sometime. You're going to be staying with us for at least six weeks. What are you going to do, avoid it for ever?'

I look down at my plate.

'I gave Cam your note,' says Vicky.

'My note?'

'I found it with mine. Was that OK?'

My voice comes out thick. 'What did she say?'

'I haven't seen her since. But you'll know tonight, won't you?'

* * *

The yard always seemed really far away but tonight we seem to be there in a couple of minutes. I zone out from Rory and Vicky's conversation and let all the landmarks I used to count march past me – bus stop; Orange Hall; crossroads.

Then we're there.

The sweep of headlights picks out a new gate across the farm trail. I don't think I can get out of the car. *You need to start facing up to things*, says Mr Dermott's voice in my head. *I faced up to Barry*, I tell him, *and look where that got me.*

Ah, says Mr Dermott in that you-can't-argue-I'm-a-teacher-and-I'm-right voice, *but it didn't just get you a cracked head, did it? Look at you – you've got Colette back, Vicky's forgiven you, your mum's getting sorted out, and what's this about you and Seaneen?*

But this, now, seems the biggest thing. I lean against the car while Rory locks it. My legs feel shakier than they did on the way up to Barry's flat and I feel sicker than when I downed the bottle of vodka. Vicky turns to me as if she can guess. 'Come on,' she says. 'You'll feel better when you've seen him.'

I swallow hard and follow them. Rory's holding Vicky's hand but when she notices I'm lagging behind she reaches back and takes mine in her other one.

Everything is the same. The stack of brushes against the far wall of the barn; the big round bale of haylage; the horses blinking in the sudden glare of the electric light. Above all, the smell – haylage, shavings and dung.

He's at the back of his stable, pulling at his hay net. Every time I've seen him in my head for the last month he's been struggling, bleeding, sweating, dying on the road. And now here he is, standing, eating, snuggled up in a yellow tartan stable rug. He turns to look at us and blows out through his nostrils.

'He's still resting his leg, isn't he?' Rory says, appearing at the door.

Vicky suddenly gives a whoop that makes Flight goggle his eyes and back away with a snort. 'Oh my God, Rory! That's his *good* leg. That means his bad leg's feeling better. Oh Flight, you clever boy!' And she throws her arms round Flight's neck.

I reach out and touch his shoulder. It's softer and fluffier than it was before Christmas. 'Can I … can I see?' Part of me doesn't want to, but I know I have to.

Vicky nods. 'It's under his rug. Pull the back end up – look, over there. It's nearly healed over.'

Maybe, but it's still a huge, ugly gash of imperfection on this lovely animal. I touch the skin around the closing wound very, very gently, like Seaneen touched the cut on my head earlier. 'I'm so sorry,' I whisper. I don't know if I'm talking to Flight or Vicky, but Vicky puts her hand on Flight too, over mine, and says, 'I know. Me too.'

We stay there for a bit until Vicky pulls her hand away and straightens the rug. 'It's going to take time,' she says, 'and patience. The vet says he needs to be walked in hand every day to stop his leg stiffening up. And then if he ever gets back to work we'll have to take him really slowly.' She twists a strand of his mane round her fingers as if she's making up her mind about something, then she blurts out, 'You can help if you want.'

'Cam won't want me …'

Vicky shrugs. 'If you want to speak to Cam she's probably in the tack room.' She raises her voice. 'Rory! Could you bring me one of those apples?'

My feet force me across the cobbled yard to the tack room. I can see her through the window, bent over a pile of saddlecloths, her red hair glinting in the light, the same colour as Flight's coat. She jumps when she sees me.

'Well,' she says. Her voice is very cool. Not giving anything away.

I swallow. 'I came to say... I ... em... I just wanted...' The words are out of reach. I shake my head and try again. 'I'm sorry.'

'I got your letter.' She goes on checking the stitching of a green saddlecloth that I remember is Kizzy's. The tack room walls are harsh white under the bare light bulb.

'Also, thank you. For everything you taught me.'

'You're welcome.'

The leather smell from the neat racks of saddles is delicious and unbearable. Even the sweaty smell of dirty saddlecloths. I stretch out a hand and finger a soft leather bridle on its hook.

'Is that all?' asks Cam. Her voice is a wee bit warmer.

'No.' I can't believe I'm going to ask. 'I know I've no right to ask you this. But is there any way you'd ... No ...' I know it's hopeless. 'It's OK, forget it. I'd better head on.'

'No,' she says. 'Ask me.' She puts down the saddlecloths and comes over to me. Her green eyes are challenging. Does she want to hear me ask to give her the satisfaction of telling me to piss off? I wouldn't blame her. But if she does I haven't lost anything.

'Can I come back and work here?'

She doesn't answer. I twist the reins I'm holding. I realise I should have said please but it's too late now.

'Declan, I trusted you. You let me down.'

'I know.'

'I gave you a chance in a yard full of valuable animals when most people wouldn't have had you near the place. Oh yes – I knew about the joyriding. I've known from the start.'

'So how come you…?'

'It doesn't matter. The fact is I don't know if I can ever trust you again.'

'I swear you can.'

'I didn't think you'd ask me to my face,' she says. 'I didn't think you were brave enough.' Her face relaxes. 'OK, if I give you a month's trial – no wages, all the dirty jobs and no riding until I think you've earned it – could you stick it?'

I square my shoulders, trying not to wince. 'Yes.'

'I mean it about the dirty jobs – you're going to be lifting more horse shit and cleaning more tack than you ever imagined.' She looks me up and down. 'When are you going to be fit to start? You're pretty crocked up, aren't you? Not much use to me like that.'

'Couple of weeks?'

'That'll do. Now scram. I have horses to get ready. Oh, and Declan?' For the first time she smiles. 'Welcome back.'

And I head back to the shed where Vicky and Rory are waiting for me and the horses are chewing their haylage like they have all the time in the world.